"He made bail last night while we were having dinner."

"Oh, great! We'll never see him again."

"Wrong," the detective said. "He's in the morgue."

"Say what?"

"Someone bashed in the back of his skull."

Three Strikes And You're Dead!

A Brad Powers Mystery

By J. Scott Payne

ARGON PRESS

Three Strikes And You're Dead

Published in the United States of America
by Argon Press

Cover design by H. William Ruback,
InColor Digital Design, LLC

Cover Photo courtesy of Shutterstock.com
Copyright Real Deal Photo

ISBN: 978-0-9908831-2-8

Library of Congress Control Number:
2015939364

Kidnapping, Murder and Torture
In the Heartland

Brad Powers, retired U.S. Army counterintelligence investigator, hopes for a second career as a small-town cop in Indiana. His plan goes on hold when he becomes entangled with two women, one a predator and the other her prey. He finds them to be the keys to an unsolved murder 20 years past.

He also finds himself to be the murderer's target.

Also by This Author

A Corporal No More
A Novel of the Civil War

To my daughter, Lee – the little lady who,
from her first minute, gave real meaning
to my life.

Three Strikes And You're Dead

Chapter 1
3:30 a.m. July 19, 1993

After a 40-minute drive, the big sandy-haired man eased himself from the cab of his grimy pick-up down to the gravel parking lot. Arthritic knees forced him to take mincing steps at first. He squinted and half averted his face from the headlight glare of the car facing his truck. He shaded his eyes with broad, work-thickened hands.

"All right," he said toward the figure he could barely see behind the headlights. "We've got to talk." More fluidly now, he began striding toward the car. "Come on! Come over here and meet me face-to-face!"

The glare robbed his peripheral vision so he didn't see the figure move behind him, but it would have been too late anyway. The aluminum hardball bat already was accelerating through its 8-foot arc.

The crunch of a shoe pivoting in gravel registered in his mind, but a millisecond later he was dead. With a muted *bink* the bat's sweet spot crushed the base of his skull. His knees landed first, then his full length, face thudding last into the gravel. The body's weight expelled air from its lungs in a long rattling sigh.

The assailant bent down to fish the billfold from the corpse's khakis, then turned the bleeding body onto its back. A gold chain snapped as the killer jerked it from the body's neck. Next, three rings were twisted and pulled from the left hand's limp fingers. The killer crammed the billfold's contents, except the driver's license, into a side pocket along with the jewelry.

The murderer's feet crunched back to the car. The bat rang as it dropped into the trunk. The trunk lid slammed. The feet crunched to the driver's door. The car headlights switched off, leaving the scene dimly illuminated by moonlight. The feet returned to the body. The empty billfold fell on the dead chest

"Dammit, will you get your ass over here? I can't do this all by myself!"

7

Another car door slammed and a set of feet moved across the gravel to the body. The new figure shook out a heavy plastic drop cloth, settling it to the gravel beside the corpse.

"You hit that one right out of the park."

"Just shut up."

"Well, it's what we had to do to score."

"You're not the one that got to do it, so quit yakking about it. I'm going to need a drink."

"No. You've got to drive back and and be at the plant in the morning. Just like nothing happened."

"Aw, for Christ's sake, I'll be whipped."

"Forget it. You'll be rich."

It was a chore to roll the big corpse's floppy dead weight into its plastic cocoon. With straining breaths they barely managed to boost the body up onto the truck's open tailgate. Sliding it forward in the truck bed was much easier.

Three minutes later, both vehicles were en route to town.

Chapter 2
The Present Day

Looking at Brad Powers through rheumy eyes the old veteran eased his position in the wheel chair. "Hey, boy, is this your last visit with us?"

Powers grinned at "boy" and ducked the question. "You want some sugar in that coffee, Captain?"

The old man rolled his wheelchair to thump against the dining table. "Did you bring some real sugar? That artificial crap can kill you. I'm 98. I need all the help I can get."

"Don't worry, Burt," Powers said. "I've got the real McCoy here." He pretended to peer surreptitiously around the big dining room and the nearest server pretended to be oblivious. Completing a ceremony evolved over seven months, Powers fished a small white sugar packet from his inside jacket pocket. He shook the contents into the lower end of the packet, peered around again, and tore open the opposite end.

"The whole thing, sir?" Burt had blood sugar problems but he said he was damned if he would use artificial sweetener.

The old man gave a tight grin. "Damn right, the whole thing. And hurry before they catch you."

As Powers poured he said, "Now I suppose you want me to stir it for you?"

"Well, hell yes! What else have you got to do?"

Powers grimaced. "Well . . . not much anymore, that's for sure." He began clacking the spoon round and round in the ugly recycled plastic mug.

"Oh, Burt, that was such a rotten thing to say." A heavily veined hand groped for Powers' left wrist, giving it a firm squeeze. "You owe Brad an apology."

Powers turned his broad smile on Gwyneth, a blind 80-year-old who had a sweet and tender wit. "Awww, Gwyn, it's okay. That's just how Burt and I talk. He was Army and so was I."

"It doesn't matter," she said, with a rare chill in her voice. "You don't say things like that to a friend who has just buried a wife . . . even an ex-wife."

"I'm sorry, guys," Burt said.

Gwyneth Hofstra and Burt Jensen had been Powers' companions at the same 4-place dining table each Sunday noon for the past seven months. He met them the first time he wheeled Rae, his former wife, into the big dining room.

Gwyn and Burt, old friends, took a quick liking to Powers. He listened. He chatted easily with them. He heeded when they tipped him off about certain foods on the home's menu. The underside of the crust on the cherry tarts often has blue mold. Chew the meatloaf verrry, verrry carefully because sometimes it contains birdshot. Never under any circumstances, order the pork and dressing entree.

Rae rarely spoke, huddling within what little remained of herself thanks to protracted alcoholism and advancing Alzheimer's. Powers suspected Rae may have been jealous at first. For though he attentively fed and talked with her, he also chatted with Burt and Gwyn as he doctored Burt's coffee and cut Gwyn's meat.

As the life in Rae's face died over the months and the disease muted her, Burt and Gwyn supported and encouraged Powers. On rare occasions when she spoke to Powers, the old couple backed out of the conversation.

They tried to comfort him at the end when Rae began refusing food, clamping her teeth in an iron grip on the spoon . . . even when he tried to slip her favorite, blueberry yogurt, into her mouth.

Neither ever asked Powers why he helped care for his ex-wife. He suspected the patient grapevine knew her history. For certain, they knew she was one of the home's big majority: residents who otherwise received no visitors. Ever.

Powers, a retired Army chief warrant officer, first arrived at the home – The Wellness Center -- in September. He moved to Southland in part to start a new career, and in part to support Rae because no other relative would or could. Their son, who isolated himself from his mother years before, now was out of touch as an Army special ops sergeant in the Mid-East.

As Powers, Gwyn and Burt shared their first meal after Rae's funeral, Powers said he planned to stay on in town and would drop by from time to time.

"Ahhh, don't waste your time on a bunch of old farts," Burt said. "You just turned 47? You're still a kid; got a lot of life left in you."

"Speak for yourself, Burt," Gwyn said. Then, wistfully, "It would be nice to chat."

"Oh, I'll be back. I've still got a ton of work to do in Rae's Garden. I may even get a job here in town." Powers kissed her cheek, catching the lavender scent. He shook Burt's hand.

"You're a good man," Burt said in his gravelly voice.

"Drop by when you can," Gwyn said. "And when you work in her garden," she added, smiling, "please beware of global warming. They're blaming it for the late frosts."

Powers chuckled, crows' feet crinkling. With a pronounced limp, he marched from the dining room -- head up, shoulders squared, a stocky, barrel-chested man with slate-gray eyes. He stopped at the nurse's station on Rae's wing. Amanda, the CNA from Malawi, beamed when she saw him but tears quickly welled up in her doe-like brown eyes.

"Don't you start that crying, now," Powers ordered. "Else I'll start, and then we'll have a flood."

"Oh, Mister Brad," she said, wrapping her arms around him and leaning her head on his chest. "I hope you come see us some time."

"I will," he promised, patting her back then kissing her forehead. "Especially you, 'Manda. You were so wonderful for her. Rae always knew she had a friend and I'm grateful to you . . . more than you'll ever know."

Powers sniffed and wiped his eyes as he limped out across the parking lot. It felt like leaving behind friends in a prison.

✒ ✒ ✒

Chapter 3

Powers stepped into Station No. 5 at the pistol range next door to Detective Sergeant Robert Daniels. The sergeant, a rangy man with a seamed face and a fringe of gray hair, gave Powers a wintery smile. "You sure you want to be seen with me, Bub? They say I'm a rogue cop. But, who knows? If they boot me out, you could be the Southland PD's newest detective."

Powers snorted. "Are you kidding? I listed you as a reference on my job application so now I'm *associated* with you. I bet now they wouldn't hire me as a janitor. But whatever. Do you think you can shoot that wimpy 9 mm as well as I can shoot my .45?"

"The winner buys?"

"Yeah," Powers said. "You buy me beer if I win. If you win, I buy you coffee."

"Don't rub it in, Brad."

Each put on his ear muffs, racked a round into his pistol's chamber and began firing.

After shooting two magazines each, they reeled in their targets and began a genial argument whether 30 shots from Daniels' 9 mm would have done as much damage as 16 shots from Powers'.45 caliber. Both men had clustered their hits in the silhouette targets' heads.

"Look," Daniels said, "either one does the job. Two shots from my nine stopped that bank robber. Of course, now I'm in a sling for it and your job application is in limbo."

"No actually my job application is in the toilet," Powers quipped. "But don't sweat it. I've got my Army pension. So, how's the investigation going?"

"Hell, Brad," Daniels sighed, "I don't think they're ever going to wrap it up."

Six weeks earlier Daniels wounded a bank robber who turned out to be armed with a toy replica of an assault rifle. The state police were investigating whether Daniels was justified in using lethal force.

"For God's sake, the robber is healed enough to be released from the hospital. He's in jail awaiting trial, but the bastards keep grilling me. 'Couldn't you tell that so-called rifle was plastic, Sergeant?' So I ask what difference that would make. M-16s are half plastic to begin with. I told them to ask the bank guards why they were lying flat on the floor with their hands clasped behind their heads and their eyes squeezed shut.

"It didn't impress them."

Powers nodded. "Believe me, I know, pal. With bureaucrats, it's like talking to a wall."

Chapter 4

Kneeling beside the sidewalk, Powers swore aloud in frustration and let his head and shoulders slump. The damp March breeze was freezing his hands. Worse, his pocket knife was much too short to cut through the giant root ball of an Empress Wu hosta.

It was foggy, too. So foggy that even his spade looked a bit ghostly 10 feet away in the hole from which he dug the muddy bushel-sized mass. Worse, a faint rhythmic thump carrying through the fog told him somebody was coming. Glancing behind him, he saw a vague figure in the fog. *Crap!* He was embarrassed about anyone seeing his pathetic attempts to divide the plant.

He resumed trying to slash vertical cuts through the center of the root ball. It felt like trying to cut concrete. Feet scraped and paused behind him then came a contralto suggestion. "Maybe you'd have better luck with a kitchen butcher knife or a cleaver."

Great! A damn know-it-all.

"Well . . ." he turned toward the voice, giving the meanest look he could muster . . . "if I happened to have a cleaver or butcher knife I'd use it."

He was instantly contrite because his glare fastened on the saddest pair of eyes he'd ever seen . . . pale blue eyes belonging to a pretty six-footer in a long black raincoat, jeans and down-at-the-heels running shoes.

"Sorry!" she snapped, whipping away at high speed down the Ninth Street sidewalk.

"Hey, please!" he called. "I didn't mean to sound like that. Please wait!"

She stopped, still facing away, holding both hands beside her hips, palms parallel to the sidewalk. She pushed her hands downward. "Forget it!" She resumed her long-legged march.

Minutes later, Edna Hasselbeck stopped after being hauled up the Pierce Street sidewalk by Cooper, her ever-eager Beagle. As

Cooper hypersniffed among the weeds and hosta sprouts. Edna said, "She purely cut you off at the knees, didn't she, boy?"

"Hey, Cooper! Hey, boy!" Scratching the dog's ears and getting several licks in return, Powers turned to her. "She sure did. But I guess it's my fault: I kind of jumped down the lady's throat. Do you know her?" He began scratching Cooper's back and the pooch stretched, groaned and shivered in canine ecstasy.

"Nope. She just comes tearing past every couple days. But it isn't your fault. She's always like that. Seems like she's got trouble."

"Why do you say that, Mrs. Hasselbeck?"

"Boy, didn't I tell you to call me Edna? Just 'cause I'm a old lady don't mean I got to *feel* like a old lady. No, we get other walkers here now and again, but most of them's polite enough to at least wave or say hi. But the thing is, she won't never speak or meet your eyes. I think she's walking like that to shake off some demons."

Powers and Edna were talking in a wedge-shaped garden in the apex of a small vacant lot.

The plot formed the inner corner where Ninth and Pierce intersected on a sharp rise. It was the only vacant property in a long-settled neighborhood of old, well-kept two and three-story frame houses, with neat lawns, sprouting beds and neat shrubs all set to bloom in a month.

A small wooden cross, leaning about 10 degrees out of true, proclaimed *Rae's Garden* in black paint faded to gray. "You ever going to get a new sign?" Edna asked.

Powers mused. "No. I think I'll just repaint it one of these days. It's about the only thing left of her here."

# # #

Two mornings later, Powers heard and then saw Ms. Walker — his mental name for her. This time she was coming up the Ninth Street sidewalk at a frantic pace, hands pumping high, head tilted slightly to one side, breath trailing in the frosty air.

He got up from his knees with difficulty and tried to greet her. "Ma'am, please let me explain. This little garden belonged to my late ex-wife. I'm trying to restore it . . ."

15

Face set, eyes like stones, she turned the corner without a word and headed down the Pierce sidewalk.

Two days later, like clockwork, she approached the corner again, this time ascending the Pierce Street sidewalk.

Remaining on his knees, Powers seized a wooden handle jutting from the ground and pulled his antique Army bayonet out of the earth. Hefting it by the blade, he hurled it across her path to stick chest-high, audibly vibrating, in the trunk of the Chinese elm between sidewalk and curb.

She gasped and stopped, both hands to her chest.

Chapter 5

"I took your advice," Powers said cheerfully, getting to his feet with difficulty. "Didn't have a kitchen knife or cleaver. But this old bayonet is great steel, 15 inches long and razor sharp."

"Are you threatening me?"

He shook his head, spread his hands and smiled, "Good Lord no, Ma'am. Far from it."

He doffed his black ball cap with the gold Army star and held it across his chest, giving a clumsy bow.

"Despite my grimy attire and unfortunate ugliness, Ma'am, I intend you no harm. I only wished to tender my most profound . . . may ah say pro*found* . . . apologies for receiving your very valuable suggestion in such a churlish way. Is there any chance at all you can forgive my terrible manners? What can I do to atone for my transgression?"

Arching an eyebrow, she said, "Atone? Transgression?"

He grinned. "Not terms you expect from a grubby gardener."

"Not exactly," she said.

"Well, at any rate, Ma'am, I'm sorry to have startled you, but before you go on, I hope you will accept my apology for the way I spoke to you the other day. I really, *really* appreciate your suggestion. It's making this little community project considerably easier."

"Community project? I thought you said you were doing it for your wife."

"No, no! This lot belonged to my ex-wife," he stressed, pointing to the faded wooden sign. "She's gone now – Alzheimer's."

"I'm so sorry," she said, still with a touch of frost.

"Thank you," he nodded. "But it's over, thanks be to God. A blessing for both of us. I'm still adjusting and the gardening seems to help."

She nodded and began walking away but then she stopped and turned back to Powers. "I wonder . . . could you use one other small piece of gardening advice?"

"Certainly. Do you think I should switch to bib overalls from jeans?"

She gave the smile again.

"No. It's just that I see you have a lot of tulip bulbs in the box there. I strongly recommend that you not plant them now."

She told him tulips planted in spring usually do poorly and often don't survive. She advised him to keep them in the fridge and plant them in autumn for next spring

"Hoo, boy," he said, donning the cap and thrusting his cold hands into his pockets.

"So my plans for this season have to wait. Well, what do you suppose I can plant . . . safely, I mean?"

The question animated her. Standing hip-shot in her rain coat, she held up one mittened hand and, with a finger in the other, totted off marigolds, zinnias, petunias, nasturtiums . . . all could be planted soon . . . too many for him to remember.

He held up a hand abruptly. "Whoa! Wait a minute."

She stopped, looking alarmed.

He smiled at her again and stooped to wipe his muddy hands on an olive drab towel hanging on the rim of his bucket. He stepped toward her.

"I'm Brad," he said, extending his right hand. "Brad Powers. And thank you so much for all this information."

She returned a real smile and took off the right mitten to give his hand a firm grip. "I'm Myra. You're welcome. And your hands are freezing!"

"My pleasure, Myra" he said. "And, yes, they are really cold. Now I've got to get home and clean up, but I hope you'll swing by again to backstop my gardening. I'll have pencil and paper next time to take notes. I'm too old to remember everything you told me."

As he began putting his gardening tools in the pail, she said, "Uh, Brad, don't forget . . ." and pointed at the bayonet.

"Ah, yes! See what I mean about my memory?" He wiggled the bayonet free from the tree trunk. "Thanks Myra." Wiping the blade as she turned to leave, he asked, "Oh by the way, do you think can you forgive me now?"

She stopped, turned back and tilted her head, giving another smile, a beauty, which brightened her face in soft loveliness.

"We'll see."

Chapter 6

After a hot shower at his apartment, Powers felt as if his core temperature might almost be back up to 90 degrees. But his mood was sour. With job prospects dim, he mulled whether it was time to move on. But the wanderlust that usually seized him was missing. *Might be nice to get to know that Myra.*

He dropped that thought and debated trying to cheer up Daniels by inviting him for a drink someplace. But Daniels wasn't drinking as long as Internal Affairs had his neck on the chopping block.

Powers dressed and drove to the first tavern he saw, O'Neill's Place. By the time he'd finished his second Foster's, he knew the joint was a mistake. A large mixed group seated at a long table was practically shouting to be heard above deafening big-screen TVs overriding each other with football, tennis and soccer scenes.

Ready to leave, he took a deep swallow to finish his third beer when someone traced a fingernail lightly across his upper back. He arched forward, catching sight in the bar mirror of a tall blonde.

When he turned, she smiled, giving a slight twist which seemed to accentuate every curve of a *Sports Illustrated* bathing suit figure. She shouted, "A man with shoulders as broad as yours ought to be part of my team."

Powers swallowed. She was edging just over middle height and middle age, and making the mistake of trying to look 18. The jeans looked painted on. Cascading blond curls didn't quite hide her strained knit green top. The swell of her tanned breasts framed an onyx pendant on a gold chain. She radiated sexuality.

"What team is that?"

"The local team I sponsor – the Southland Sluggers. We're mixed men's and women's baseball . . . baseball, not softball. We're always looking for power hitters and you've got the build. Why don't you come over to our table and get to know us?"

"Uh, Miss . . . "

She yelled, "I'm Carlene," and grinned, slowly twirling one of the curls by her right breast.

"I'm Brad," he shouted back. "I'm not much of an athlete now. I got chopped up a bit in Iraq and so I can't run worth a damn."

"No? That's too bad." She looked at him sideways, batting her green eyes and running her tongue along her lower lip. She moved close to his ear. "But I bet you can really swing. Come on over. It's our first meeting of the season." Nodding in the direction of the table, she gave a pout and supplemented it with more eye batting. "Please?"

Oh, what the hell? He climbed down from the bar stool.

She bumped him twice with her hip on the way to the table and then backed into him, holding the contact, ostensibly to make way for a passing waiter. *Damn, a reverse lap dance.*

She shouted his name to the group and, giving the waiter a $100 bill, ordered refills of the three beer pitchers standing among the pizza and wings trays. Her team waved and yelled. Powers wasn't sure whether they were greeting him or applauding the beer. She waved a big round-faced man out of the chair next to hers and invited Powers to take his place.

The man – built like a bruiser -- stood indecisively until Carlene darted a quick dirty look at him. With a hurt expression, he wandered to the far end of the table and found a vacant spot between two girls. One nudged him hard enough to rock him in his chair. He glanced at her and then and stared down at his beer glass on the table.

"Who's that?" Powers asked.

Carlene dismissed the question with another wave. Two minutes later, she was peering at Powers as she ran her hand up his thigh.

He leaned close to her. "Sorry, Carlene. I appreciate the gesture, but the leg is bad. It doesn't have much sensation. And I'm not sure you should be doing that."

She pulled her hand back. "Why? Afraid wifey will find out?"

"Nope. She's dead."

"Sorry about that. I bet you get lonely."

"Sometimes," he said. "What's with the guy you just shooed away?"

"Him? Pfffft. He's just one of the players and he sometimes gets the wrong idea."

He took one of the new pitchers, filled her glass and topped off his own. "Am I getting the wrong idea?"

She smiled and looked into his eyes.

After an hour and many beers, the gathering broke up. Weaving slightly, Powers escorted Carlene to her green Jaguar. They kissed as he opened the door for her. "Where are we going?"

"It's not far," she said.

He followed in his old red Jetta.

Chapter 7

Carlene dismounted from Powers, stood up naked beside the bed and stretched. Switching on the bedside table lamp, she gave Powers a peck on the forehead. "Boy, what a work-out! Mister Man, you are a real stallion!"

Looking up at her, he said, "So do I get a blue ribbon? Best in show?"

"Oh, don't be such a sourpuss," she said. "It's just postwhatsit depression. Go to the bar in the living room and fix yourself a drink."

She stretched again, fists reaching overhead above the edge of the sheer bed canopy. Powers soberly decided he had never seen a more beautifully sculpted body. She looked luscious, but at the same time lean and hard with beautiful curve definition, like a classic marble statue.

"Lady, you have one incredible build," he said.

"Yeah, I know. Lotta work. Thanks. I've got to hit the showers." She padded across the carpet to the bathroom, saying, "Later" as she closed the door. Seconds later, he heard the shower start to run.

"Well, Powers," he smirked. "Guess you don't rate a shower. So, it's wham, bam, thank you, man."

He sat up in the bed, still feeling the effects of all the beer. Looking around the huge bedroom, he focused on a massive glass-fronted cabinet. It looked to him like some sort of Victorian furniture, not out of place in an old Sears home with 12-foot ceilings.

Through its beveled panes he made out delicate filigreed shelves bearing a hodge-podge -- tiny Japanese netsuke figures, a miniature brass cannon, intricate Bavarian wood carvings, Lladro porcelains. A frosted glass ballerina was doing an arabesque above a flintlock pistol pointed at a Steuben glass elephant, all under the serene gaze of a big brass Buddha.

It seemed like everything else in the house – high-end clutter. Earlier when she led him through the living room, she virtually danced and twirled, breathlessly calling attention to her fabulous possessions – a dozen paintings with horribly mismatched frames, a period marble bust of the Roman emperor Vespasian, antique vases and furniture ranging from Heppelwhite to retro 50s.

"What a mess." He looked away from the cabinet and twitched the sheet aside. *I guess this stallion now can go out to pasture.*

He dressed quickly and gave the living room a quick inspection as he headed for the front door. In the dim light of two table lamps, it looked to him more like a museum warehouse than a living room. Passing through the front door, he glimpsed more clutter on the broad front porch.

He was faintly surprised to see a third car off to the side of the driveway. *Somebody else living here?*

When he got to his apartment, he showered until he exhausted the hot water. He found it hard to get to sleep. *Forget it. Too much to drink. Just a quick roll in the hay.*

To divert his mind, he began debating whether to bother any longer with his application to join the police department. He submitted it a month ago and had yet to receive a response.

Daniels said it was laziness on the part of his boss, the chief, about whom he painted a sorry picture.

"I hate to say it," Daniels told him, "but when people used to refer to the police as pigs I think they have our chief in mind. He's getting so fat it's a chore for him to get out of a squad car. I bet he can't walk a block without stopping to catch his breath. But the real problem is that he is just lazy as sin."

According to Daniels, the department's uniforms and detectives were hoping for better times while unofficially trying to coordinate their work with the county sheriff whom he regarded as a superior law officer.

Chapter 8

It was cold and drizzling two days later and Powers was happy to see Myra coming up Ninth. Her head bobbed into view first, then shoulders and torso, then her whole form, the rain coat flapping at her knees, water droplets bejeweling her floppy knit cap.

"Pardon me if I seem forward," he told her when she stopped at the garden, "but my knees are starting to kill me and I'm cold. Any chance I could buy you a cup of coffee up at the corner? I could take some notes which I really can't do here in this drizzle."

She leaned as if to continue her walk but then stopped and smiled. "Oh, why not? I could use some hot coffee."

"Good! Here goes." Supporting his weight on opposite sides of the bucket's rim, he boosted himself to his feet. "Creeeeak," he said. He stowed the garden tools in the bucket.

He found it hard to keep up with her as they walked two blocks to the McDonald's on the state highway. His problem wasn't so much his game leg, but that she was almost a head taller and walked with a hard 36-inch stride.

"I thought I was in pretty good shape," he puffed. "But now I don't know."

"I'm sorry." She slowed. "I walk a lot," she said, voice flat.

"I gathered that," he said. "Well, I'm back here in your wake, so order me a black coffee and save a chair for me."

She turned to walk backward, streaked auburn hair swirling around her face. "Wait a minute, you piker!" she said, pointing at him, eyes dancing. "I thought you were going to buy!"

"Well," he puffed, pretending to be out of breath, "I would . . . if I had . . . enough wind . . . to order."

She giggled and touched his shoulder. He liked seeing her seem to come alive and he liked the humor behind that tease.

And her touch quickened his heartbeat.

# # #

It didn't take Powers long to penetrate Myra's reserve as he questioned her attentively about flower types, repeating her advice, taking careful notes and asking pertinent follow-up questions.

Powers' Desert Storm wounds 15 years earlier left him useless for further duty as a platoon sergeant, but he had enough college credits to qualify for a transfer to the Intelligence Corps. The Army assigned him to train at Ft. Huachuca in Arizona. As a counterintelligence agent he interviewed hundreds of people in background and security violation investigations. In the process, he discovered and honed an unsuspected talent: he became a superb listener with quiet, simpatico focus.

He always pursued the How, What, When, Where and Why, but never with those blunt words. He eased into most queries with, "Help me understand . . ." or "I can't quite grasp what you mean . . ." or ". . . now am I correct in assuming that . . ."

As with Myra now, he would tilt his narrow, scarred face just so, nodding to show complete understanding of the speaker. He prompted her with "I-see-what-you-mean" noises, elaborating to show he understood, making her feel he was catching on, making her want to explain further.

Myra reversed the conversation by asking the why of the garden, and about his ex-wife. It intrigued her that he still had cared for Rae though the couple divorced 20-plus years earlier.

"That's 'cared for' pretty much in the clinical sense," Powers said. "I think 'felt sorry' is the better term." He explained that by the time Rae's last live-in cleared out, she had exhausted all her goodwill with her siblings and cousins.

His marriage with Rae had been tortured and brief. "We eloped. It wasn't long before I realized that her binge drinking was a necessity . . . a habit. It just got worse. So we divorced.

"She remarried occasionally, but I stayed wedded to the army. At first I was stationed near her so I was the cheapest babysitter she could get . . . luckily that was mainly when our boy was two to six years old."

Myra nodded with sympathy. After another few minutes of chit-chat -- watching her alternately glow with humor and go blank -- Powers began to suspect Myra had considered divorce for some time.

She said that once her daughters were established at a college or university, she hoped to get back to painting and to do some traveling.

"Travel is great," he said. "I'll never forget the Louvre."

"You're kidding," she said.

"No," Powers said. "While I was on convalescent leave, I spent a week in Paris and made five day-long visits to the Louvre."

"I've only been there once," she sighed. "Standard tour – check out the Mona Lisa and race past 5,000 paintings so you can get back to the bus on time."

"Yeah, and dodging the Gypsy pick-pocket brats out front."

"Right," she grimaced. "But what really was terrible was seeing people selling porn at Notre Dame, not just outside, but right there inside the beautiful nave of that church . . . and during services, of all things."

He rolled his eyes and nodded. "Believe me," he said, "there was none of that at the Brandenburg Museum in East Berlin."

"I've don't know anything about it."

"Most people don't," he said, warming to the subject. "The commies kept people away from it all those years after the Wall went up. It's the most magnificent collection of ancient Greek art and artifacts anywhere," he said. "Unbelievable what the Greeks did in art 2,400 years ago . . . you just can't grasp it . . . well, you could with your background, but it was just incredible to me."

Myrna glanced at her watch, said "Oh, my God! I'm way late." She jumped up and pulled on her mittens with an apology.

Powers waved and grinned when she looked back through the closing door.

"I want to hear more," she called.

Chapter 9

In their next meeting at the garden, Powers contented himself with learning that Myra's name was Windom, maiden name Purdy (teased incessantly as a high school basketball player – "gangly, but Purdy"). She spoke little of her husband other than to say he ran a small manufacturing company. She was the majority stock holder through a bequest from her father. He and the father's widow – whom, she emphasized, was neither her mother nor step-mother – also were part-owners.

"I gather your father was pretty young when he died."

"He was murdered."

Powers' mouth dropped open. "Good Lord. I'm sorry."

"It was terrible," Myra said, "and they never found out who did it."

"Did it happen here?"

"Yes, Brad, right here in quiet little Southland. I don't think the police did much of a job. At first they said it was a robbery. But then they dropped that idea and, in the end, just seemed to forget the whole thing. The insurance company didn't pay the claims for the longest time because they were so suspicious.

Tears welled in her eyes. "Brad," she went on, "I'm sorry, but can we just drop the subject? I still lie awake nights wondering why it happened. I'd just as soon forget it."

"I won't say another word about it," Powers said. "But tell me, do you have children?"

Myra brightened, saying that her 17-year-old twin daughters were serious students with high ACT scores who would head off to college in autumn.

Powers asked about her favorite poet but didn't recognize the name. She wrinkled her nose at hearing he liked Kipling. But then she smiled when he added, "My favorites are Yeats and Carl Sandburg."

"A career soldier who likes poetry?"

"Oh sure," he chuckled. "You see, it helps pass the time when you're huddling in a foxhole waiting out a mortar barrage or praying for air support or what-not."

She looked at him uncertainly. Adopting a cracker accent he said, "Now looky here, Little Lady, sometimes us knuckle-draggers do like to raise our eyes up from *Dukes of Hazzard* re-runs and dimly try to appreciate the finer things."

For the first time, she laughed aloud and, he thought, with a hysterical edge . . . as if she hadn't genuinely laughed for a long, long time.

Later he smiled to himself, thinking a 10-minute chat with Myra was far preferable to 20 minutes of striving and sweating with Carlene the Screwing Machine.

# # #

That afternoon, Daniels called to ask Powers to join him for a celebration drink. "They finally cleared me, Brad. I'm still a desk jockey until the mandatory suspension winds down, but I'm in the clear. No charges will be filed against me."

"That's great, Bob. So where do you want to go?"

"Anyplace but O'Neill's," Daniels said. "It's like trying to talk inside a boiler factory and I'm already hard of hearing."

"I don't like the company there, either," Powers said.

They nursed their beers in Jake's Pub, the only background noise being the muted thump and clack at the pool table in the back of the tavern. Powers asked about the Chester Purdy murder.

"Where did you hear about that?" Daniels said.

Powers explained he had learned of it from Myra Windom, Chet Purdy's daughter.

"Well, it's certainly our unsolved town murder," Daniels said. "The media called it the Case of the Southland Slugger."

"Why did they call it that?"

"I've never seen the case file," Daniels said. "But from what I hear, the coroner found that the murder weapon was a bludgeon, probably a baseball bat. So you know how the media types are, always trying to look clever. So they came up with 'slugger'. Supposedly, it was a robbery because some expensive jewelry was taken, but from what I hear none of it ever turned up."

"So rather than a robbery," Powers said, "maybe someone just flat wanted the victim dead."

"Yeah, maybe," Daniels said. "So what's the Purdy woman like?"

"Oh, pretty bright, I'd say. And well-educated. Artsy-fartsy, but very quiet, even subdued. Got twin daughters. And she's a compulsive walker; seems to have troubles."

"Well, if I get a chance I'll look up the file. Why don't you keep your ears open around her?"

Powers took a swig of brew. "Will do. She drops by the garden every day or two. I doubt if I will hear anything because she said she doesn't like to talk about her dad's murder. But if I do hear something, maybe it will help my job chances."

"Well maybe, maybe not," Daniels said. "I've heard the chief is very, very touchy about that case. I'm sure not letting him know that I'm looking at it."

"You wonder why," Powers said. "Maybe because the PD never solved it?"

"Could be." Daniels said. "It will be interesting to go over the file, but I'm not going to start asking questions while I'm still on suspension."

"Do you think you could get me a copy?"

"Are you crazy, Brad? Just simmer down for now, buddy."

Chapter 10

Powers bought an old curved concrete garden bench and nearly ruptured himself lifting it from the car trunk and dragging it into the garden. He thought it would give Myra an excuse to linger and talk so he might learn more for Daniels' investigation of the old, cold Southland Slugger case.

She obligingly perched on the bench as they chatted. He turned down her invitation to help so, as they talked, he groveled on the ground, yanking and levering up weeds and crabgrass.

It wasn't long before Edna let Cooper pull her up the sidewalk to the garden.

Powers was on all fours amid the hosta sprouts when Cooper bored in, giving his face a big wet lick. Powers sputtered in protest and wiped at his face with the back of his hand, leaving a muddy streak. Edna and Myra grinned at the show and chatted briefly.

When she led the pooch away, Edna gave Powers a sneak wink and grin of approval.

Powers bagged what seemed like 50 pounds of weeds and last autumn's leaves. Dropping the refuse in his car trunk, he took a break. He sat on the bench as far from Myra as possible. His gentle questions steered her to the source of her apparent misery: her husband had been having an affair for a long time, and no longer bothered to conceal it.

Powers shook his head. "Stupid bastard!"

Startled, she looked directly into his eyes for perhaps the first time.

"The idiot is married to the brightest, sexiest woman in the Western Hemisphere. How could he possibly want anything more?"

She stiffened and started to rise from the bench. But then her eyes welled with tears. She sat back down, waved off his apology but accepted his handkerchief. "It's the nicest thing anybody's said to me in 15 years, even if it's not true."

31

"Oh, it's true," he said. "As a former agent with the U.S. Army Counterintelligence Corps, I'm a trained observer. I recognize these things."

She chuckled as she dabbed at her eyes.

"Now that's better," he said, in an avuncular tone.

He asked if she'd seen a lawyer, but she said she wouldn't consider divorce while her daughters depended upon her.

"They're the only reason I'm staying in a dead marriage," she said. "I put up with it for the sake of their stability. Especially at college, it's a very dangerous time for girls. There's so much pressure on them at school and they don't need their home anchor giving way."

# # #

That same evening, Daniels dropped by Powers' apartment and gave him a copy of the Chester Purdy murder case file.

"Damn, Bob. Aren't you taking a hell of a chance doing this?"

"Yep," Daniels said, "so for Christ's sake, promise me you won't say a word about it to anybody but me. I just thought that since you're talking with the Windom woman, you may come across something that would help with the case. Now not a damn word, buddy, or you and I will split the blanket."

"You got it, Bob. Not a word."

As soon as Daniels left, Powers started by skimming the file. He was disappointed to find it sketchy.

It recorded that at about 8:15 a.m., June 19, 1993, Thelma Lyle discovered Windom's bloody corpse when she pulled her car into a Southland municipal parking lot.

She had arrived early to catch up on work at the offices of Feiler & Dring, Attorneys at Law. The body lay face down beside the open driver's side door of his pickup.

The first report surmised that robbery may have been the motive because the victim's wallet, lying beside him, had been emptied of everything including his driver's license which lay on the body.

His watch was missing as were rings which survivors later identified as two wedding bands and a signet diamond ring. Also missing was a gold chain and pendant, a wedding present from the widow, which she later claimed the victim wore habitually. The missing pendant bore an inscription: "To Chet -- love, Carlene."

The medical examiner estimated death had occurred after midnight but not where the body was found. A blow to the base of the skull by a baseball bat or similar bludgeon, had lacerated the scalp and torn spinal and cranial arteries, causing massive blood loss as evidenced by the saturation of the victim's clothing. No spattering or blood pool, however, was found on the truck or the pavement under the victim. The pickup, wallet and driver's license were wiped clean of any fingerprints

Contacts with snitches on the fringes of the criminal community elicited neither rumors nor anyone bragging concerning the assault and theft.

The investigation seemed stymied from the start.

Chapter 11

The next time Myra came by the garden, Powers tried to keep the conversation on safer subjects such as art. He confided that his ultimate desire was to tour the Hermitage in St. Petersburg. "I hear the Russians claim that it makes the Louvre look like dog meat."

"I hear it's almost in a state of collapse," she said.

Powers pained Myra when he let slip his dim view of what he called junkyard art. He challenged her to defend scrap-iron Picassos or red-lead Calder sculptures – he called them "alleged sculptures" -- compared to works such as Houdin's Voltaire, or the marble statues of the renaissance or ancient Greece.

She took up the challenge, contrasting the Greek adoration of The Ideal and Restrained Beauty as opposed to modern concerns with a messy, complicated world.

Respectfully, Powers argued back that today's world is no messier than Greece of the Peloponnesian War or France before the revolution. His thought was that the true contrast lay between real artists and phonies. He savored the play of excitement in her features, as she rebutted him.

"You know, this is like going to college," he said, beaming at her.

"Kind of like hanging out in the student union?"

"I guess," he said. "I never got to do that. But it's like being back in my books as a student."

He said he was considering attending a college now that Rae had died. He explained he had amassed nearly 90 credit hours while in the Army, most of it by correspondence. "I loved it. I wished I'd been stationed some place long enough to spend two or three years on a language."

She arched an eyebrow, *"Parlez-vous Français?"*

"Leider nicht!" he said, shaking his head. *"Ich spreche nur ein bischen Deutsch.* And I picked up some Korean and Russian. You know – enough to ask how to get to the bathroom."

She chuckled, so he responded in mock pomposity, "Madam, that information can be critical sometimes."

"Mr. Powers, you are a card."

"No, I'm a warrant officer." Then remembering an old Jonathan Winters monologue he added pompously, "That's *Chief* warrant officer! Don't ever forget it! Cost my family plenty. I didn't spend 10 years in college for nothing."

She snapped a parody of a left-handed salute. *Wow,* Powers thought as she walked away. *I might talk with her about the case again, but I don't think this is the sort of conversation you get with a criminal.*

# # #

That evening, Powers had his nose back into the Southland Slugger case file.

The investigator reported that the interview with the widow was difficult because she was hysterical. At the time of the murder she was visiting relatives in Pennsylvania, returning home on a red-eye flight that arrived in Indianapolis about the time the body was discovered.

Carlene Purdy had waited almost three hours at the airport for her husband to pick her up, calling the home repeatedly, getting no answer. The household answering machine verified her calls. She hadn't called for a taxi because she said taxis are "nasty" and taxi drivers are "creepy."

Her call to the Purdy company offices at 9 a.m. elicited the information that Purdy hadn't arrived and nobody in the office knew his whereabouts.

Okay, why didn't anybody at the plant know about the murder by then? Why didn't the cops show up out there five minutes after the body was found?

At 9:05 a.m., Carlene Purdy called the police who dispatched a cruiser to the airport. An officer took her to the funeral home – which doubled as the town's morgue -- to identify her husband's body, and then to the couple's home.

In other interviews later that same day, the victim's daughter seemed shocked but coherent and cooperative. She had spoken to the victim by telephone the previous evening and, though sounding somewhat terse, he spoke of no special concerns or worries. She believed her father to be well-liked and to have no enemies. She was surprised that robbery had occurred since he rarely carried more than a few dollars.

The son-in-law said the victim, his immediate superior, seemed normal throughout the preceding day, repeatedly expressing anticipation about his wife's return. Both daughter and son-on-law claimed to be home the night of the murder, going to bed about 10 p.m.

Subsequent reports indicated that alerts to pawn shops and jewelers in Indianapolis and across state lines and in Chicago revealed no attempts to fence the jewelry in question. Likewise, no charges ever were attempted on the missing credit cards. Asked for assistance, police in Pennsylvania spoke with relatives who verified that the widow had visited them.

So somebody went to the trouble of checking her alibi, but why were they so pokey about getting out to the plant?

Chapter 12

Merely turning the pages to look through Powers' resume almost seemed too much of an effort for William Ackers, Southland's police chief. He rolled basset eyes up from the papers to Powers. "Why d'ya want . . . to be a detective?"

Powers thought the overflowing ashtray by the chief's hand explained the pause in the question.

"Exactly what it says in my application, Chief. I worked for 15 years as an investigator for the Army. I got pretty effective at the work and I like it."

Ackers inhaled heavily, straining the buttons of his blue uniform shirt. "Why do you want to be . . . on this force?" He posed the question with deeply labored breathing, lips touching in a muted "pt" at the start of each exhalation.

"Well, sir, I've lived here seven months helping my late wife. It seems like a nice quiet town. Nice folks. And my best buddy from the Army is on your force."

"Daniels, right? And he gave you a letter of recommendation."

"That's right, sir. We went through Ranger school and jump training . . ."

"Jump training?"

"Yes, Chief. We both volunteered together to be paratroopers and were in the same infantry squad in the Panama invasion. I carried the pig and he was a rifleman and grenadier."

"The pig?"

"That was the troops' nickname for the M-60 machinegun."

Ackers lit a cheroot, blowing smoke in Powers' direction. "Were you any good with it?"

"The pig could be very temperamental, sir, but I kept mine squeaky clean and it never let us down. And both Daniels and I got home without a scratch."

With a small smirk, the chief asked, "So how did you get that groove between your eye and your ear?"

"That's my souvenir from Desert Storm."

The smirk remained. "So . . . you weren't shooting so well by then?"

Nettled, Powers said, "I was shooting just fine. We were doing long-range recon two days before the invasion. The LT – our lieutenant -- didn't want to waste time scouting the overpass that we were approaching. But one of Saddam's squads was up there and cut loose as we passed underneath. I took a bullet in the leg. Not all that bad, but later one of them fired an RPG that hit the abutment just above where the medic stashed several of us wounded."

The chief pursed his lips. "Did your commander survive?"

"Barely."

"How about the enemy."

"They're now cavorting with Allah and their 72 virgins."

Thinking to lighten the conversation, he said, "You know, I've often wondering whether Muslim doctrine holds that those virgins remain virgins after the departed jihadist has his wicked way with them."

The chief simply stared at Powers. After a few more puffs on his cheroot, he said, "We don't go in for shooting very much here in Southland."

Powers grinned. "Well, sir, the absence of gun-play is one of the features that has appealed to me most about this community. Like I said, I enjoy the town because it's a quiet place."

The chief remained blank-faced. Then he changed course.

"Now when you question suspects, do you shout and pound the table?"

"Usually not," Powers said. "But I guess it depends on the suspect and the crime. I try to ask them simple, precise questions. When possible, I prefer to relax them so that they feel as if we're just chatting. It's amazing how much people will say when they feel at ease."

"Tell me about your most difficult investigation."

Powers related the discovery of classified aerial photographs in the municipal dump in Seoul, Korea. He explained how that it took weeks of round-the-clock interrogations before the thief, an

American civilian agent in Soviet pay, was uncovered and eventually arrested.

"Did you break the case?"

"By myself? No, sir. It was a team effort all the way."

The chief looked at him coldly. He pulled another file from the side of the desk and opened it.

"Well, Powers, Daniels is reinstated and we don't have a slot for a third detective right now. But we might be able to work you in starting September – that's when the new fiscal year begins."

"I see," Powers said. He tried not to show his disappointment.

"The city commission has kept our budget static, so you'd have to come on board as a reserve officer, directing traffic at sports events, funerals, and maybe some investigative work in between. You know, you'd get paid when you'd actually be called in to work. I . . ."

Powers smiled, "Sorry, Chief, but I've got to say no to traffic control. My leg won't take the standing. If you can use any help in investigations, I'll be happy to . . ."

"Let's be clear," the chief interrupted. "We don't need any loose cannons on this force."

Powers started to do a slow burn again. *Loose cannon? What's your problem?*

"We've got very little serious crime anyway," the chief droned on, "and we solved our only two murders."

Powers said, "Really, Chief? Well, what about the Purdy murder – the so-called Southland Slugger case?"

The chief's face turned a dull red. "How the hell do you know about that?"

"I had a lot of time on my hands during my ex-wife's illness," Powers said. "So I read the old newspapers. I'm sorry if I'm wrong. Have you actually closed the case?"

The chief heaved another deep breath. "Powers, I think you're just a wise-ass. Civilian police work is a whole lot different from the military. We don't need any hotdog amateurs here in my department."

Furious, Powers stood up and started to leave, but stopped and looked at a photo on the wall. It was a tall policeman in dress uniform – Ackers, less maybe 20 years and 100 pounds.

"Gee, Chief, is that really a picture of you? It kinda looks to me like your singing muscle has slipped."

Ackers slammed his fist on the desk, setting off little wavelets throughout his upper body flab.

"Powers, you get the fuck out of here!"

෴   ෴   ෴

Chapter 13

With Myra's help, Powers started setting out a flat of mixed marigolds – the sovereign remedy, she claimed, to keep rabbits from devouring the garden. It helped him forget the disastrous interview.

As they worked, she said, "Brad, I'm sorry, but something about you doesn't ring quite right to me. I wouldn't think most professional military people speak so articulately. And why do you like gardening, of all things? What's your story?"

He sat back on his heels, enjoying the sight of her hair hanging either side of her face as she worked on all fours digging and planting.

"Well, first off, Myra, the military isn't made up of all grunts. It's like any other profession with the usual percentages of geniuses, dumb-dumbs and lazy time-servers. But, where to start? I was orphaned when I was seven and they put me in a foster home."

Myra looked up and frowned in concern. "Oh, I'm sorry to hear that."

"Oh, don't be," Powers said. "My foster parents were a wonderful old couple. They had a huge garden with everything from peas to peonies."

He spoke of weeding and hoeing beside his foster father during his first summer, probably killing more radishes and tomato plants than weeds. "But he was very patient as I learned the ropes.

"Then on summer nights, we sat on an old steel glider out on the patio, citronella candles burning to keep skeeters away. We shelled peas and pulled the cords from string beans as we listened to the Kansas City Royals game on WDAF.

"I remember seeing the fireflies rise up out of the yard. They came up in millions, or maybe billions . . . just like a second Milky Way growing around us."

"It sounds lovely," she said.

"It was. But their greatest gift was insisting that I go to church with them. That's where I learned to speak decently."

"How so?"

"They were Episcopalian, so that exposed me to the most beautiful English ever written – the Eucharist and Evening Prayer from the old Book of Common Prayer. Didn't appreciate it at the time, of course.

"But that language and the King James Version, both from back in the sixteenth century, set the tone of writing and speech from London to Calcutta and New York to Sydney -- and in most American church denominations, I might add. And it certainly gave me my own verbal treasury.

"Of course, then the church went off to Woodstock and dumped all that beauty," he added bitterly, "but that's another story."

Chapter 14

The next morning over coffee, Powers vented for 10 minutes to Daniels about his reception by the chief.

Daniels sympathized. "The man's a tub of lard and just about as useful. And I think you made a permanent enemy. Your remark about the photo . . . wow! It was taken when he joined this department as a rookie."

Powers chuckled. "Man, that was on a galaxy far, far away and many pounds ago."

Daniels urged Powers to apply for a private investigator's license. "You ought to do it just to cover your butt," he said. "And then you'd sure as hell be able to officially get into the case file on Chet Purdy's murder. List me as a reference for your application," he added. "I bet Rosa would let you list her, too."

"Rosa?"

"Our landlady. Do you know anybody else here in town?"

"Just Burt and Gwyn at the nursing home."

"Who's Burt?"

"Burtram L. Jensen, a retired Army captain."

"Holy shit, Burt Jensen! You know him? He was a town hero. I believe he got a silver star in Korea. Right after the war he served four terms as sheriff here. And he's in a nursing home, now? Crap! But if he's still got all his marbles I bet he'd give you a recommendation, too."

"Oh, he's sharp as a tack."

"Good. So, drop everything and work on that PI license. You can get the application on line and just take it from there. With Burt signing on, I bet Bill Crockett would grant you a probationary license."

"Bill who?"

"Bill Crockett, our current sheriff. He's about one-fourth the size of our lard-ass chief with about 10 times the brains and energy.

Crockett is a Desert Storm vet, too. I'll call him and let him know what's up."

"Thanks, Pard. I appreciate it. And maybe I ought to go out and buy that novel about Sam Spade."

"Oh, I don't know," Daniels said. "Maybe you ought to try a Mickey Spillane or one of the Travis McGee books."

∾ ∾ ∾

Chapter 15

After submitting his application to become a private investigator and receiving a probationary license, Powers drove to the garden. He began chopping up the soil in a hole he had dug for the garden's crowning glory, a Japanese maple. Myra arrived soon after.

As he worked, she looked at him tentatively.

He stopped and looked back at her. When she still didn't speak, he said, "Is something wrong?"

She still hesitated. "Well, I'm curious about your life, but I hear it's bad form to ask veterans about their time in combat."

Powers took off his cap and said, "Oh, I guess it's a bad idea if you don't mind getting bored to death."

"Was it bad for you?"

"Combat was terrifying before it started and after it was over," he said. "But during it you're just too damned busy to be scared.

"The worst thing in the infantry is losing buddies. Next worst is the constant suffering – the heat, the dust one day, thigh-deep mud the next, the ticks and leaches, big jungle sores, or else you're blinded by a sand-storm and trying to dig foxholes in dirt that's rock-hard.

"But pretty soon you find out which people around you are dependable and -- the big secret -- that they depend just as much on you. That stiffens you – makes you part of the team. Pretty quickly you settle down, keep your head and do your job.

"But, Myra, here's the really, really big secret. It occurred to me after our son was born."

"What's that, Brad?"

"I think combat for a green soldier is a lot like a woman's first childbirth. You've heard about what's ahead of you. You're scared, no matter how much training you've had or all the breathing classes you've taken. And you have absolutely no choice about it. You've got to go through with it one way or the other."

He told Myra that after his son's birth, he heard several moms on the maternity floor. "They talked exactly like veterans just back from a fire-fight. The veteran moms were just a little bit cocky. And yet they give reassurance to the brand-new moms about what they've been through and what they face with these new babies they've got."

"That's amazing," Myra said. "I see exactly what you mean. It was tremendous, lying there with twins in my arms and talking with nurses who'd once given birth right there in the same delivery rooms."

"There's one other secret," Powers said.

"What?"

"I think combat is far worse torment for the wives and relatives at home than for the troops in the line. I've been finding this out with Matt. You just have to wait with no idea at all about what's going on. I think that's one reason I never ever even thought about marriage again."

# # #

Powers told Myra that after his divorce he applied for all the special training he could get: demolitions, sniper-scout, long-range reconnaissance.

"It took the Army about five months in Germany to pull me through my Desert Storm boo-boos. This is one of my souvenirs," he added, tapping the eye-to-ear scar on the left side of his face.

"That must have been terrible."

"Let me tell you," he smiled, "it was almost worth it, when you consider getting to spend all that time in the Louvre. The only bad thing was having to climb those three tiers of steps with a bum leg and a cane to get a close-up look at the Winged Victory."

He told of his reassignment to the Intelligence Corps and spending the remainder of his career as an investigator overseas and in the United States.

"Well, that sounds interesting," she said.

"Yes, in terms of meeting new people. But doing background investigations can be pretty dull. We were just trying to verify people's lidmac."

"Their what?"

He laughed. "It's one of the Army's 10,000 acronyms. The letters LIDMC stand for Loyalty, Integrity, Discretion and Moral Character, as if you can find such things nowadays.

"Well," he said, "I've got to break this up." He began putting his gear in the bucket. "Time for lunch at the nursing home and then I've got to get home and feed the birds and let the cat in."

"Let the cat *in*?"

"Sure. He needs his sleep after prowling and yowling all night."

As he headed for the car, she said, "Did you forget something, again?" She was dangling the trowel from her hand. He had left it on the bench.

"Oops! Man, am I losing it. Thanks, Myra."

"See you soon," she said, dimpling, as she arose from the bench and turned down Ninth for home.

As he went to the car he followed her with his eyes. It struck him that she no longer seemed quite so withdrawn and depressed . . . and that maybe she was beginning to look forward to their meetings. Suddenly it surprised him to realize he was warming to the idea of spending more time with her . . . a kind of anticipation he hadn't enjoyed for decades.

Just as he closed the car door, she turned.

She waved.

He drove down the slope and stopped level with her and grinned.

"Hey, little girl, can I give you a lift?"

"Thanks, Brad," she smiled, suddenly starting to swing her arms dramatically. "But I need the workout. This is how I stay the sexiest chick in the world."

"Wait a minute! I didn't say 'world,' I said 'western hemisphere'."

She stuck out her tongue at him.

❧ ❧ ❧

Chapter 16

"This really was a pretty wimpy investigation," Powers said when he and Daniels met again at Jake's. "The president of a local industry is murdered and the local cops don't seem particularly driven to find out who and why."

"You're right," Daniels said. "I came on board five years ago and heard a little about the case, but never had the chance to look it over before. Really sloppy work even though the murder gained a lot of local notoriety."

"Yeah. And the file doesn't tell who did the investigation. I sure wouldn't want my name on it."

"Right," Powers said, "it's kind of like an Obama investigation of the IRS. It started and then just kind of drifted away in the fog. The least we can say is that robbery definitely wasn't the motive. The jewelry never turned up and nobody ever used the credit cards."

"Yeah," Daniels said. "I agree with your idea that somebody wanted Purdy dead. And leaving the body right out in the open in town? They wanted his death known. The question is who gained from his death."

"That's obvious," Powers said, "but it doesn't prove a thing." He also said he thought it was crazy that nobody from the force went out to the plant immediately to separate people and start interviewing them.

"I had the same thought," Daniels said, "and something else struck me. We hear that the widow and Windom had been having an affair, maybe for years. So maybe Purdy's second marriage wasn't turning out to be all that happy. I mean, this is a small town. Word could have been getting back to Purdy that his trophy bride actually was a booby prize."

"Booby prize. Good one," Powers laughed. "It could be that Purdy was getting wind of the fact that Windom was sleeping with some of the girls in the steno pool, too."

"So who's to say Purdy didn't confront Windom and literally got himself whacked?" Daniels said.

"Right, and all the more reason that the next day Windom was telling the cops how Purdy was panting to see his bride return from her trip."

# # #

When Myra came by the garden the following Sunday, Powers invited her to join him for lunch. "I want you to meet a couple of friends of mine – they remind me of my foster parents."

She seemed put out when he parked in front of the Wellness Center. But after he introduced her to Gwyneth and Burt, she relaxed.

Gwyn bore herself as a kindly duchess and Burt even became courtly. "You should come here around more often, Miss Myra," he said in his gravelly voice. "You dress up the joint."

Myra smiled as she watched Powers go through the coffee-sugar routine for Burt. Powers started to cut Gwyn's Salisbury steak, but Myra gave him a mock scolding and took over. "Brad, those bites are much too large for a lady."

After dessert, Myra excused herself for a trip to the powder room. Gwyn turned to Powers. "I can't make out her features, Brad, but she's a lovely, sweet woman. And I think she likes you."

"Yeah, she's a peach," Burt said

"We're just gardening buddies," Powers said. "I'm pretty much a loner. Have been all my life."

"No," Gwyn said, "you're definitely not a loner. You're just alone and you've been alone so long it's a habit. Time for you to think about that."

"Well for heaven's sake, Gwyn, she's married and they have two college-age girls."

"Young man," Gwyn said, "you bide your time. She'd be very, very good for you."

"Well, I guess I can dream," he said.

After lunch, Powers took Myra to the nurse's station, but Amanda had the day off. As Powers drove them back to the garden, Myra was saying how much she liked Gwen. They halted at a stoplight and seconds later, Carlene pulled alongside them in her Jaguar.

Powers cringed. *Oh, God no.*

Carlene spotted him and gave a big smile. "Hey, Brad! Brad? Why did you leave without even having a drink or saying goodbye? I wanted to show you around the place . . . oh, hey, Myra! I haven't seen you in in a coon's age! How are you?"

Powers felt the temperature in the car go subzero.

Carlene waved and pulled away and Myra unfastened her seat belt and made a dead silent exit from the car.

"Myra! What are you . . .?"

She didn't bother to shut the car door.

⊷ ⊷ ⊷

Chapter 17

Cursing, Powers pulled the Jetta to the curb and watched Myra disappear at high speed around the corner. She was headed home. He rattled his thumbs on the steering wheel and then butted it with his head.

"Ahh, to hell with it!"

He accelerated down the street, turned the corner and was surprised not to see her tall silhouette. He drove slowly and then caught sight of her cutting diagonally through a park on the east side of the street.

He pulled to a stop near the park's north boundary. He alighted and began walking as fast as he could, hoping to cut her off before she reached the east end of the park. It turned out to be very tough going in tall wet grass on uneven ground. After 50 yards his leg was complaining viciously.

She looked toward him from 100 yards' distance, turned her head away and seemed to redouble her pace. He tried to increase his own speed and kept his eye on her.

Suddenly he was in space.

With a thud and a strangled yell, Powers landed on a steep slope. He tried to dig his fingers into its rock-hard dirt, but rolled out of control down to a rounded concrete ledge, then off of it to fall onto craggy limestone rocks – the bed of a small creek lined with 5-foot rock walls, a storm drain in bad weather.

"Ouch! Damn! Damn! Damn!" Powers was hissing with pain everywhere. "God almighty!" A bleeding scrape on his right forearm was covered with dirt and there was a tear in his left pant leg knee. He got to his feet and stepped on a flat rock to cross the little waterway. It turned under his weight, dropping him into the creek itself.

Now soaked, he leaned forward to get up and saw blood drops falling from his head onto the rocks and into the water. Lightheaded, he sat back into the creek with his arms on his knees and began laughing bitterly.

"What could you possibly find to laugh about?" Myra was looking down at him from atop the creek bank's wall. Her frown showed pure scorn.

"I'm laughing," Power said, "because everything that could go wrong has. I feel like a walking example of Murphy's Law."

"Do you know you've cut your head?"

"No," he said morosely, putting his hand to his scalp. "But if you can hum a few bars, maybe I can fake it."

"This is no joking matter," she said.

"You're telling me," he said, now looking at his bloody hand. "I'm still not clear what happened."

"What happened is that you blundered over Blindman's Dropoff into Jersey Creek. Every kid who ever played in this park knows to avoid . . ."

"Myra!" he grated, "that's not what the hell I'm talking about. Why did you just take off that way? Without a word, even?"

"Well isn't it obvious, Mr. Powers? You're sleeping with my father's widow."

Powers' jaw dropped. "What?"

"You didn't know?"

"Carlene was married to your Dad? Hell no, I didn't know! I ran into her . . . no, actually she ran into me. In a bar. She wanted to recruit me for her baseball team and the next thing I know . . ."

"Spare me the details," Myra said, climbing down into the creek bed. "Idiot!" she said under her breath.

"You're right. I feel like an idiot."

"I meant me!" she snapped. "I'm an idiot for ever speaking to you. Now let me help you out of here. These rocks are terrible to walk on. I've still got scars from when I was a girl playing here. Look at you . . . the whole right side of your head is bloody."

"I've got a first aid kit up in the car," he said.

"Well, let's get you up there," she said, reaching down to give him a hand.

"Thanks."

"Don't take it personally. I trained as an LPN. I'm still blistering mad at you."

"I sensed that."

She helped him up the west wall and to climb over the berm above it. When he was able to stand upright, he said, "Myra, you're not as mad at me as I am."

"I doubt it."

"Look, let's just say my encounter with that person – the only encounter – was a sterile, meaningless, animalistic mistake. And I was half-drunk. Had I known what she was like, I wouldn't so much as looked at her. If she were the last woman alive, I'd be content as a celibate."

"Methinks thou protesteth too much."

"No way, Myra. She is utterly empty and she made me feel empty. And I couldn't believe the hodge-podge she lives in. She has whole collections of those figurines – I think my foster mom had some. They were called Hummels or Lladros or something like that. And right there among them she had a flintlock pistol beside one of those ceramic tankards – you know, a German beer stein -- and some jades from the orient -- one was a Kwan Yin. And then some of that leaded glass, Steuben glass, and plus those gnarled seven dwarfs-type carvings from Bavaria. The whole joint was more like a damned tourist trap than a home."

"Well," Myra said, "you've got that right about the bitch."

When they reached the car, she had him lean against his car as she applied Neosporin to a large gauze pad and taped it to his head. "I think you may need stitches."

"We'll see," he said.

"I'm not kidding," she said. "I worked at the plant for a while and that's a pretty wide laceration."

"Well, I'll get it checked," he said, "but I'm going home to shower off this gunk from the creek. Then I'll see if it's still bleeding."

She took a water bottle from the car and rinsed the dirt from his forearm scrape. She rolled up his pant leg to clean his knee and took a deep breath when she spotted the long, deep crescent scar on his calf.

"My God, that's big! What the hell happened here?"

"That's a souvenir from some nasty little jihadist."

"You're lucky you don't have a prosthesis," she said.

"I think you're right. And thank you again, Miss Nightengale, for patching me up."

"You're welcome, you sap."

"Yes. You're right. But, Myra, please, please, please keep coming to the garden. Please."

"Maybe."

Chapter 18

Powers agonized next day when Myra didn't show up at the garden. The day after, however, she did return. She kept returning every other day and, as the weather warmed, so did she, seeming more friendly and also tending to stay longer.

As they chatted one oppressive May afternoon, the southwest horizon turned tar black and the light took on a greenish hue.

"Brad, don't look now," Myra said, as a fitful breeze stirred and thunder grumbled in the lowering sky, "but we're going to have a heck of a thunderstorm. I think I'd better head home."

He nodded. "I think you're right. Be careful." He started packing up and by the time he got the car loaded, she was out of sight. Big drops started thudding into the dust and splatting on the sidewalk. Then the skies opened with a windy deluge. He jumped into his car and drove catch up with her. She already was soaked. He yelled through his window, "Come on, Myra! Let me give you a lift."

A flash of lightning and instantaneous crack of thunder spurred her to accept the invitation. The wind-whipped rain pounded the little car with a monsoon roar. Rain cascaded up from the pavement, virtually hiding it under a dappled skin of water.

The downpour had plastered her hair to her head and face. "I must look like a drowned cat," she said, raising her voice to make herself heard.

He sat quiet for a moment. "Now I don't want you to get the wrong idea," he said, "but may I suggest we swing by my place?" She stared at the water pouring down the windshield and didn't reply. "I can put on coffee," he said, "and I promise I'll stay two arm-lengths away at all times and we can talk."

She was silent for a minute and then smiled. "What a line! I bet you even arranged for the thunderstorm."

"Damn, Girl, you do catch on quick! But how about it? Or should I just drive you home?"

She seemed to shudder. "Nope," she said glancing at him, "I gratefully accept the invitation."

He pulled into the drive at the old frame house and braked opposite the side door. Handing her a skeleton key, he said, "Basement apartment. Just go straight down the steps. I'll park under the lean-to and be right behind you."

She scrambled to the door. Just as she opened it a big striped cat streaked inside ahead of her. She gave a little jump and glanced at Powers with a delighted smile on her dripping face. Powers parked in the garage and sat in the car a moment. *Bob wants me to investigate this lady? I think she's okay.*

He tried to run through the rain with what he called his gimpy gallop.

He was wringing wet by the time he reached the screen door, cringing at the loud squawk of its old-fashioned coil spring. Standing in the little living room, she was plucking nervously at the front of her blouse, soaked to transparency, pulling it away from her chest.

"I was beginning to think you weren't coming in," she said, frowning.

"Sorry." He went through the bedroom door. "I'll be right back." He returned, tossing a beach towel to her and draping a bath towel over his head.

Turning away to rub his buzz cut dry, he said, "If you like, Myra, go into the bedroom and close the door and see if one of my shirts or even the terrycloth robe in the closet will fit. Meanwhile, how 'bout some coffee? And do you like it strong?"

"Strong is good," she said.

Minutes later, she emerged from his bedroom buttoning one of his dress shirts. "Thank you for the change of clothes," she said. "I didn't need the robe. My jeans didn't get that wet." She hung her wet shirt on the entry door knob.

"Hey, good fit!" he said. "The sleeves are just the right length."

"Yes, I think the length of my arms compensates for breadth of your shoulders."

"My pleasure . . ." Powers glanced at her as she tilted her head and began patting her hair dry. The sight rattled him. He hadn't seen a woman do that in decades. "I'm sorry I can't offer you a hair drier," he said.

"You don't look like you'd need one," she grinned. "Maybe I could borrow a comb in a bit?" She pointed to the cat. "And who's your buddy here?"

"He's the Midwest's biggest mooch. I call him Bowser. I'll go get the comb."

"Bowser? But that's a dog's name!" She seated herself at the table, continuing to dry her hair.

"I know," Powers said, returning with brush and comb. "But Bowser doesn't care. There's no telling what his real name is. He just comes and goes. Drops in to sponge off me and then sacks out.

"I've never used the brush," he added as he handed it and the comb to her. "It's factory fresh.

"Anyway, Bowser's a tough guy. Three times I've seen him ambush dogs around here. Also stalks my birds out in the driveway."

"Your birds?"

"Yep, I put cracked corn and sunflower seeds out beside the drive every morning. Blue jays and cardinals show up and, every now and then, Mr. and Mrs. Grosbeak, plus about a thousand sparrows. It's quite a show. And when I'm reading, their constant twitter is . . . well, it's relaxing."

The cat approached the table, tail up. When Myra chirruped, he jumped up, tilted his head and butted it along the side of her face. "Wow, is he friendly!"

"Well, of course. He recognizes beauty when he sees it."

She snorted in derision.

"Do you have cats?" Powers asked as he counted scoops into the coffee pot basket.

"I did as a girl, but Herb hates them. So . . . no."

Chapter 19

As Myra stroked Bowser, she looked around the room which was neat and Spartan. CD player. No TV. She stood to take a close look at his book shelves; stacked bricks and planks right out of the 60s and all biographies and histories. Though he had several country discs, she discovered Powers also shared her taste for Bach and Beethoven.

"Brad," she said, "I don't see any blues or jazz here. I thought maybe you'd like Jimmy Hendrix."

He glowered and adopted a venomous Russian accent: "Bah! I am spitting on Hendrix . . ." and gave a pretend whak-tooie into the carpet. She let out a peal of laughter. Their eyes met as he laughed with her but then she bewildered him by bursting into tears.

"Whoa, Myra! What's the matter?"

She bowed her head. "I'm sorry, Brad," she gasped. She wiped her eyes. "Herb and I once could laugh together like that. Your joke created a very beautiful moment and very painful memory. It never happens anymore – hasn't for years -- and I wonder what I did to destroy that."

He replied in a quiet voice. "Myra, stop blaming yourself! We all are flawed. We all make mistakes. But the man has an absolute jewel of a wife and he's a fool. He's the one who's done the destroying."

As she calmed he said more quietly, "And I don't even know who Hendrix is."

She shook her head, grinned and sniffled, looked around the room. The closest things to décor were two framed photos: a faded, badly focused snapshot of an elderly couple, the other of a young man in camouflage battle dress holding an assault rifle. He had a hard, humorless version of Powers' narrow face.

"Oh, I recognize that," she said, pointing to the bayonet spiked upright in one of the shelves. "I must say, Brad, your apartment . . ."

"I know, I know," Powers said sheepishly as he closed the lid over the filter basket and pushed Start. "It's your basic paneled basement that needs a woman's touch. Rosa keeps wanting to put some little shrine down here -- St. Lazarus of Tijuana or something like that -- but I had to resist."

"Who's Rosa?" she said, not quite achieving a casual tone.

"Rosa is my landlady. She's Mexican, a citizen now and a widow. She has two daughters in college. I rent here on the recommendation of an old buddy, Sergeant Daniels of the Southland PD. He rents another apartment from her, the second floor of her own house, about three blocks away."

"Excuse me a minute." He went to the bedroom, removed his soaked golf shirt and pulled on a dry one.

Returning, he said, "The one thing she could do for this place would be to install a modern screen door. This one drives me nuts because it squeals so badly when you open it – scares my birds." Myra nodded politely, but her attention was on the cat which had flopped onto its side, stretched to its full length and was doing a noisy purr as she rubbed the fur beneath its jaw. She asked whether the policeman had designs on Rosa.

"I doubt it," Powers chuckled. "He's a 3-time marital loser. But the reverse may be true -- Rosa may have designs on him."

He placed mismatched coffee mugs on the table. "Being's how I live alone," he apologized, "I don't really have a decent set of dishes or cups. I just pick up things at Goodwill as I need them. Simpler that way."

"So you can take off without any hassle."

He seated himself across the table from her. "Well, yes. I've had to move so often over the years that I travel light. I don't have any real ties except Matt," he nodded toward his son's photo. "And he's beyond reach for now. In fact, ever since my divorce, I've kind of avoided any ties. It's easier. My only reason to stay here is the possibility of a job, Rae's garden and a few friends."

"What job?"

"Police detective."

"And what friends live here in town other than Burt and Gwyn?"

"Well, Bowser and Sergeant Daniels. Bob and I were buddies in the same infantry squad for two years and in the Grenada operation. You can't get much closer to someone than that."

He paused.

"And now there's you, of course. So, I'm in no rush to take off. Besides, I've got no place to go except maybe some college."

"Brad?"

He looked up as she reached across the table and gave his hand a quick squeeze. "I'm glad you're not rushing away. You're kind of good to have around."

"Thanks. I have to say I've really enjoyed talking with you and . . . well . . ."

"Yes?"

"Well, I don't know quite how to put it, Myra. But when you and I talk, I really find pleasure in it." He looked down, scraping with his thumbnail at a blemish in the table top. "To be blunt, I enjoy you." He glanced at her and looked down again. "This isn't easy," he said. "I don't think I've ever talked like this to anyone. Ever. I wasn't kidding when I said you are sexy . . . I'd be lying if I said I weren't physically attracted to you. You're stunning.

"But you're at your most beautiful when you talk and smile. And it's just exciting for me to be with you in any old way. I get very antsy anticipating whether you'll walk by my garden today, or whether I've got to wait another day."

She didn't respond for a moment. She dabbed at her eyes and said, "Nobody's talked to me like this for years. In fact, you're the first person I've been able to talk to at any length for I don't know how long. Herb just pries constantly," she said. "When we're in company, he dominates conversation. When other people ask me questions, he butts in with an answer. He just can't shut up.

"At first, years ago," Myra added, "my self-esteem was gone and I guess I needed that kind of support – except now it feels like control and it drives me crazy. He picks up our mail at the post office. He won't let me answer the phone. I guess he's afraid one of his girlfriends is calling. He even butts in when I talk with our girls. My walks are the only me time that I get. So, Brad, this isn't easy for me, either."

"I guess I understand that," he said. "For me, it's like being a kid all over again." He looked down at the hand she touched. "And this probably sounds juvenile, but if you were a *Playboy* magazine, I'd buy it off the rack because of the cover art. But then I would really want to read – and I stress 'read' -- the whole thing, every word, front to back. And I'd take my time; read all the cartoons, even the ads."

She dropped her eyes. "What about the center fold?" she asked in a cold tone.

The coffee maker beeped and Powers arose to get the carafe. "The center fold could wait." He poured her coffee and then turned to his cup. "At least it could wait until I finish reading."

He watched the coffee rising in his cup as he poured, so he didn't see the blush that heated her face.

Chapter 20

The following day, Powers was on his knees again in Rae's Garden which actually was starting to look like a garden. Hosta shoots were unfurling all around him in assorted greens, yellows and even purple. Buds were starting to brighten the marigold border.

"I don't know about this stuff, Myra." He was reading the pet warnings on a bag of diatomaceous earth. The garden shop's clerk recommended it as the remedy for slugs which, in a day or two can transform a broad hosta leaf into a sieve. The warnings, however, indicated that it could harm pets if they inhaled it.

"Folks walk their pooches up here all the time," Powers added. "And Cooper – well, Cooper always has his nose going over the ground in among the hostas like a vacuum cleaner. What do you think?" He plunked the bag next to her on the bench.

Reading quickly, Myra expressed mixed feelings. "If you take the warnings on aspirin seriously, you'd never put one in your mouth. They're always overstated to cover their butts for lawsuits." She told Powers she once tried a garden magazine's recommendation for non-toxic slug control. It involved filling either empty sardine or tuna cans with beer. "The slugs love the stuff."

"You're putting me on!" Powers said, looking up with widened eyes.

"No kidding," she said, leaning to hand the bag back. "They ooze up over the edge into the can and drown in it. I suppose they die happy, but it's a nasty mess to clean up, especially in summer heat."

"Yeah, I can believe that," Powers said. "Ruins the beer, too, I bet." Myra giggled. "Well, I better take this back to the store and see if they've got something else."

She said goodbye and resumed her walk. Powers got up and turned to his car.

A long squeal of tires on pavement startled him.

A rusty white van swerved in a U-turn and then accelerated to bounce up over the Pierce Street curb and stop, blocking the sidewalk 10 feet in front of Myra. She halted in surprise.

A big-bellied oaf in a paint-stained T-shirt and khakis heaved himself out of the driver's seat, pushed open the sliding side door and then grabbed Myra's wrist. Powers started a lurching gallop toward them. Myra yelled and wheeled her arm in a sharp circle, breaking the man's grip.

"Bitch!"

He grabbed her coat lapels and began pulling her toward the van. She screamed and bent forward, backing one arm out of the garment. He grabbed her hair and she screamed, in pain this time.

Ten feet away, Powers yelled, "Hey, Bluto! Think fast!" With all his weight behind it, he hurled the 5-pound bag over Myra at the man's head. The assailant looked up just as it slammed into his bearded face. The blow rocked him back against the van and broke his hold on Myra's hair.

Blood running from his nose, Bluto yanked out a switchblade knife with his right hand and turned toward Powers. With blood now pouring over his lips and bared teeth, he snarled, "You son of a bitch . . ." and stabbed down toward Powers' face.

It was an amateur's move.

Powers blocked the man's forearm with his own, seizing the knife-hand wrist with both hands. He raised the man's right arm, wheeled his back against the man's torso, then inverted the arm, yanking its upside-down elbow hard onto his own shoulder.

Bluto yelped and dropped the knife.

Powers continued his turn, now gripping the wrist with his left and jabbing Bluto's throat with his right. Bluto convulsed, choked and dropped to his knees. Powers raised the arm, levering Bluto face down onto the sidewalk.

Keeping the arm high, he grabbed the back of the belt and heaved the man away from the van, keeping him face down. Coughing and sputtering, Bluto groped for the knife. Powers yanked the wrist hard toward the opposite shoulder, eliciting a pop and a strangled yell.

Myra was ashen, staring at Powers, the inside-out coat dangling from her arm.

"Run up to that house and call 9-11," he ordered, still holding the assailant's wrist. He turned back to the would-be mugger and gave him a vicious kick in the center of his thigh, convulsing him again. He then booted the knife 10 feet away. "Stay flat, or I'll *really* make you hurt!"

Myra was back beside him.

"Myra! I said call the cops!"

Her voice shaking, she pointed to the house, "Edna already did call."

Bending the assailant's hand towards his own wrist in a come-along grip, Powers said "Okay, then run and get inside my car and lock the doors."

"N-n-n-no, I think I'd rather be here right beside you."

She gave a quavering sigh and leaned into his shoulder. He reached around her waist and pulled her against him. She tilted the side of her head down against his and both exhaled noisily, hearts still pounding to the adrenaline rush.

"We make a pretty good team, eh?" he growled.

She raised her head. "Yes, Brad. But, my God, why would he do that?" she asked, voice tremulous. "Why?"

"He's not talking right now," Powers said. "But, by damn, we'll find out."

Chapter 21

A police cruiser rolled up, flashers blinking and parked diagonally behind the van. A stocky red-headed officer alighted and trotted up to them, hand on his pistol grip. "Okay, what's the trouble here?"

From her front porch Edna yelled, "Denny? *Denny?* I saw the whole thing and I called it in!"

She paused for breath. "Denny, that fat rat there on the ground tried to mug this lady after he damn near hit her with his van. And the little guy there," she pointed at Brad, "that's him, the gardener, he saved her by purely wiping up the sidewalk with him. Never saw nothing so fast. He oughta be on the force with you and you need to take that mugger in and lock him up."

"Okay, Grandma! I got it. We'll need a statement from you." He turned to Myra giving half a grin, "Does that pretty much sum up what happened here?"

Myra and Powers, still trying to catch their breath, both nodded affirmatively. The cop looked appraisingly at Powers. "So, you're the hero?"

Seeing the nametag, Powers said, "No, Officer Hasselbeck, I'm no hero. But I didn't like what was happening. He was assaulting this lady; no two ways about it."

Powers gave Myra a squeeze and dropped his arm from her, at the same time pushing the man's hand toward the policeman.

Hasselbeck nodded and pulled out his handcuffs. He bent over the assailant and recited the Miranda rights as a second cruiser rolled up.

The man gave a hoarse scream when the two officers pulled him to his feet. He began coughing again and then, in a faltering yell, demanded an ambulance. They eased him into the back seat of Hasselbeck's cruiser locking him inside.

The officer retrieved the knife from the sidewalk, put it an evidence baggy and noted down their contact information.

After stepping to the porch to speak for a second with Edna, Hasselbeck returned. "Sir, my grandma tells me you're okay. I need you and this lady to come to the station immediately to give your statements."

"I know exactly where it is," Powers said. "Sergeant Daniels and I are buddies. I'll drive us right there."

"Sir, I think it probably would be better if you just let me follow you in my cruiser."

"Your call, Officer. I'll leave when you're ready."

"Thank you, sir," Hasselbeck nodded.

As the second policeman went to interview Edna, Powers opened his car door for Myra. Once around the car and in his own seat, he tilted his forehead against the wheel and took a deep breath, waiting for Hasselbeck to get into his cruiser.

Myra said, "My, God, Brad, what *are* you? Don't get me wrong. I'm very grateful. But all this time I've been talking with a nice quiet gentleman gardener and then in a lightning flash you're some kind of super ninja gorilla."

Powers bit his lip as he pulled away from the curb. "It's just training, Myra. I'm a quiet guy and I don't like fighting. But if you try to hurt someone I love I'm going to come down on you like a ton of bricks."

"Love? You love me?"

He nodded his head jerkily. "Well . . . yeah. I do."

"Oh God." She crossed her arms and turned away to stare out her window.

After driving a few minute in silence, Powers asked, "Myra, did something seem odd to you about what was happening back there? I mean, was it really . . . ?"

"Odd?" she yelled at him. "Are you kidding? *Odd?* This madman comes out of nowhere and attacks me. So little Mr. Greenjeans does a Superman number on him and then says he loves me? Odd? I'd say it's damned crazy! Just an ordinary day in the neighborhood . . ." She started sobbing.

He reached over to put his hand on her shoulder. "Hey, easy now. It's all over."

She slapped his hand away. "No it isn't all over!" she snapped. "Stop it! Just drive, damn you! Get me to the police station. They can take me home."

"But . . ."

"No buts! Just go!"

৶   ৶   ৶

Chapter 22

Myra ordered Powers to stop in front of City Hall. As Hasselbeck's cruiser passed, she got out, slammed the car door hard and, with neither glance nor word, marched up the steps to the front entryway.

Jesus! Women!

Powers parked in the public lot beside city hall and watched as Hasselbeck pulled Bluto from the cruiser in the police lot behind the building.

Bluto seemed to have recovered his voice and was yammering to Hasselbeck as the officer, patiently nodding, walked him up the open lattice steel stairway to a broad steel lattice platform. They turned to the right-hand door to the police station and, a second later, were buzzed in. The left-hand door led into city hall itself.

Powers brooded for a moment about Myra's tantrum. Then he locked the car and walked to the stairway and climbed painfully to the police station entrance. The door buzzed open when he got to it. He saw no sign of Myra.

"Hello there Detective Sergeant Daniels," he said.

Daniels, eyes as level as a ruler, looked up over his glasses from filling in a report. "Oh no, I'm still in uniform. It's still just Desk Jockey Daniels." He rolled his eyes and jerked his head toward the half-open door to the chief's office.

He continued work on the form.

"So," he said, finally fixing his gaze on Powers. His eyes weren't friendly. "What the hell just happened out there, Mr. Powers? First, in comes this badly rattled lady saying she's supposed to give us a statement about a mugging.

"Then, Officer Hasselbeck reports in with some mook who is making noises like a basket full of kittens. Between whines, the guy is demanding a lawyer and a doctor. Hasselbeck was laughing. Said the prisoner talks more like a muggee than a mugger. Said you're a good doobie. Seems the mugger somehow got his shoulder dislocated."

68

"Yeah, he tripped and fell," Powers said. He outlined the assault in detail. "Now two more things, Bob. First, this lady is Chet Purdy's daughter."

"Oh, really!"

"Yeah, really. And second, Bob. It was not a mugging."

The door to the office opened all the way and Chief Ackers waddled into view. "Oh? And who says it wasn't a mugging?"

Powers bit off an angry retort. He took a deep breath.

"Chief, it just wasn't. It occurred in broad daylight in a residential neighborhood. The assailant was using a car. He made no attempt to steal a thing. He wasn't after her purse because she wasn't carrying a purse. He literally was trying to pull her into his van . . . by the hair! I think the guy targeted her and was trying abduct her. He was either on drugs or under orders. Where is she, by the way?"

"Shut your goddamned mouth," the chief said. Panting, he added, "You don't ask . . . questions in my station." He turned on Daniels. "What the hell is he . . . doing here . . . anyway?"

"Sorry chief, but he's a material witness to an assault. In fact, he arrested the assailant."

Daniels immediately rounded on Powers. "But the Chief's right," he snapped, winking so the chief couldn't see him. "We're the ones who do the questioning so just sit your ass down until we're ready to take your statement."

He turned back and leaned close to the chief. Powers overheard some of his whispers. ". . . doc doesn't want you getting excited . . . I'll handle it . . . angina? . . . maybe take a nitro tablet . . . it'll be okay . . . get it all taken care of."

With his hand on the chief's back, Daniels steered him to his office and closed the door. He returned to Powers' side.

Whispering, he said, "Glenda Subczek has her back in the interview room. Glenda's a tough, sharp cop. We call her Glenda the Good, but punks here in Southland call her Gestapo Glenda.

"Anyhow, she's getting the lady calmed down and taking her statement. The lady was pretty upset and she made it clear she didn't want you around."

"Shit!" Powers sighed, "Well, no good deed goes unpunished."

"Boy, ain't that the truth?" Daniels said.

"How about a drink after your shift?"

"I dasn't drink until my suspension is up; the IA guys still could do another little CAT scan on me. But I could go for a shake and a hamburger."

"Health food, hunh? Okay, let's do it." Raising his voice to conversational levels, Powers said "So who's going to take my statement?"

"Oh, hell, you've written maybe a thousand investigative reports. Just go over there to Glenda's desk and draft it on her word processor. I'll look it over for unanswered questions and I'll witness your signature."

# # #

WITNESS STATEMENT

At approximately 1:30 p.m., this date, the undersigned, of 1415 Ransome Street, Apartment 1, Southland, Indiana, observed an eastbound white Chrysler Town and Country van (license number and VIN unknown), execute a U-turn and cross onto and halt upon the north sidewalk in front of 920 Pierce Avenue, Southland.

The driver, an obese white male Subject, approximately 6-2, brown hair, brown eyes, short trimmed beard, emerged from the vehicle and opened its sliding side door. Subject then seized the wrist of Myra (middle name unknown) Windom (street address unknown), believed to be a resident of Southland, and appeared to be dragging her toward the vehicle's sliding doorway. Windom resisted and Subject seized her hair, continuing to pull her toward his vehicle, when the undersigned threw a bag of gardening product at Subject, striking his face.

Subject released Windom and attempted to stab witness with a switchblade knife, was disarmed by same, subjected to citizen arrest and released to the custody of Southland Police Officers Hasselbeck and Pratt who responded to the scene after a witness, Edna Hasselbeck, 920 Pierce, called the 911 police dispatcher.

(signed) Bradley H. Powers

When he read the draft, Daniels said, "Good. That's short and sweet. I want you to insert 'CWO4' and all that crap under your name and reprint it. I think it'll do just fine for the department. Do that and you're free to go. Stay in town, of course. At least this time nobody can sue the department for cruel and unusual punishment."

"Will someone be giving Myra a ride home?"

"Yeah, we'll take care of it."

Powers typed in:

> Chief Warrant Officer 4 (Ret)
> U.S. Army Intelligence and Security

When he handed over the report he said quietly, "Okay, Desk Jockey Daniels, please do me a favor and fill me in on the background check on Bluto. I think there's a lot more to this than meets the eye."

"Okay, you got it, Brad. Now get out of here before the chief comes out here again and has a real heart attack . . . oh, and thank you for your service."

Powers gave a wry chuckle. "Yeah, yeah! Sure. You too, Bozo."

He gave a dejected wave as he left.

℥ ℥ ℥

Chapter 23

Elbows on the speckled Formica countertop at the Blue Willow cafe, Daniels sipped his milkshake and said casually, "Hey, that Myra Windom is one good-looking lady. Great body, too."

"I wouldn't know," Powers lied. "Never seen her without her raincoat or windbreaker." He glanced at Daniels' sardonic smile. "You trying to needle me, Bob?"

"Nope, Pard. I just see an old fart suddenly acting like a love-sick teenager . . . a scar-faced, baggy-eyed, broken-nosed, gray-headed teenager with advanced male pattern baldness."

"Oh, hell, Bob, you've been looking in a mirror . . . but she's a nice lady, or seemed like it."

"A nice, exciting lady, Brad."

"And a very nice lady who seems to have some really serious problems."

"Oh? And you're going to solve them?"

"Maybe. Tell me what you found out about Bluto."

After giving Powers a long jaundiced look, Daniels pulled a small notebook from his uniform shirt pocket.

"Well, Charles Aloysius Forrest, age 28, 6-1, 344 pounds of pure flab, born Detroit, current residence – aside from Cell Six at the jail – is Apartment No. 2, 211 Temple Ave., Southland. He's currently on unemployment, laid off from Purdy Precision Castings.

"Chucky boy has himself a rap sheet: mostly garden-variety drunk and disorderly, fighting, pleaded to one grand theft auto, put on probation, arrested for attempted burglary and two assaults with intent to do great bodily harm, not convicted.

"This low-life has done some jail time, and this Windom escapade could put him away in prison for a while. But all-in-all he's pretty much a bottom-feeder. Based on my contact with him, I'd say he has the mind of an active child of 12."

"Did he say why he did it?"

"No, he's suddenly got one of them match-book school lawyers to represent him, so he's keeping his yap shut."

"He got a lawyer that fast? Who wired that?"

"Good question, Brad. I wasn't in a position to ask, but I'll try to check into it. By the way, you really put young Mr. Forrest in a world of hurt. They say he may need shoulder surgery so he'll probably sue you for damages."

"Screw him. I've got two witnesses who'll testify that he tried to stab me first. So it's a pure case of justified citizen arrest."

"Good," Daniels said. "But where'd you learn all that kung fu stuff? I don't remember it from when we were in the Army.

"Oh, after Rae and I divorced, I took a bunch of outside classes in self-defense."

Daniels grinned. "Woooo! I better keep my Smith and Wesson off safety when I'm around you."

"Bob, it wouldn't do you a bit of good. I'm faster than a speeding bullet."

Daniels grinned. "Okay, wise guy. But can you leap tall buildings in a single bound?"

Powers chuckled. "Nope, but if I take a run at it, I can hop over one of those little decorative plastic garden fences."

Powers asked Daniels to mull over the case again as a veteran investigator.

"Look, Bob, even if Forrest is dumb as a box of rocks why would he risk that big a felony out in the open? Something's screwy. I bet somebody hired him – promised him $10,000 or maybe a year's supply of smack or coke. And I wonder if it's got anything to do with the Purdy case."

"Because of the daughter? And because of his lay-off?" Daniels mused. "I'll keep my ears open, but I can't get involved in it while I'm on suspension."

"Got you," Powers said, giving a sympathetic nod.

Daniels frowned. "Now that you mention the Purdy case, I just remembered something that made my pointy little ears perk up and get all tingly."

"Yeah, what's that?"

Daniels said that minutes after Powers left the station, Myra's husband came charging in, demanding to take her home immediately.

"Well, I told him she was giving a statement to an officer of the law in connection with an official criminal investigation and that he could just sit his butt down and wait a few minutes.

"He started bleating about her right to a court-appointed attorney and I told him she didn't need a goddam lawyer since she wasn't charged with a crime, but that if he wanted to blow a wad of cash for nothing, to be my guest. I told him to place a call over to Dewey, Cheatum and Howe. I said, 'Those bozos'll cheerfully bill you $400 an hour to come over and hold your hand.'

"Well, that calmed him a little. So it wasn't too long before Glenda brings Mrs. Windom out of the conference room. And without so much as Hello, Goodbye or Kiss My Ass, Hubby grabs her by the arm and hustles her out of there. No hug. No kiss. No 'are-you-all-right-darling?' No nothing."

"Well," Powers said, "I do get the impression that it's not what you'd call a very happy marriage."

"So what?" Daniels asked. "Even if my meanest ex was in the station, I'd sure as hell ask if she was okay. If it had been Rae, you would have too."

Powers nodded and then asked what Windom looked like.

"Oh, he's a good-looking dude. Well over six feet. Big hands and wrists and looks lean, like he's in good shape. I'd say he spends a lot of time at the gym and lots of money on his coyfewer."

"His what?"

"His haircuts, dummy. He's got that iron gray Hollywood hair. Perfect, like that George Clooney guy."

Daniels said something else had caught his attention. He said Windom's arrival surprised Officer Subczek.

"Glenda told me afterward she had offered the Missus a ride home and the Missus accepted. But the Missus never made a phone call while giving her statement. And she didn't have a cell phone with her."

"Yeah, so?"

"So how the hell did Windom know his wife was at the police station? Did you call him?"

"Nope. I've never seen or spoken to the guy. I wonder why he was so eager to get her out of there."

"Yeah," Daniels said. "Kind of creepy -- especially since they're both part of that old case. I'm wondering, the way he acted, if Windom fits into this assault somewhere."

"Like I said," Powers responded. "There's more to this than meets the eye."

Chapter 24

The basement steps creaked as he descended them. At the bottom he ducked beneath a nest of cobwebs by the naked light bulb. He wiped at his face. "Why do we have to meet down here? Place gives me the creeps."

She rolled her eyes. "Because, dummy, nobody can see us or overhear us."

"Yeah, okay. So how soon does Herb get here?"

"Should be just a minute. He'll be tighter than a goddamn banjo string, so don't egg him on. I'll do the talking."

"Okay Carlene," he said, "so now what do we do?"

She let out an exasperated breath. "Please, Billy. Let's just wait 'till he gets here. Obviously, we've got to revise the plan."

They looked at each other when they heard the faint slam of a car door. Billy rubbed his hands together and let out a deep breath. "Just relax," she grinned. "I'll get him calmed down and it won't be long before we're out of here, living in the sun."

"God, I hope so. I'm ready."

"Me, too." She reached over and patted his knee, then took his hand in both of hers. "Don't worry, Kiddo. It's going to be okay."

They heard rapid footsteps cross the kitchen floor upstairs. The door to the basement stairway opened and Herb came down the steps in a rush.

Failing to duck, he got a face full of cobwebs. Billy grinned as Herb said, "Awwww, shit!" yanking out a handkerchief to wipe off his face and head.

Billy snickered. "It's not funny," Herb said.

"Sorry. No, it's not funny. Same thing happened to me. Carlene's housekeeper ain't doing her job."

"Okay," Carlene said. "Let's get down to business. Herb, does she suspect anything?"

"No, she just thinks Forrest was trying to mug her. She was real relieved to be home safe."

"Well, we still have a problem."

"What?"

"Well, Herb, like your plan flopped – big time. Forrest didn't follow the directions and wait until she was in the park. So instead of a dead wife you now have a fellow conspirator who got the hell beat out of him and then thrown in jail.

"What's worse," Carlene added, "her little tough-guy savior knows it wasn't a mugging. Lard Ass called and told me the hero is going to be a problem and Forrest will, too. So we need to take care of that. We need to get Forrest out of the pokey and then get them both out of the picture."

Billy opened and closed his meaty fists, "So . . ."

"So . . . first off, Herb, as Billy's former and deeply concerned employer, you need to call the legal beagle and get him bailed out ASAP. Then, Billy, you need to meet him for a beer and, well, you know the rest."

Billy nodded. "Okay. But what about the tough guy?"

"If we just disappear with Myra one day soon, the problem disappears too."

"Dammit, Carlene," Herb said, "I've thought this over again and I've decided I don't want to rush that. There's still almost 400 thou that we can get. That buys an awful big house in Argentina or Brazil."

"Christ, Herb. Do you know how much money we've got stashed already?"

"Not enough, Carlene. You've spent a hell of a lot of our retirement money on stuff that we're just going to have to leave behind in your storeroom. Did you ever think about that?"

"Damn you, Herb! Have you forgotten that we've got three little paintings worth almost $5 million. They're as good as cash in the bank. We just need a few days to get them into the hands of a broker so he can auction them. Don't be greedy about peanuts."

"Greedy! Greedy? Don't you talk to me about greedy, you bitch!"

She grabbed a dusty mason jar and hurled it at him, striking him in the chest with a solid *thunk*. It bounced to the concrete floor and shattered.

Wildom jumped to his feet, fists clenched.

"HEY! Stop it! Both of you!"

They both looked at Billy, surprised.

"I'm not kidding," he said. "When you two start screaming at each other it scares the shit out of me.

"Now, like Carlene said, we're *this* close, so let's please pull together or we'd going to be all the way up Shit Creek without a paddle and not a penny to our names. I've already done some time and I *ain't* gonna do no more! Now settle down!"

Everybody took a deep breath.

"You're right," Carlene said. "So, we've got the Forrest problem scheduled. Let's see what we can find out about this Mr. Brad Powers. Maybe there's some way to cool him down for a bit.

"I'm sorry that I called you a bitch," Herb said.

"No, you're right, Herb. I am a bitch.

"And I intend to be a very rich bitch."

❧ ❧ ❧

Chapter 25

Even though it was after 2 a.m., Powers was wide awake. He snatched the phone in mid-ring.

"Hello!"

She spoke in a whisper, "Brad?"

"Myra, thank God that you called. Listen, I apologize that I upset you . . . "

"Hush, Brad! Just let me talk a minute. *I'm* sorry. So much happened so fast, and then when you said what you said . . . well, there are things you don't know yet. But I'm so, sooooo grateful for the way you rescued me. I was terrified!"

"Well, Lady, you didn't do too badly yourself, the way you broke out of his grip."

"They didn't call me Mean Myra for nothing when I played basketball. But, Brad, I just wanted so say that . . ." she gasped and a male voice snarled, "Enough, you bitch . . ." The connection broke.

"Myra? Myra?" he pleaded, knowing it was useless. Her husband had surprised her and cut off the call. He slammed phone into its charger. "Damn it! Damn it! Damn him!"

In the agony of frustration, he couldn't help picturing the foaming rage Windom would inflict upon Myra. He gave a mirthless laugh. Who could be more brutal or less forgiving than a marathon cheat and control freak imagining that his long-suffering loyal wife dare talk with another man?

With no possibility of sleep, Powers opened the top drawer of his dresser and got out a flat wooden box, battered, oil-stained and scratched. He sat down with it at the table, flipped up the little brass catch and raised the lid. He lifted the 1911 .45 service pistol from the green felt liner.

He ejected the magazine and laid the weapon on a tattered old T-shirt. After checking the chamber, he let the slide forward and rotated the barrel bushing, careful to ease the recoil spring and its plug from beneath the muzzle.

He gave a grim smile. The first time he field-stripped a .45 was in a Quonset hut classroom at Fort Leonard Wood 20-some years earlier. His pistol's spring and plug had arced gracefully across the classroom and bounced off Charlie Reese's shoulder.

Reese cried, "Medic! Medic!" and the whole class cracked up. So did the instructor, a hard-ass platoon sergeant. And as he laughed, he ordered Powers to drop and give him 30 of his best push-ups.

Field stripping the pistol now was a comforting, mechanical process requiring no thought. His fingers automatically extracted the slide stop, pulled the slide off its rails and reached for the barrel.

As he worked, he mused about the intensity of his rage over what happened . . . the deep feeling of loss.

Maybe Gwyn's right that I'm not a loner but just alone. But for a month I haven't felt alone. I've had a companion. I don't want to lose that. I don't want to lose her. Don't want to be alone, I guess.

As Powers fretted about Myra and he half-consciously began to formulate an investigation.

After a bit, he muttered, "Okay, you bastard. This is war. I'm coming after you, man. I'm going to track down every damn thing about you. Evvvverything."

# # #

Trying to calm himself, Powers paced, first thinking about Rae's Garden and what to do about the slugs.

Calmed, he mentally reviewed his conversation with Daniels. He remembered Daniels saying Windom was the CEO of a small plant that produced steel castings for the defense industry.

Daniels believed Myra's father founded the operation and that Windom, then a vice president, took over management after the father's murder. Daniels had heard the company laid off some workers sometime in the past year, but that wasn't front page news. Every company seemed to be doing the same.

Powers reassembled the pistol, lowered it back into its felt-lined nest and returned it to the dresser. Relaxed now, but knowing he'd be unable to sleep, he brewed coffee and began listing places to go, people to see and items to check on the internet.

He finished his list and a series of spin-off questions as dawn became visible through the basement windows, slowly lighting the yew hedge between the driveway and the neighboring driveway. He could make out little shapes – birds -- beginning to flit among the branches.

Powers threw cracked corn out on the drive for the birds and fixed oatmeal for his breakfast.

He got out his lone business suit. After showering and shaving, he donned the same blue oxford cloth shirt Myra wore after her cloudburst soaking. As he buttoned it, he inhaled her scent which still clung to it. He selected an understated tie and, as usual, had a hard time buttoning the top button.

Chapter 26

Tops on his list was a simple drive-by at the factory. He saw that the company grounds lay along the south bank of the river. An old residential neighborhood lay snugged to the opposite side of the street which edged the property. Powers guessed employees built their homes adjoining the plant back before zoning laws existed.

The main production building was a two-story brick structure with east-facing saw-tooth roof windows, showing it to date from World War I. Some of the factory's stubby stacks looked rusted through.

A half-block 3-story brick office building, thick with ivy, adjoined the chain-link gate to the company grounds. Its front double doors were sagging open on their hinges beneath a concrete lintel bearing an elaborate Old English engraving, *Burgess Castings Ltd.* Many street-side first and second-story windows were broken. Chest-high thistles and 20-foot sumacs choked the narrow verge between the building and the rusty chain link perimeter fence.

A more modern but stained wooden sign, *Purdy Precision Steel Castings*, surmounted the gate in the chain-link fence. The rails of the spur running through the plant gate were rust red.

Place has seen better days. Not much maintenance budget. He turned the car to head downtown

He spent the rest of his morning hunting for information, first at the Chamber of Commerce, next to the office of Manufacturer's and Employer's Association, then the local AFL-CIO Hall, the Community Foundation, the offices of the Community Chest. Early in the afternoon, he visited the Junior Achievement director. He also paid a visit to the morgue of *The South County Daily Post,* now a tri-weekly that no longer published each day and either didn't want to admit it or hoped for better times.

Finally, he went to Southland's library and spent the afternoon skimming intensely boring on-line material about recent trends in light manufacturing. In the end, several items turned out to be interesting.

# # #

Light-headed after a sleepless night and long day, Powers drove to the local supermarket and found a special on frozen dinners. He was nearing the cash-out lanes when he spotted Myra and two young women walking in from the parking lot. The twins were tall, blondish copies of their mom, though without her strong face.

He caught Myra's eye and then rolled his eyes toward Gardening. She winked.

Ten minutes later she found him pretending to read directions on weed killers. He turned anxious eyes on her.

"I've only got a minute," she said. "The girls think I've gone to the john."

"Did he hurt you?"

She closed her eyes and shook her head quickly.

"He yanked my arm and bruised it, but that's all. He bellowed and stormed and threatened me. Accused me of sleeping around . . . that's a laugh and a half. I haven't had . . . well, never mind.

"His shouting woke up the girls and really scared them, so I'm spending time with them to reassure them. But I won't be doing any speed walking for a while."

"I'll miss you badly, but I'm glad," Powers said. "You shouldn't be outside alone until this is cleared up. But is there somewhere we can meet, say for an hour or so? I've been nosing around and have some information and maybe you can help me clarify it."

She frowned. "Information? About what?"

"I'm an investigator, remember? And remember when I asked if something seemed odd about that attack?"

She nodded warily.

"Myra, that was no mugging."

"What? Why do you say that?"

"Myra, muggers usually are cowards and sneak thieves. They lurk and then make a dash for purses or wallets. This character had something else entirely in mind . . . he was after Myra Windom -- the person, not the purse. In fact there was no purse, right?"

"Right. But what are you getting at, Brad?"

He told her of meeting with Daniels, how Daniels had him relate again what happened, step-by-step. Daniels repeatedly questioned Powers about the assailant's act in opening the van's sliding door. No, it didn't pop open when the van bumped over the curb. Yes, the assailant got out of the driver's seat. Yes, he first turned to the slider door and deliberately yanked its handle toward to the rear, so that it slid open. Yes, and only then did he grab for Myra.

"Afterwards Daniels said he agreed with me that it seemed like an attempted abduction rather than a mugging."

"Good Lord," she said.

"Here's what's grim," Powers said, voice low and fixing his eyes on hers. "Daniels asked me, 'What did Bluto plan to do once he got Myra inside the van?' He said, 'She's a strong, healthy woman who wasn't going to just sit there and let him drive away with her. He had to silence her or incapacitate her some way . . . and the only thing he had to silence her was that knife.'"

Myra turned pale. "My God!"

"See my concern, Myra? My gut tells me this was planned – either abduction or killing -- something that somebody planted in Bluto's tiny brain. Aside from that, I've come across some things that you and I should talk about."

"What things? This is already scary enough," she said.

"Yes, it is. But we don't have time to discuss it now and we really don't know yet exactly what's going on."

"You're right. I've got to go." She bit her lip. "I'll try to call or text you this evening."

"No," Powers said. "Don't do anything like that from home. Not where anyone can see or overhear you. That means the girls, too. You don't want to put them in the position of having to choose between Mom and Dad. Myra, above all, please, please be careful. I don't want anything to happen to you. I'm not trying to stake any claim. I have no right to. But I meant exactly what I said in the car."

"You do? Seriously?"

He nodded. "I'm damned serious. Granddaddy always told me there's no fool like an old fool, so maybe I'm an old fool. But no matter what you may think about me, I want you to know I'm like a singed cat -- better than I look.

"No argument there, Brad."

"Well, the point is that you've got a defender if you need him. Think of me as your gimpy old semi-retired knight – the armor is dented and has some surface rust, but the lance is still sharp. So is the sword."

She gripped his hand and her eyes reddened. As she left, she said "Brad, you're one of the few good things in my life."

Chapter 27

Powers awoke the next morning needing coffee badly because nightmares made his sleep fitful.

His nighttime horrors generally related to Desert Storm. The Storm Mare, as he entitled it, was a repeater: an RPG flying past his face with time so slow that he could make out its Cyrillic lettering from some Soviet ordnance plant. "But I'm not a tank," he cracked to his buddies. Then he felt his grin disappear as he caught sight of the follow-on shot, the one that cratered the abutment.

The brilliant flash, then nothing. He came to, seeing the world through a red wash; his wounded buddies, two of them, tossing in agony, coated with concrete dust through which blood began to pulse. He knew they were screaming, but he couldn't hear. He tried to reach for them, but his hands wouldn't work.

He started the coffee and, as it brewed, lathered with cup and brush. *Real soap, not half air like that canned crap.*

As he angled his head to shave, the light gleamed on his scars. They reminded him of watching with one eye as the medic plucked steel shards and concrete chips from his biceps and forearms, then the betadine sting . . . nothing compared to the furnace roaring in his leg.

He doused the memory in an extra hot shower, afterwards sipping his first cup of coffee. He raised his cup to his son's photo. *Here's to you, Sarge. Take care.*

After a second cup, Powers phoned Daniels at the station and asked for a meeting.

"Yeah, okay, honey," Daniels said with unwonted cheerfulness. "I don't get off 'til 3, so we can drive over . . ." His voice became muffled as his hand covered the mouthpiece. "For Christ's sake, Chief, this is my daughter! She's in town and I haven't seen her since Christmas!"

After a pause. Daniels asked, "Honey, are you still there?"

"Yes, Father Dear," Powers replied, doing his best to perform a falsetto voice.

"Okay, sweetheart, why don't you come to the apartment and we can go from there? Maybe go out and get some din-din. Love and kisses. Got to get busy 'cause this paperwork never lets up."

"Daddy," Powers said, "you're making me gag. Oh, and by the way, Daddy, as an actor, you'd make a great plumber."

Chapter 28

Powers drove back past Purdy Precision Steel Castings. He turned into the neighborhood two blocks past the gate, pulling to the curb in front of a lawn where a tall, wiry black man was vigorously pushing an old-fashioned reel mower.

Powers walked onto the yard. The man, wearing a red and gold USMC T-shirt, stopped and came to meet him. Powers said, "I haven't seen one of those mowers since I cut my granddaddy's lawn about 35 summers ago. Must have been in junior high. It sure looks in great shape."

"It is, Mister. Now I warn you, I ain't buying nothing."

"Well, I ain't selling," Powers smiled, extending his hand. "Name of Jenkins. I'm a field agent with the State Environment Protection Commission. I wanted to ask whether you're ever troubled by pollution from the Purdy plant."

The man shook hands and said, "I'm Charles Wilson Jefferson. You puttin' me in some report?"

"Naaah! This is just a walk-around," Powers said. "Might never be a real report."

"Welllll," Jefferson rubbed his mouth, "if you'd been here five years ago, I probably would have griped some, because we did get fly-ash drifting out of the stacks. Really pits the paint job on your car. But they're running so slow at the plant now, don't nobody take much notice.

"Now 25 years ago," he added, "it was lots worse than that, but I wouldn't have said nothing then because I worked at Purdy. Wouldn't want to lose my job."

"Would they have fired you for talking to us?"

"Oh, hell no! Chet Purdy was a fine man and he didn't play that way nohow. No, I woulda been worried what some brand-new air pollution gizmo would cost in jobs. I swear, ever' new regulation you busybodies pass means folk be getting laid off."

"Well, Mr. Jefferson, it's for the public good."

"Yeah, well, Mr. Jenkins, I ain't got much good if I can't make a living, now do I?"

"Mmmmm, you've got a point," Powers said.

"Damn right, man."

Jefferson said Purdy rescued the company in 1970 when it was almost on the rocks.

"Back then we sometimes had to wait a day or two to cash our paychecks. Well, Purdy come in and bought the company which was only a grayiron foundry – you know, cast iron things like engine blocks. Burgess Castings, it was called. He fired all them jackasses. Then he sunk a bunch of money into it and put her back on her feet."

He said the firm spent nearly four years changing over from cast iron products like manhole covers and fire hydrants to small precision steel castings – drive wheels, shaft mounts and the like.

"It really got the place to humming," Jefferson said. "But then he got killed and his dumb-dumb son-in-law took over. Herby Windom might be a Wharton grad-you-ate, but he's an educated fool. Don't know shit from shinola about this business. Company's just been dying little by little ever since. Had a big lay-off three-four months ago and I hear they's another one coming.

"So Windom isn't a castings man?"

"Mister, onliest thang he knows is chasing pussy. The company started slipping when Mrs. Purdy died. Long, long bout with cancer. It really wracked up old Chet, and then his daughter run off. Big tall gal. Real nice kid. Did some nurse work in the plant. But after her momma died they said she just seemed to go a little crazy. Maybe got into drugs and I don't know what all."

"Was she a hippy or something?"

"No. See, after Purdy lost his wife, he done a damn fool thang. He started sticking his dick in the pencil sharpener."

Powers exploded with a laugh, "He *what?*"

"Chet started humping his secretary . . . maybe even while his wife was so sick. Well, she couldn't have been a day older than his own daughter, and he ended up marrying the bitch. And I do mean bitch. I've had to work for her."

Powers looked puzzled. "I don't get you."

"Well, when I retired say 'bout five years ago," Jefferson said, "Windom axed me to stay on part time as kind of a night watchman and janitor. But, about the onliest work I was doing for a year was renovating the first floor on the far side of that old headquarters building which was pretty much abandoned. Built kind of an indoor warehouse – it's about 4,500 square feet -- for all the shit that woman totes here from all over the world."

"You're kidding!"

"I am not, Mr. Jenkins. She's got paintings from Europe, some real beautiful furniture – stuff made of teak and heavy as hell – from the Philippines and Thailand places like that. And it's climate controlled – it's got dehumidifiers; air conditioners for the summer and furnace for the winter. All covered with real heavy plastic drop cloths. The best locks on the doors that you can get. You'd think she'd want them paintings out where she could see 'em. But she seems to me to be some kind of a pack rat, you know what I'm saying?"

"A hoarder?"

"That's the word."

"Damn," Powers said. "Seems like a hell of a waste."

"Telling me, man. I even had to expand and rebuild a bathroom for her effing majesty – she called it a powder room. Pink stool and sink and tub – tile floor, too. And a little kitchen nook with a microwave.

"That's when I found out she could be just as mean as a snake. Everthang had to be just so or she'd turn into a devil. That pretty face would just start to crinkling into something like you'd see at the bottom of a goddamned dumpster. Now, of course, the rest of the building is all rotted to hell and about to fall down, but they don't give a shit . . ."

Jefferson stopped speaking and stared at Powers.

"Mister, how's come we be talking about all this?"

"Beats the hell out of me, Mr. Jefferson. I always like a good yarn, but I'm mainly concerned about residential pollution complaints. You know anybody else around here that I should talk to?"

Jefferson swept his arm in a grand gesture around the factory's little neighborhood. "Don't much matter. You're going to hear pretty much the same thing from everbody."

"Well, much obliged." Powers turned back toward the car, but then stopped. "Say, before I go, where did you get that mower?"

Jefferson chuckled with pride. "Bought it at a garage sale for five bucks. I'm an old mechanic, so I tore it all down and rebuilt it. Had to put in one new bearing, and I keep it oiled and sharpened and it keeps my old joints exercised."

"Is that the original paint job?"

"Yeah, mostly. I had to do some touch-up."

As Powers walked to his car, he turned. "You know, Mr. Jefferson, you ought to get it appraised as an antique. Probably be worth something someday."

"You think I could put it on Ebay or something? Maybe I'll get me appraised too."

Chapter 29

Powers stopped at four other homes in the neighborhood. Nobody answered the doorbell at the first residence. Two old men said they wouldn't speak with another damned salesman and ordered him to leave their front porches before they called the cops.

At the fourth house, a stooped old lady, a secretary retired from Purdy, invited Powers in for coffee.

Miss Wilhelmina Medlin said that disgust nearly made her take early retirement from Purdy Castings.

She said it had become obvious to her back then that a new secretary, Carlene Mouton, was having an affair with the boss. She said once the woman won Chet Purdy's favor, she virtually stopped working and was hinting to co-workers that they'd best do her typing and filing while she talked on the phone and worked on her nails.

"Carlene was what the men used to call a bombshell," Mrs. Medlin said. "She had absolutely lovely features. But she was coarse and cheap, too. And, it wasn't just some silly secretarial fling."

She sipped from a delicate flowered cup.

"I think I remember that Carlene was only 19 when she got the affair started. She was no starry-eyed, giddy girl, but a hard, calculating little slut."

Powers blinked at that description.

"I'm serious," Miss Medline's lips quivered in indignation. "All of us dressed very tastefully . . . we wanted to build up that company, not play games. That is, all of us but Carlene. She was practically falling out of those scoop-neck get-ups that she wore every single day and I swear her skirts looked painted on. Certainly didn't leave a lot to the imagination. It seemed to me sometimes like she was ready to get up on her desk and do a strip tease right there in the outer office.

"And in the end," Miss Medlin said, "she got exactly what she was after – life on Easy Street with the boss."

Mrs. Medlin said that ever since her husband's death, the Widow Purdy seemed to buy new sports cars every year and to travel a great deal. "I hear she's always out of town on cruises or trips to places like Bermuda or Puerto Rico or Guadeloupe or Paris. She's nothing at all like Chet's first wife . . . not one bit."

She sipped again and dabbed her old eyes.

"Ginger Purdy -- now there was a real lady, Mr. Jenkins. At first, back in the 70s, while Chet was getting the company on its feet, Ginger worked right in the steno pool with us.

"And let me tell you, mister, she was a crackerjack. And even though she supervised, she never needed a cross word that I ever heard. Never told anybody to do something she wouldn't do or couldn't do better. Her daughter, a lovely girl, too; worked in the first aid station in the plant and was good at it. The foundry guys always were getting minor burns and cuts and Myrna was real efficient at treating them. She was a sweet girl . . . and that's another tragedy."

"What do you mean?"

"Well, supposedly Herb Windom saved Myra after she ran away. We heard that he found her somewhere out in one of those communes on the West Coast.

"Well, he married her and then brought her home. They did sort of a reverse elopement, you might say. That was just about a year before her daddy was killed.

"But I can't believe it's been much of a life for her. Being married to Herb," she leaned forward and whispered, eyes glittering, ". . . well, let's just say that he's a handsome devil, a real charmer and being a husband and a father never stopped him from trolling that secretarial pool.

"And before I left, I heard he even was taking up with George Purdy's young widow."

"Wow!" Powers said, "Well, after her loss maybe she was just reaching out for comfort."

"Reaching out, yes," Miss Medlin said in acid-dripping tones. "But loss, my foot. I'll just say this much, and my girlfriends agree: she didn't have the decency to even pretend to cry during Chet's funeral.

"Mr. Jenkins, I grant you . . ." Miss Medlin frowned and her eyes narrowed, ". . . that at the funeral, her bosom certainly was heaving.

But she definitely was *not* mourning. She had herself on exhibit . . . in a black scoop neck dress instead of a red one

"And that young policeman who escorted her at the funeral was practically snorting and pawing the dirt."

Chapter 30

Just as Powers pulled into the single-lane driveway at Daniels' apartment, a short figure bustled out the side door directly into his path, waving an apron and losing one of her flip-flops.

"Senor Powers! Senor Powers! Please . . ." she paused to hop on one foot as she slipped the fugitive sandal back on the other, ". . . please not to park yet! I must get out my car to go to the chop."

"What are you chopping for, Rosa?"

She laughed, running her hands over her midnight hair. "Oh, you crazy loco gringo. I go to the *store*! I must chop for Senor Daniels."

She zipped back into the house as Powers backed out and parallel parked. Grinning, he stood beside the driveway curb cut. Rosa Hinojosa owned three rental properties and Daniels and Powers were among her tenants. She was short, energetic, smart as a whip, pretty, slightly pudgy and very bossy – a tendency she cheerfully leavened with flashing eyes and a snowy wrap-around smile in which one gold canine glinted.

Daniels rented the second-floor apartment in her home.

As she backed her car level with him, Rosa stopped and said, "I told you so many times you please say my name 'Rossa' not 'Roza.' Okay? And my last name, Senor Brad? How do you say it?"

"Let's see. I forget. Oh, si, si! It is 'High-no-johza,' right?"

"No! No!" she rolled her eyes and laughed delightedly. "So terrible! You please say it right, please: 'Ee-no-hassa'!"

He held up his palms in a surrender gesture. "I'm so sorry, Senora. But why are you buying food for Bob? He can buy his own."

"Oh, but Senor Roberto, he is so skinny. He does not eat enough. So I fix a good Mexican dinner for him tonight."

"So, you actually know how to cook Mexican food, like tacos and such?"

She glared at him and answered in firecracker Spanish, then gave her smile. "You eat with Roberto tonight? I cook for you, too? Tonight we have poblano rellenos."

"Wonderful! Muchas gracias! Does that mean you're going to raise my rent?"

She laughed and drove off. Powers walked up the drive. Using the pain-free right leg to mount each step, he climbed the outside stairs to rap on Daniels' door.

"Come on in, you gimpy old bastard. What took you so long?" Daniels, seated in a recliner, pointed for Powers to take the threadbare wingback chair.

"I was just chatting with your girlfriend, Bob."

"Ooooo, don't you start that stuff, Brad! I've screwed up my life three times with women. Not gonna do it again."

"Now was that your wives' fault or your fault? What the hell, man? Rosa's a sweet lady."

"You're right, my friend. She's sweet . . . and she has a whim of carbon steel. But we're here to talk about your girlfriend, not a lady that wants to be my girlfriend. So what have you found?"

"Who said I've been looking around?"

"You look whipped and excited at the same time. So that tells me you've come across something. So why don't you sum up?"

"Well, not much that's concrete." Powers said business and labor people gave him the sense that Purdy Precision Steel Castings was in quicksand. It was losing clients and sales force because new carbon fiber technology was outmoding some steel products that Purdy introduced in the 70s. Yet management seemed indifferent. It seemed to have no strategy or long-range plans. No commitments to any community outreach and no community involvement at all. Employee morale supposedly in the tank.

"Annnnnd," Powers added, "the boss supposedly has a case of chronic satyriasis. All his screwing around with the ladies in the office reportedly is breeding a big civil rights action by the state."

"So what?" Daniels said. "You haven't mentioned a single criminal act except possibly sexual harassment. It may be criminally stupid to run a business into the ground, but it ain't against the law."

"But, Bob, you've got to admit it's a funny pattern," Powers said. "And I've still got this feeling there's some connection between the company's problems and cheap muscle attempting to abduct the founder's daughter who happens to own the majority of the stock."

"Well, Brad, you can't make an arrest on a feeling or take a feeling to trial. And don't forget that she's also the boss's wife. She could be part of the problem."

"Hey!"

"Hey, yourself," Daniels snapped. "You're starting to investigate something in which you have an obvious personal interest. That's poison. You need to step back or, better yet, back all the way out of it."

Powers rubbed his head in frustration. "Yeah, Bob, you're probably right."

"Okay. Just so you keep it in mind. Now," he grinned, "how do you plan to take it from here? I think you need to follow the buck, see where the money is . . . and figure out who's after the money."

"Well, there's one other thing, Bob. Herb Windom apparently has been doing the bump for a long time now with Purdy's widow."

"Holy shit! Are you sure? The bastard must take goat gland extract. He's already laying everything but the Atlantic Cable and then he's doing her, too? He must be some kind of sexaholic."

"Can't prove it, Bob, but you get the same innuendo right across the board here in town . . . chamber, the labor boys, you name it. Apparently it's a relationship of long standing and they don't bother to be very discreet. Which makes me want to ask whether you've had a chance to look at the file on Chet Purdy's murder."

"I haven't yet. I'm still trying to keep the damn department current on paperwork."

As the pair started bouncing theories off each other, Rosa drove into the driveway. After an hour shooting holes in each other's ideas, Powers stood up to stretch. "Man, what is that smell?"

"Oh, that's Rosa grilling her peppers for dinner."

"Wow. You are one lucky son-of-a-bitch."

"Well, you're having dinner with us, so you're lucky too."

Rosa called to them from half-way up the stairs. "You hombres come down to dinner, now, no?"

"We come, yes!" Daniels boosted himself out of the recliner.

After they descended the stairway to the driveway, Powers opened the side door for Rosa. As she entered, she asked, "So what you are talking about so much?"

"Oh, Herb Windom."

Rosa stopped dead. She turned to them, eyes squinted and face set in a bronze mask. "I hope you shoot him! And his puta! They are filth!"

Daniels and Powers met each other's eyes.

Chapter 31

"Puta?" Powers asked. "Isn't that Spanish for 'whore'?"

"Yes!" Rosa said. "Exactamente! I mean Windom's whore."

"Who?" Powers asked, voice rising in alarm.

"Whoa, wait a minute, Brad," Daniels said. "Rosa," he went on, "there are two Purdy women. One is a very tall lady with dark hair and is married to Mr. Windom. The other is the blond widow of Mrs. Windom's father, Chet Purdy."

"Si! Yes! I speak of that widow -- Carlita, Carla, something like that. The widow. She is la rubia, a blonde, and . . ." she made push-up motions with her hands in front of her chest . . . "and is always showing too much of her tits."

"Whew!" Powers said, puffing out his cheeks in relief. "I thought you meant Myra."

Daniels gave a quick flash of amusement and turned back to Rosa. "Why do you call Windom and Carlene 'filth'?"

"Because Carla, Carlene, whatever, hired my daughter, Luisa, two, three years ago to clean . . . so she could earn money for college, you know?"

"Yes? So?"

Rosa explained that Windom came to the house almost every afternoon to drink with Carlene and, Luisa believed, often to share her bed.

On many occasions, the pair argued furiously – usually about money, with Carlene sometimes throwing things at Windom: a shot glass, a TV remote, a bedroom table lamp.

Once, Carlene bragged to Luisa that she had known "that high and mighty" Windom when he was a just a dirt-poor punk in the projects in "Feely."

Powers quirked an eyebrow at Daniels.

Rosa said Luisa one day groused about changing the soiled sheets on Carlene's king-sized bed so often and Carlene luridly suggested that Luisa might like to help soil them.

Rosa explained that, at first, Luisa wasn't quite sure she had heard Carlene correctly, but the next day erased any doubts.

Windom came to the house and, with Carlene's encouragement, tried to entice Luisa to join him and Carlene in sex. With Carlene looking on and smirking, he pinched Luisa's bottom, tried to fondle her breasts and tried to kiss her.

"My Luisa, she is very frightened," Rosa said, "but she is also very smart woman. She pretends to be interested but says she cannot make love because of her period . . . they must wait two days. So Windom and his puta go together to the bedroom and Luisa leaves the house and must walk home."

Tears rolled down Rosa's cheeks.

"My poor little Luisa. It was very cold and very snowing that day and because she's afraid to ask them for a ride, she walked all the way right to here, almost 13 kilomet – maybe eight miles. She cried for hours when she get home. Sometimes I wonder if he raped her but she was too afraid to tell."

Rosa's face contorted. "He is a beast. If my Phillipe still lived he would . . . you know castracion? He would be castrato . . . make noises like a girl."

"I think we get your point, Rosa," Daniels said. "Now, Rosa, this is important. You said Carlene told Luisa that she knew Windom when she was young? You remember that?"

"Oh, yes. She said that."

"And where? You said 'Feely'?"

"That big city . . . Philadelphia."

"Interesting," Daniels said to Powers.

"Damned interesting."

"Rosa," Daniels said, "if you get the chance the next time you see Luisa, see if you can find out whether Windom actually did assault her. I think we could make the bastard pay for it."

ᦉ ᦉ ᦉ

Chapter 32

Rosa's stuffed peppers were moderately spicy and very flavorful. She tried to talk with them during the meal, but Daniels and Powers ate in virtual silence, each trying to fit her revelations to the case.

After dinner, they scandalized their hostess by clearing the table. She tried to block them as they carried dishes to the kitchen, so they began lateralling plates and silverware to each other and then forward passing napkins over her outstretched hands.

She still was yelling and Powers laughing when Daniels brought things back to earth. He asked whether either Herb Windom or Carlene had bothered Luisa after she quit.

"Oh, yes, that puta, she called two or three days later very angry because Luisa did not come back for cleaning. Luisa listens for about two minutes and then said she would never go in the house again. She is finish!

"Then the Senor Windom sees her in the store one day and scared her bad. He said she better keep her mouth shut or he would make big trouble for her. When I hear about this, I want to call the policeia but Luisa just wants to forget it all."

"Where is Luisa now?" Powers asked.

Rosa flashed a proud smile. "She is at St. Mary's College near that Notre Dame. I think she is safe."

"And your other daughter?"

"'Yes, Julia, the older."

"And where is her school?" Powers asked.

"She studies for the computer science at Indiana University."

# # #

After dinner, Powers and Daniels returned to the upstairs apartment. Daniels tried to capsulize what they knew so far.

"We've got no real evidence of anything, but a lot of funny relationships.

"Herb and Carlene apparently know each other long before he first comes to town.

"So maybe Windom hires on at Purdy as a controller or vice president and somewhere along the line in there he gets Carlene on board and they target Chet Purdy. Or maybe she just sets her sights on Chet, a man who's heartsick, unhappy and lonely because his wife is dying of cancer. So, is this something Herb researched and then pushed?

"Oh . . . and was Windom the vice president for marketing? Operations? Finance? Anyway, Myra runs off – maybe because her mother died, maybe because Chet married Carlene. Maybe just because. Not clear on the timing.

"So Herb plays the hero. He goes off and manages to find her, maybe seduces her (Powers shifted uncomfortably in his chair) and then elopes with her. Then a year later, give or take, Chet is murdered, and Windom steps into his job – and into the widow's bed, too."

"If he wasn't there already."

"Right," Daniels said.

"These aren't just coincidences, Bob. They're facts and I think they show some real connections."

"Yeah, maybe. Maybe not. Let's assume Windom killed Purdy to wind up in his job. That's still no connection with Forrest or his attempt on Myra."

"Except that Windom might want to get rid of his wife," Powers said, "so then he'd be the majority owner."

"I don't think that tracks, Brad. Why would he want sole control of a company that he seems to be driving into the ground? There's no real evidence of anything illegal now. There is just a scent or several scents to start following. The point is, we just don't know enough yet."

"It sounds like I'd better try to find out about Herb Windom's financials," Powers said.

"Oh really! Without a court order?"

"Well, you've got Myra's social security number, right?"

"Yeah. So what?"

"Well, you can develop a lot of information with the spouse's number – including the husband's. And plus that, I've got an army friend who owes me a big, biiiiig favor. He works in the Chicago field office of the Intelligence Corps."

"Brad, I'm still a cop. Don't say another word about that."

Powers gave Daniels a grin. "Don't say another word about what?"

"Just be damned careful," Daniels said sourly.

Chapter 33

Powers started the day obtaining a reciprocal Indiana permit for his State of Kansas concealed weapon permit.

Then he placed a call for Special Agent Revis Ramsey at the Chicago Field Office of Army Counterintelligence. It turned out the Army had reassigned Ramsey as the special agent in charge of its Champaign Resident Office. When he got Ramsey on the line, Powers said, "Hey, Beavis, how's Butthead?"

"Dammit, Brad, ain't you ever going to drop that? My name is pronounced 'REV-iss' not 'REEV-iss'."

"I know," Powers said, "but I just love to hear you bitch. And by the time I get off the line, I bet you'll really be bitching."

"Oh Lord! What's up?"

"Well, do you recall back at Oberammergau when I covered for you concerning a certain indiscretion you committed with Colonel Snagglepuss's Bavarian cream puff?"

"Shit, I knew you'd bring that up one day," Ramsey said. "You looked so damned smug about it, and you never did tell me how you headed the old man off."

"It was easy, buddy. I just told him he sure as hell wouldn't want Mrs. Snagglepuss to see the telephoto 8X10s I had of him with Big Bertha. The good colonel just about blew a gasket. Made all kinds of threats, but I didn't care 'cause I was two weeks from discharge.

"Anyway, I asked him whether his wife would like to see a photo of Bertha taking a wild ride on his baloney pony. He caught on real quick."

"So you had pictures of them rolling in the hay."

"No. But he didn't know that."

It took a full minute for Ramsey to quit laughing. "Okay," he said, still chuckling, "what's this going to cost me?"

"Well, I've been saving it for a special occasion and this is it." He told Ramsey he wanted all the background information that he could get, including finances, on a Southland industrialist named Herbert M. Windom and a life-long liaison named Carlene Moulton Purdy, Social Security numbers to follow.

"Okay, Brad, and what's the Army's security interest in this?"

"His company maybe does some defense work."

"Maybe?" Ramsey exploded. "You want me to break every law in the books, don't you? I could end up in Leavenworth for life and one dark night."

"Damn, Revis, he was right."

"Who was right?"

"The guy who said gratitude is the most fragile emotion."

"Dammit, Brad, this could be serious trouble for me. These people are civilians, for God's sake!"

"Please, Revis, quit your pissing and moaning. It wouldn't be the first time, and you're a first sergeant now with more contacts in the Army than the fucking president. Just do it behind the scenes."

"Yeah, but . . ."

"Look, I bet you can even call in a favor or two with some of your boys who graduated to the FBI.

"For what it's worth, I think there's a valid federal criminal case and it may even have a tax evasion component. And, man, I saved your ass! Snagglepuss would have assigned you to a mess kit repair battalion on Diego Garcia for the rest of your miserable life."

Once Ramsey calmed down, it took five minutes to explain the issue and the connections in the case.

"Okay, Dude," Ramsey said. "But none of this goes by email. It's all unofficial off-computer typewritten snail mail in a plain brown envelope. And no copies on this end."

"Makes sense to me, Bevis."

∾ ∾ ∾

Chapter 34

Once off the phone, Powers drove to the laundromat. As he used up his quarters and folded his clothes, he mused about Myra. The more he thought about her, the more uneasy he became. He could see no reason for the attack other than to abduct or kill her.

On the way home, he stopped for lunch at a Greek restaurant which previously caught his eye. Once indoors, however, Powers was abashed to find it an upscale establishment . . . a place frequented by lawyers, judges and business executives. His jeans and T-shirt made him feel conspicuously underdressed.

In cool tones, the hostess at the front desk said, "A table, sir?" She was formal in an elegant white blouse, black ribbon around her neck and black skirt with black hair and big black eyes to match.

"I'm sorry but I guess not," Powers said, "I'm new in town and I didn't realize how posh this establishment is. I'd better come back another time."

"Posh." she said with a big smile. "What a nice word. We thank you. But please, don't leave. We don't want any new customer to leave without tasting our cuisine. Perhaps you would feel more comfortable in the bar -- it's much more casual."

"Why, thank you. I'll try that." He grinned, raised his hands and said "Opahh! You have solved my problem."

She beamed. "Opahh, indeed, sir. You like Greek food?"

"I love it. I've enjoyed many meals in both Corinth and Athens."

"Oh, wonderful," she said. "Our head chef is from Athens."

"Excellent," he said. "You have made my day."

He took a seat at the bar. The hanging soft-white lights did little to brighten the dim room. The bartender, who didn't look old enough to drink, reacted with ill-concealed amazement to Powers' order for ice water. He seemed slightly mollified when Powers also ordered a Greek village salad

Half way through his salad, Powers felt a sharp attack of déjà vu -- a fingernail tracing gently across his back, shoulder to shoulder.

It was Carlene again.

"No man with such broad shoulders should have lunch without a real drink," she said. She held out her hand. "And I'm sorry you left before we had time to get better acquainted."

Her hair was up in a long ponytail this time, and she was in a business suit – and this time a gold pendant lay in the deep valley between her breasts.

"What will you have, Brad?" she said, smiling and giving him a bold stare.

Powers swallowed with something of a gulp and said, "Thank you, but it's way, way too early in the day for me."

"Oh, my," she said with a pout while batting her eyes. "Well, you can't have a Greek lunch without at least drinking an Elliniko café." She looked at the bartender. "Don't you agree, Antonio?"

Antonio's eyes brightened. "Yes indeed, Ma'am. Elliniko coffee for the gentleman. And what will you have?"

Powers studied her more closely as she ordered. "Vodka tonic. Grey Goose, of course. And put a shot of cognac in his coffee."

"Of course," Antonio said. "Right away." He fixed her drink with a flourish, placed it on a napkin before her, and headed back toward the kitchen for the coffee.

"We didn't take the time to talk before," she said, smirking. "Aren't you new to Southland? It's a very small town, but I didn't recognize you. But then I'd just come back from The Continent."

"How wonderful for you," Powers said. "I'm here to settle my wife's estate."

"Ohhhh, that's right. You said she died," she said, her voice expressionless. After a pause she added, "You're built like an ox. Are you sure you couldn't be a pinch-hitter?"

"Sorry to disappoint you, Carlene," he said, closely examining her facial skin, suspecting he discerned faint face-lift scars. "Never had much time for sports until I was in the Army. I played some football and was a pretty good right guard, but it was just intermural stuff between battalions."

"But I must say, Brad, you do have the athlete's physique. I recognize it." She gave a throaty laugh and delivered the twist again.

"Well, I never played baseball."

"Your loss." No pout this time. "But like I said, it *is* a small town. Maybe I'll see you again. Enjoy your coffee."

She turned abruptly and marched with her drink toward the dining room. He followed her with his eyes. Her waist was narrow and her very tight skirt showed hips with a runner's concave indentations. Her calves looked hard as rocks. *Whooeee, is she in shape! And even sexier when she's wearing clothes.*

Antonio arrived with Powers' coffee. "Oh, darn! She left?" Antonio seemed to be a worshipper. Powers told Antonio to skip the cognac. Powers sipped, finding the coffee ultra-strong.

"Quite a babe, isn't she?" he said. "But I think I'm too old to interest her."

"Too bad," Antonio said. "She's a widow, you know." Then he leaned close and whispered. "I'm not supposed to talk about customers, but man isn't she hot? And I hear she's rich, too."

"No kidding?"

"Yeah, she's got real expensive taste. Whenever she comes in for a drink, she orders only the costliest vodka. You know, like Grey Goose. Or maybe sometimes she'll have Napoleon brandy. And sometimes she'll buy drinks for everybody. Always pays with big bills.

"Funny thing about her, though -- sometimes she eats the pretzels we have here on the bar. But like she'll only eat unbroken pretzels. Same with potato chips. I once gave her a basket that was maybe half broken chips, like from the bottom of the sack, you know? Man, she blew her stack. Cussed like our and threw the bowl right on the floor.

"Oooops! Gotta go." Antonio moved off to fill orders for two new customers. Appetite gone, Powers left the coffee and cash on the bar.

Won't eat broken potato chips. Damn!

❧   ❧   ❧

Chapter 35

He was back home mitering the corners of the clean sheets on the bed when Myra called, sounding subdued.

"Can I come over and see you?"

"Of course. Better give me five minutes so I can hide all the dirty laundry in the oven."

She didn't laugh. With something like a sob she said, "I'll be there."

Powers did a quick inspection of the apartment: laundry folded and stowed, no dirty dishes in the sink. It was a warm afternoon so he had the fan on. He opened the top dresser drawer and checked the .45 and magazines.

He paced and then stepped outside to scatter cracked corn along the driveway for the birds.

As he returned to the door, she pulled into the drive. She quickly got out of the car, head down, arms folded, purse hanging from one elbow. No big stride today -- she almost scurried toward the door. *Something's really wrong.*

He opened the screen door, wincing the thousandth time at the spring's squawk. He stood aside, making way for her to descend the stairs, but Myra came straight to him.

She dropped the purse and wrapped her arms around his shoulders, rocking her forehead back and forth against his neck.

"Hey, kiddo," he whispered, rubbing his hands up and down the long lines of her back. He stooped out of her arms to pick up the purse, put his arm around her shoulders and led her downstairs to the little living room.

She hugged him again and sniffed. "Can I ask you a favor?" voice muffled against his collarbone.

"Ask."

She withdrew from him, eyes red, and pointed. "Would you please sit down over there against the arm of the couch."

Mystified, he nodded and seated himself, left elbow on the left couch arm. She came to stand facing the couch about two feet from him. She knelt on the seat cushion and reclined across him onto her right side, into his arms, pressing her forehead against his neck.

"Please just hold me a while."

"Gladly."

After a minute, he lifted a thick strand of hair from the side of her face and smoothed it back along her head. With the fingertips of his right hand, he began messaging tiny circles on her temple. He could feel her relax and sink against him. Her breathing slowed and deepened.

God, this is wonderful. She can stay like this all day. Then he frowned. *Dream come true for me, but it must mean she's in a nightmare.*

After perhaps 15 minutes, she pulled herself upright and swiveled to sit beside him. She stared at the wall for a second.

"Brad, thanks for understanding and not taking advantage, which you probably could have gotten away with. But I needed that snuggle."

"There's plenty more where that came from," he said quietly. "Any time. But is this something you can talk about?"

"Yes."

∾ ∾ ∾

Chapter 36

Elbows on her knees, Myra lowered her face to her hands, her mane spilling forward. Then she raised her head, pushed her hair back and gave him a bleak look.

"It's horrible, Brad. You see, before daddy was killed, he set up a trust for me. He made Herb . . ."

"Your husband?"

"Exactly. Daddy made him the trustee because he felt I was too flighty. I ran away from home — first as a teen, and again after Mom died and he married that slut . . . well, I guess Dad was afraid I might just blow my whole inheritance.

"Maybe at one time I would have, Brad, but that was two decades ago.

"After the girls were born, I decided I would dedicate the trust first of all for their educations and then for their children after that. I've always had a modest income from the trust but I've never touched the principal.

"The trust gives me a regular allowance — it started out at $2,400 a year and now, 20 years later, it's up to $6,000. I can ask for money for any reasonable purpose, for a car, tuition for girls, but can't withdraw a big sum without Herb's permission."

"Do you mind me asking how much is in the trust?"

"Not at all, Brad. Originally, it was nearly $1.5 million."

She turned to look at him. "It should have grown a lot since then, but now I think much of it is gone."

"How do you know?"

"I don't for sure," Myra said.

"But here's the thing that has me scared about it," she said. "I started to talk to Herb this morning about making plans for college — about budgeting for room and board and tuition for the twins. I made it clear I want them in the best schools and don't care what it costs.

"Well, My God! He immediately got all stiff and tense. He said he thought they should go first to a community college for at least a year, or even two years maybe, supposedly so they can get acclimated to college life." She mimicked a pompous baritone, "He told me, 'After all, I didn't start off at Wharton.'

"Well, Brad, both the girls are serious students! They both earned college fellowships when they were high school juniors. They're not party girls, for God's sake.

"When I pointed that out to him -- as if he didn't know it -- he really started to get defensive. So I told him that if he was going to be such a bastard about it, I wanted a full accounting because the money is mine, after all. And I said that if he didn't cooperate, maybe I'd see a lawyer about going into court to revise the terms of the trust.

"He just blew sky-high!

"I've never seen him carry on like that before. He's not used to me standing up to him. He got very belligerent, absolutely foul-mouthed -- but under all that swearing and bluster I could see that he was terrified.

"Anyway he kept yakking about his sacred promise to Daddy and that how he chooses to manage the trust was none of my damned business.

"And then he stormed out," she said. "And now I don't know what to do."

"Haven't you received annual reports about the trust?" Powers asked.

"I used to," she said. "But I always was bad about math and those sheets looked like just a blur of solid numbers. They didn't mean anything to me and, after four or five years I just told Herb not to bother any more. Stupid of me, I guess."

"Okay, Myra, but that info has to be on file somewhere and we really ought to eyeball it."

"Yes. You're right." After a deep sigh, Myra said, "What I'm wondering is whether he's being blackmailed and using the trust to pay off somebody. God knows he's done enough stupid things and slept around enough . . . more than I probably know about.

"But look, Brad, when you and I spoke at the store the other day, you told me you were looking into some things and that you wanted to talk with me about them. Is this the time? And is the trust something that's tied to all this?"

"Myra, I didn't know about the trust until this minute, so that's an entirely new factor. I've got to check a few more things – might take a week or two for me to get all the information I need. And then I'll lay out everything I know. I don't want to say anything yet because it might be completely off base."

"One other thing, Brad. Maybe I've become completely paranoiac, but I have a queasy feeling."

"What do you mean?"

"I think someone's been following me."

Chapter 37

Powers walked to the dresser and tucked the Colt into his belt at the back of his Bermuda shorts, leaving his shirt untucked to conceal it. Myra's eyebrows rose and her eyes widened.

"Don't worry," he said. "I'm not setting out to shoot anyone, but I am going to take a quick walk around the block. I want to have a look at what cars may be parked here. Give me 10 minutes."

When he returned he said he'd seen nothing unusual. He asked whether she was driving straight home.

"No, I need to stop at the grocery store to pick up a few things."

"Good. I'll wait here a bit and then drive there, too. I'll be in the parking lot. Why don't you park way, way out in the lot? That makes it easier to spot anyone who might be taking a special interest."

Powers told Myra to take her time and to shop as she ordinarily would. Then he instructed her once back in her car to drive to a new parking place in the lot and to stop and turn off the engine – to stall for a few minutes by putting on make-up or pretending to make a cell call. He also instructed her to drive home slowly by an unfamiliar route.

"Why?"

"Because if someone is tailing you, he probably knows your usual route. So you don't want to be predictable. Do something different and he may make mistakes."

# # #

He parked clear across the lot from her car, a gray Honda CRV. He slumped in the seat of his Jetta, pretending to doze under his Kansas City Chiefs baseball cap as he kept his eyes scanning the lot.

It was nearly 45 minutes before she wheeled her cart out the parking lot's center lane to the CRV. She opened the hatch and begin loading groceries into the trunk. Powers spotted a beefy man in overalls and dark ball cap get behind the wheel of a maroon Dodge van two lanes beyond her auto. He shut the door, put both hands on the wheel and sat.

As soon as she got into the Honda, Dodge started his engine.

"Come on, honey," Powers muttered. "Now take your time. Make him wait so I can be sure."

She did. She started the car, drove about 100 feet to park in a different slot. She refreshed her lipstick and then took a moment to brush her hair.

"Good girl."

Dodge had driven to a new parking place and cut his motor. He sat until she keyed the Honda's ignition. Then he started the van again.

Powers jumped halfway out of his skin when his cell phone rang. It was Myra.

"Am I doing this right?" she whispered. As he watched, Dodge turned off his motor again.

"You're doing great, girl, but why are you whispering?"

After a pause she giggled. "I don't know. Silly I guess. Or nervous."

"That's alright, Myra. Now just remember not to drive straight home. Meander around a bit."

"Yes sir, sir." As she backed from her place, Dodge started his van again.

Dodge kept his distance as Myra drove to the lot exit. He steered for the right lane of the exit, the one she normally would have taken, but Myra swerved, turning left out of the lot. Dodge, three cars back from her, had to cut across traffic, was blocked briefly and then had to accelerate to keep her in sight.

Following the pair, Powell called Daniels on his cell. When the detective answered, Powers said, "Daddy, if you have a minute can you run a car license for me?"

"Of course, sweetheart. What is it?"

Powers read the off number. Daniels called back immediately, but with a question. "Just exactly where are you, Darling?"

"At the moment, Father Dear, I'm southbound on Taft about a block behind the vehicle in question."

"Well, that's very interesting," Daniels said. "The vehicle you're following is . . . wait, it's a maroon Dodge van, right?"

"Right."

"Well, Honey, it's registered to your friend Bluto."

"Is that right? Well he ain't driving it."

"For sure he's not," Daniels said. "He made bail last night while we were having dinner."

"Oh, great! We'll never see him again."

"Wrong," Daniels said. "He's in the morgue."

"Say what?"

"Someone bashed in the back of his skull."

❧ ❧ ❧

Chapter 38

Powers tried to mull over Daniels' news as he concentrated on keeping pace with the van and Myra's Honda.

The van driver made no attempt to close with her Honda and, on long stretches, fell back.

What the hell is going on?

Powers was inclined to dismiss Bluto's demise, the slob being just the type to get himself killed in a bar fight.

Turning his thoughts to Myra, he could see no reason for anyone to tail her unless her husband was in a true panic about the trust. Powers speculated that Windom might arrange a tail in concern about whether she was visiting a lawyer.

But that didn't explain why he would have her followed beginning a day or two before their argument about the trust.

He jumped as his cell phone shrilled again. "Brad, it's me. Is somebody following me?"

"Yep, but he's keeping his distance, Myra."

"Oh God, this is scary."

"Myra, I don't think there's anything to worry about at this point. If he gets too close or tries something, I'll be on his tail just the way I dealt with Bluto.

"By the way, Girl, you did a great job in the parking lot. Made him stand out like a sore thumb." He didn't tell her Daniels' news about Forrest's murder.

"Okay, Myra, we've led this guy around enough for us to spot him and know what he's doing, so why don't you head home now? I'll keep you in view until you're safe inside the garage and have it closed. Then I'll be in touch."

In 10 minutes, Myra turned into the driveway of a sprawling brick ranch home on what looked like a 3-acre lot. The place looked expensive. But its landscaping and the home itself had a down-at-the-heels look that reminded Powers a little of the Purdy Precision

Castings campus -- it appeared to be in need of some serious maintenance and repair work.

The van drove past without slowing. Powers followed the Dodge from a block away until it turned onto Main and headed toward the center of town.

He turned back to drive past Myra's house, arriving just in time to see her with an armload of groceries hitting the button to close the garage door.

He turned toward home, getting on his cell to ask Daniels for a meeting to run some new information by him.

"I'm off work early," Daniels said. "I just got some great news. So where do you want to meet?"

"Why not my apartment?"

"How soon will you be there?"

"It'll be about two minutes. I'm just getting ready to turn onto Ransome now," he said, stopping to make a left.

Still holding the phone to his ear, he had time to say, "Oh, my God . . ." as he glimpsed the grillwork of a pickup truck inches before it slammed into the driver's side door of his Jetta.

The collision fired the airbag deafening Powers as if he were hearing a pistol shot in a closet.

Stunned, ears singing and with his left arm and side on fire, Powers fumbled for his seatbelt release. He shook his head and yawned repeatedly to clear the whine in his ears.

He couldn't hear Daniels yelling over the cell phone which now lay on the floor by the clutch pedal. He glimpsed the other driver, tall and broad-shouldered, ball cap pulled low over his eyes, descending from the battered truck.

The man, carrying a two-foot length of pipe, was looking Powers in the eyes as he walked quickly toward Powers' battered Jetta.

Oh-oh! That don't look to me like PVC.

With both hands, the man raised the pipe high over his left shoulder, corded muscles standing out in his forearms as he prepared to bash in the windshield.

But then finding himself staring into the muzzle of Powers' .45, he stopped in his tracks.

He turned and ran.

Powers tried to make a mental record of the man's appearance, but suddenly felt very weary. His head sagged and he slumped back into the seat as unconsciousness settled over him like a quiet fog.

Chapter 39

His first awareness through the ringing in his ears was the faint regular beep of some hospital monitor; then voices saying something about vitals being good.

He started to speak but could barely move his mouth against the rubbery outlines of a mask.

Okay. Let's do inventory. He flexed his left foot. *Okay.* Then he tried the right. *Good.* Now the left knee. *Oooops, that hurts, but not too bad. Wait, that knee always hurts. Right knee? Good.*

Okay, 50 percent working order so far. Something hurts in the chest. Shot again?

Through the ringing he heard somebody's voice, "Coming out of it."

He tried to open his eyes but immediately squinted them shut because the overhead lights were so bright. *I must be in ICU.*

He started to reach for the mask with his left hand, but couldn't move the hand. So with the right he pulled the mask away from his mouth and opened his eyes again.

"This isn't Iraq, is it?"

"No, Mr. Powers," a slender nurse with short salt-and-pepper hair leaned over him. "It's Southland, Indiana. You're at Bledsoe Memorial Hospital. And please replace the mask. Now, can you tell me what year it is?"

"Gee, lady, that's kind of a personal question."

She gave a pained smile. "Mr. Powers, please stop trying to be a wise-ass and just answer the question."

He chuckled and the movement of it hurt the left side of his chest, causing him to say a quick "Ouch!" He recited the day, date and year. "And I know the name of the jerk in the White House, too. So what's wrong with me?"

Then the wreck came back to him in a flash.

She started to speak and he interrupted, "That's okay. I remember now. What's my condition?"

"Apparently it's pretty good," Daniels said, looming into view. "The driver ran off and abandoned the . . ."

"Please, Detective," the nurse said, "would you just back off let us do our work first?"

"Okay, Doris, okay! You are such a nag!"

"That's your side of the story," she said. "You always twist things. That's why I divorced you. Now, Mr. Powers, are you experiencing pain?"

"A bit. I think I may have a broken rib or two."

"So on a scale of 10, 10 being the highest, how would you rate your pain?"

"Oh, about 15, Mrs. Daniels."

"It's not Mrs. Daniels any more, thank God. It's Doris Arends, B.S.N. Do you want something for your pain?"

"No, but I do want to talk with your ex."

She snorted. "Macho peas in a pod," she said and left.

"Boy," Daniels told Powers, "you need to work on your bedside manner." Pointing at the left side of Powers' face, he added, "And man, oh, man, have you got a beautiful shiner. I bet that's sore. Now, tell me what the hell happened."

"I was waiting to make a left turn and talking to you when a damned pickup slammed into me. I think it was an old Chevy. After the crash, the guy who was driving got out and was brandishing a piece of galvanized pipe. I pointed old Betsy at his ugly mug. I remember his eyes crossing and I guess he ran off. And then I woke up here seeing your ugly mug instead."

"Can you describe him?"

"Not real well. It happened pretty fast. I remember he was big – thick through the shoulders -- wearing jeans and a gray T-shirt. Dark baseball cap pulled way down on his forehead. Hadn't shaved for a day or two. That's about it."

"You said he was brandishing a piece of pipe?"

"Yep."

"Was he getting reading to do a right-hand swing?"

"No, by God! Bob, he was a lefty."

"That's something to remember."

"Yeah, and you know, something about him was kind of familiar but I just can't place it."

"Well, keep trying," Daniels said. "It was lucky we were on our cell phones. I heard the collision and got there fast. There was no sign of the other driver. And by the way, the truck was stolen.

"This wreck tells me two things, Brad. First, you were conducting a surveillance and somebody was doing their own surveillance and caught you napping. Your instincts must be a little rusty. Second, somebody knows you're in the game and wants you out, maybe for good."

"Gee, Bob, you think? Other people have tried that and came close, but what I worry about is Myra." He told Daniels about his meeting with Myra, about the trust, the fight with the husband and about her being tailed.

"And then at lunch I had the pleasure of meeting the Widow Purdy . . . for the second time, yet."

"Oh, really? What's she like?"

"Pretty steamy. And, say, 40 trying to look 18 and doing a pretty fair job of it. She came on strong and I'm not sure whether she was trying to seduce me or recruit me . . . or both . . . again. But when I turned her off, she went away looking grim. But for now, I'm beginning to think all this points to Myra's hubby. Now, how long they gonna to keep me in this place?"

"Easy Brad. I'll find out from Doris." He punched the call button. "Meanwhile, I want you to know, what with this new murder, the chief decided to waive the rest of my suspension. I'm a detective again."

"Congratulations, Bob. I always thought you were a dick."

"Very funny, asshole. Now I was thinking I might take Glenda Subczek with me out to see Myra and hubby and let them know we're working Forrest's murder.

"We'll question them pretty closely and drop some hints that we're looking for a connection between the murder and the assault on Myra.

"I'm going to try to give Windom a bad case of the sweaty palms. He may be big and look tough, but we'll see how beefy he is in the nerves department. That ought to cool the jets of anybody with plans for immediate action. I'll be in touch."

"How did you get reinstated?"

"I told the chief I'd had it: put me back on duty or I'm retiring. He got pretty nasty so I asked if he wanted to do the investigation. Because I've been on suspension, Glenda's swamped with work. So that clinched it. It's safe to say I'm right there beside you on his permanent shit list but the last thing he wants is more work for himself.

"Oh, by the way," Daniels grinned. "Guess who investigated Chet Purdy's murder."

"Who?"

"The chief, who was practically a rookie then. Maybe that's why he did such a shitty job."

"I think I know why," Powers said, telling Daniels about his first encounter with the Widow Purdy. "I'll bet in that interview, she bewitched, bothered, bewildered and bedded him so by the time he found out what was what, she was blackmailing him. I bet he's been covering up ever since."

"Makes sense," Daniels said. "Let's keep it quiet for now."

"Damn right, Bob."

Doris stepped in to say the hospital would keep Powers for chest X-rays and overnight observation concerning a suspected concussion.

"Hey, Doris," Powers said, "may I ask a favor?" May I please have some scrub pants so my tush will be covered when I get up?"

"I wouldn't," Daniels interjected. "He's cute in that nightie."

"Mr. Powers," Doris said, "I'll get the scrub pants for you."

As she left, Daniels grinned, "Thank me later. Anything I ask she does the opposite."

Powers started to chuckle and flinched. "Ouch, dammit!"

❧   ❧   ❧

Chapter 40

When Powers looked in the mirror next morning, he got a shock. His jawline had disappeared. The left side of his neck bulged so far that the flesh nearly buried his left collar bone. *Damn, an out-of-nowhere treble chin. Instant goiter, maybe?* He ran his fingers across the area and his skin felt pebbly -- like bubble-wrap.

He buzzed the nurse's station. About 10 minutes later, a weary-looking blonde sauntered in, looking back over her shoulder and giggling. "Okay, big guy," she asked Powers, "What do you need?"

"Somebody tell a good joke?" Powers asked.

"Yes, one of the interns. The guy is a real laugh. Cute, too."

"Well, suppose you yank his ass in here because my condition has worsened overnight."

A line appeared between her eyebrows. "What do you mean, honey?" She put her stethoscope to her ears.

"I mean get the doctor. I've got lots of swelling around my neck, which I didn't last night. My breathing is a bit labored and my skin feels like it's honeycombed."

She looked at his face closely, eyes darting side to side. "You have a broken rib?"

"The radiologist said multiple rib fractures."

She ran her finger gently along his jawline. "Oh-oh. Crepitus. I'll be right back with the doctor."

"Hey!" he called to her disappearing back, "what the hell is crepitus? Hey!"

An ER surgeon showed up 15 minutes later with an orderly and a gurney. After a brief examination, he told Powers that the rib fractures had punctured the left lung and escaping air had gradually invaded his tissues during the night.

"Have you been spitting any blood? No? Good. Doesn't seem to be any hemorrhage. So it's not terribly serious now. But it will become so. Your lung will collapse and press against your heart if we don't deal with it."

"So how do we deal with it, doc?"

"We've got to put in a chest tube which equalizes air pressure inside and outside the lung. That stops the leakage which, in turn, allows the puncture to heal. It takes about a week."

"So I have to be here the whole time?"

"Yep. The whole time."

"Will I be able to get around?"

"You'll be wheeling an IV stand wherever you go. So you can get up to use the can, but otherwise we want you resting."

"Let me make a call first."

"Make it snappy, Mr. Powers."

Chapter 41

Powers was sipping a cup of ice water the next morning when Doris Arends came in trailed by flock of young women in flowered nurse's tunics.

"Mr. Powers, how are you feeling?"

"Well, Nurse Doris, there's this tube dangling out of my rib cage. And then my left leg and arm were bruised pretty badly in the wreck. So I'm a bit tender here and there."

"We're sorry about your discomfort, Mr. Powers. Do you need something for pain?"

"No, it's not that bad. Just something to gripe about since I can't do anything else. Oh, I know. I really hate plastic hospital drinking cups!" Two of the girls tittered. Doris turned to stare at them and they dropped their eyes and pursed their lips.

She turned back. "Mr. Powers, we wonder if we could have your help for a minute."

"*My* help?"

Doris turned to the girls. "These young ladies are nursing students, so as part of their training, we want them to be able to recognize and detect crepitus. We wonder if you could permit them touch those areas where you have it."

"To be touched by a bevy of beauties," Powers grinned. "Happy to oblige, ladies."

Most of the girls smiled, but Doris kept a rigid professional look.

"If you palpate these areas gently," she said, pointing to Powers' jawline, "you can feel the pebbly texture where air has infiltrated the subcutaneous tissues. If you press, you can feel it dissipate. Don't be afraid to do so because it doesn't cause pain."

Powers sat upright on the edge of the bed.

The students processed to his side to touch and press his neck and the area around his collar bone and jaw line. One of students ran her hand down over his left chest, letting it linger. He growled quietly.

As the students began leaving the room, Doris leaned close to whisper one of them would remain. She was a slender brunette with vaguely familiar features. She studied Powers carefully, eyes as expressionless as the water in his cup. She introduced herself as Jennifer Windom.

"You're Myra's daughter?"

"Correct. And I'm not actually a student here. I'm auditing before I start my pre-med studies this autumn. I wanted to meet you face-to-face."

"Why Jen?"

She frowned. "Please don't call me Jen. I hate it."

"Whoops, I'm sorry. I'll never do it again."

"If I can help it," she shot back, "you'll never see me again."

She said Myra had told the twins that Powers was a confidant and that he had saved her from a frightening physical attack. She also had told the twins about Rae and Powers' friends at the nursing home.

"You're not quite sure how to take all this, right?"

"I'm very sure. I don't like it."

"I can't blame you, Jennifer. You don't know if I'm trying to take advantage of your mom and tear up your family."

"Mr. Powers, we don't know what to think."

"Same here," he said. "I'll confine myself to saying I am very fond of your mother. She has a great mind and personality. I'm absolutely not trying to become intimate with her. I am, however, very worried for her safety."

"Are you serious?"

"Completely serious. In fact, I'd say deadly serious. I'm a retired Army investigator and I'm working with the police here. So I'm for real about this."

She tilted her head and regarded Powers skeptically for a minute. "She said you like William Butler Yeats."

"He's one of my favorites."

"Really? Okay, recite something by Yeats."

"Fine," he said. "Here's the opening from *The Song of the Happy Shepard.*"

> The woods of Arkady are dead
> And over is their antique joy
> Of old the world on dreaming fed
> Grey truth is now her painted toy
> But, oh, sick children of the world . . .

Her eyes softened. "Okay. Perhaps you are for real."

"Oh, yeah. And I'm also very frustrated being stuck in this bed with this tube hanging out of my side. Listen, I don't think I'd tell anybody but your Mom and sister about this conversation."

"Meaning you don't trust my dad? I'm not sure I do."

"Meaning I'm like you. Right now I don't know what to think. But I am going to get to the bottom of it."

"Mr. Powers, I've got to go now."

"It was nice to meet you. Please tell your mom 'hello' for me. Oh, what's your twin's name?"

"She's Ginger."

"Named for your maternal grandmother?"

"We both are."

Chapter 42

Late in the afternoon, Daniels came in and flopped an 11 X 17 envelope onto the bed.

"Careful, dammit, you hit my knee with it," Powers said.

"Awwww, too bad. Was it your poor sore knee?"

"No, it's my good knee," Powers said. "But you could have injured it. Then where would I be?"

"Right where you are now, Brad, a pain in the ass."

Turning serious as Powers started to open the envelope, Daniels said, "What you have right there is the coroner's report on Forrest and a copy of the old coroner's report on Chester Purdy."

"Oh ho! Well thank you!"

"Something interesting," Daniels said. "It seems Mr. Forrest was murdered in exactly the same way as Chet Purdy -- blunt force trauma, a straight blow from the rear. A long, narrow impact area, just like a hardball bat. It's like the Southland Slugger all over."

"Really! So how did the coroner define the actual cause of death?"

"Telescoped occipital bone. Both cases"

"That's the bone at the base of the skull?" Powers asked.

"Exactly, Brad. Bash it hard enough and it's pushed far enough forward to slam shut the foramen magnum – that's the hole in the base of your skull where the brain connects with the spinal cord. It cuts or tears the spinal cord right there – right at the base of the brain. Sort of an internal guillotine. Turns you off instantly."

Powers told Daniels he was going to inform Special Agent Ramsey at Champagne about the wreck and ask him to mail his findings to Daniels' apartment rather than his own place.

As he left Daniels said. "Oh, by the way."

"What?"

"You'll be happy to know I rescued your .45 from your car. Right now it's under lock and key in my personal evidence locker."

"Oh? And where's that?"

"My desk at the poh-leece station. I'll return it as soon as you're discharged. And now I'm off with Glenda to pay a visit to the Windoms. Happy reading."

"Bob? The pistol? Why don't you bring it to me here?"

"You know I can't do that, Brad. They don't allow guns in the hospital."

"Really, Bob? You're carrying your gun right now, aren't you?"

"Okay, dammit. I'll see if I can smuggle it in to you."

"If you don't, I'll tell Doris."

"Jeez, I said 'Okay' didn't I? So lighten up!"

Chapter 43

Powers was mulling over the old case next morning when Myra called to ask how he was feeling.

"I'm much more frustrated than uncomfortable," he said. "I just hate being stuck in this hospital."

"I miss talking with you," she said.

"Not as much as I miss you, Myra."

"Do you think it would be okay if I came up to see you?"

"I'd love it," he said. "But, as much as I hate to say this, let's err on the side of caution. Please don't come alone. I want somebody with you whenever you're away from home. Bring the girls maybe. By the way, I met Jennifer yesterday. She seems to be a very, very bright young woman."

"Both my girls are," Myra said. "But I don't think I'd feel very comfortable about bringing them. Oh, by the way, your detective friends came to see Herb and me and they made me very uneasy."

"How do you mean?"

"Well, she didn't say much, but he was kind of snotty with his questions, as if he didn't believe what we said. But I think Herb lied about not knowing Bluto or Forrest or whoever. Herb got defensive and very sweaty by the time they left. Now what if he did know him?"

"Myra, are you at home?"

"No, I'm in a side reading room at the library and the door's closed. There's nobody near me."

"Smart girl. I'm glad you're in a public place. Look, please don't let your husband know what you're feeling. I don't know that he is a danger, but when in doubt, be prudent.

"If the issue comes up, just tell him you hate those lousy cops' stupid, slimy attitudes and you wish this whole thing would just go away."

"I do wish it would," she said.

"Myra, in the end it will go away. But for now, just be very, very careful.

"Meanwhile," he added, "it is so refreshing and nice to hear your voice. It makes me greedy for more time with you."

"Herb," she said, "for me that goes double. You make me feel safe."

# # #

When Daniels showed up, Powers asked for a run-down on the interview with the Windoms.

Daniels squinted and pulled at his lower lip.

"Well, I questioned them like a very suspicious cop would -- with a strong flavoring of contempt and sarcasm under a barely polite veneer.

"Myra acted a little annoyed but Windom seemed fearful.

"When I asked if he knew Forrest. He gave me the liar's double denial, 'No sir! Absolutely not!' She did a double take at that. A wife knows when hubby's lying.

"So I asked if it didn't seem odd that both Forrest and Chet Purdy were murdered exactly the same way. I said, 'Doesn't it seem like the Southland Slugger has come back to town?'

"He said it must be a coincidence. It really opened her eyes. She'll think about that.

"I also asked three different ways whether he'd known Forrest -- like the second time I interrupted my own question by asking where he first met Forrest.

"Well, Herby boy allllmost tripped up . . . I thought he was going tell me but then he caught himself just in time. His voice got real quavery and he shrank back into his chair just like Clinton when they grilled him on TV about whether he had sex with that woman, Miss Lewinski. But then he recovered and pretended to get angry.

"So I apologized to him just as insincerely as I could. So I think you could say he knows that the law has its eyes fixed on him. I don't think he wants anything more to happen to his wife . . . at least not for now.

"Finally I asked him where he was the night of Forrest's murder. That rattled him, too. So if he had anything to do with the attack on Myra, he's gonna cool it for a while. I think she's safe for now."

"Well," Daniels said, "I better get out and chase some crooks. I'll be in touch." He pulled Powers' .45 from beneath his jacket. "Chamber's empty, magazine's full.

"For my sake," he said, "don't let Doris or the security apes know about it."

He started to leave the room.

Chapter 44

Daniels was almost into the doorway of Powers' room when he suddenly stepped back, making way for a prissy young man pushing a cart laden with bouquets and plants.

"What the hell is all this?" Powers said.

"A bouquet somewhere here for you, Mr. Powers . . . yes! Here it is. My, aren't they *gorgeous?*" The lad swirled around, extending one hand out, fingers delicately poised in the manner of a ballerina, the other holding a big bouquet of red roses.

"Mr. Powers, right?"

"Right. That's me. Who sent them?"

"Well, sir, there's no name on the card. It just reads, 'Like I said, it is a small town' with the word 'is' underlined. And, sir, it's in a *lady's* handwriting!"

Once the delivery boy left, Daniels suggested Myra sent the flowers.

"No," Powers said. "Carlene Purdy sent them. Those are her exact words to me in that bar."

"Well, that's kind of ominous. Tells me she knows all about you now."

Powers chuckled. "You know, Detective Daniels, if you keep arching your eyebrows that high everybody's going to forget that you're bald."

# # #

After Daniels left, Powers called Special Agent Ramsey at his home in Champagne. The agent was irked that Powers expected results so soon.

"Relax, Pard," Powers said. "I just wanted you to know I'll probably be in the hospital for five more days so that if you have anything to send, mail it to me at my buddy's place."

"So why are you in the hospital?"

"Some plow jockey T-boned my Jetta with a pick-up. I got some broken ribs and . . ."

"Brad, did it have anything to do with what you're working on?"

"I'd say it's likely."

"Holy shit, Brad, you got any kind of back-up? I've got some leave time accrued. I could spring loose and babysit you for a week or two."

Powers thanked Ramsey. "No need. My buddy — we were in the same squad in Panama — is a detective on the department here. He's giving me lots of back-up, so I'm not worried about another attempt. And what I really need more than ever is the information on Windom and his squeeze."

"It's gonna be on the way soon, Brad. Just try to sit tight and keep checking your six."

"I'll have my 1911 with me right here in the hospital."

Chapter 45

By the afternoon of his fourth day, Powers felt like climbing the walls out of sheer boredom.

He sourly amused himself by forming a mental picture of a patient in scrubs climbing a wall – the brick exterior wall of the hospital with an IV stand dangling from his ribs. *Maybe I could throw the stand up to the roof like a grapnel and then climb the tube.*

He had leafed through every ragged issue of *Sports Afield* and read the tattered thrillers he pilfered from the waiting room down the hall. The only choices left, which he declined, were *People* and a magazine called *Oprah*.

He tried to nap and couldn't. He turned on the room's TV, remoted through all the re-runs, commercials, game shows and, in despair, turned the device off. "Drivel, crap and bullshit."

The cleaning lady mopping the floor laughed. "I know what you means, Mister. My old man ax me 'TV cain't get no stupider, can it?' But I tell him, 'You wait, Baby. It jus' keeps on doin' it.'"

"Amen to that," Powers said. "It sets a new record for dumb every season. And if I see another freaking commercial, I'll puke."

She laughed loud and deep. "Just keep that emesis basin handy, honey, so it don't go on my nice clean floor." She laughed again as she left.

He tried to call Daniels. He wanted the detective to get Rosa to let him into the apartment to bring him his new biography about General Sherman. The department took a message.

He was staring out the window at the brick wall of another wing of the hospital when Herb Windom walked through the open doorway.

Windom stopped at the foot of the bed glaring at Powers, arms folded, feet spread dramatically apart. Powers' pulse quickened and he swallowed because his throat had dried.

Powers stared back. He had to admit the man looked impressive: tall, lean and broad-shouldered, a deep, hard chest and a chiseled TV star's face complete with blue chin.

"Let me guess," Powers said. "You've come to thank me for rescuing your wife."

"Yeah, I guess. But then she didn't have any real valuables with her."

"Just her life," Power said.

"Don't take yourself so seriously, little man." A muscle in Windom's temple worked. "And let's back up just a minute." Windom propped his big knuckley fists onto his belt. "How did you know I'm Myra's husband?"

Powers grinned and rested his head back on his left hand. He slipped his right hand beneath the pillow. "My very good friend and old Army comrade gave me a real, real good description."

"Yeah? Who's that?"

"Detective Robert Daniels, Southland PD. He said you had a movie star's 'coyfewer'."

Windom's lips curved in a brief smile, but flattened back into a compressed line. "The chief of police is my friend. I had his back in the Army and he has mine now . . . to the death, you might say."

"Golly, gee whizz and wow," Powers smirked. "Daniels isn't just my buddy, he's concerned about my safety."

"Yeah? Well, he should be concerned," Windom said. "I came here to warn you to keep your nose out of our affairs."

"Warn me?"

"Yes."

"You're *warning* me?"

"That's what I said, damn you!"

"And what if I keep my nose right where it is?" Powers asked. "You going to hire somebody else to ram me with another stolen pick-up?"

Windom turned white. "I don't know what you're talking about!"

"Sure you do. And let me tell you, it's gonna take lots more than an auto wreck to stop me."

Windom, glanced through the door and started to move toward the IV stand on the left side of the bed. He looked again toward the nurse's station, stopped and changed course. He backed up against the wall, placed his hands on the back of the room's single chair. Lowering his head, he took a very deep breath. And another.

"Got to hand it to you, Herb," Powers taunted. "You show real good control. You don't dare start beating up a patient in his own hospital bed, do you? Just too much exposure here. Or maybe you were planning to yank out my chest tube. Was that it?"

Windom flushed. He moved his hands from the back of the chair to grip its sides, giving a speculative eye to Powers.

"Don't get any ideas with that chair, Herb." Powers reached behind his pillow and pulled the .45 into view.

"Jesus, what are you going to do with that gun?"

"It's not just any old gun, Bozo. It's a Browning semi-automatic pistol, .45 caliber. Makes huge ugly holes in human chests . . . or coiffured heads. Now just you let go of that chair. Oh, hell, never mind. I think you do your hitting with a pipe or a bat, right?"

Windom blinked as if he had been struck.

Powers grinned. "Hey, Herb. Were you ever a pitcher?"

"What? Yeah, some in high school . . . a fielder in college. What about it?"

"Were you a slugger, too? Maybe a lefty?"

With a genuine deer-caught-in-the-headlights look, Windom asked, "What do you mean?"

"I mean 'Do you bat left-handed?' Just curious. Maybe a piece of the puzzle I've been working on."

"What puzzle?" Before Powers could answer. Windom sighed and said, "Look Powers, all I want you to do is leave my family alone."

"Now which family do you mean? Your wife and the twins? Or do you mean your little stable of girls down at the plant? I hear a couple of those ladies found out about each other and have teamed up with the state Civil Rights boys to haul your ass into court."

"God damn you," Windom shouted. "What are you trying to do to me? I came up here to reach some kind of an understanding with you . . ."

"Best tone it down, Herb, or they'll call for the Security apes. Now, just for the record, I'm not trying to do a thing to you. I'm not even raising my voice. You're the one doing the shouting.

"And for what it's worth," Powers added, shoving the weapon back under the pillow, "I get the impression you've been painting yourself into a corner for a long time now. I could almost feel sorry for you because it must seem like things are falling apart: business going sour; somebody attacks your wife, causing a stir; big college bills in the offing; your honeys at the plant turn rancid so you're gonna have to start paying big bucks to some greedy lawyer.

"And look -- you've got those big bags under your eyes, so you're losing lots of sleep. Your nose looks kind of puffy and it's got spider web veins so I guess you're hitting the booze pretty hard. I'm sure there's much more I don't know about."

As Powers ticked off his points, Windom's head jerked again and again in reflex.

"I'm asking . . ."

Powers interrupted sharply. "Herby! You're getting repetitious. I don't care what you're asking. I don't have a thing to give. My only concern is finding out first why some bastard tried to kill me and, second, why somebody tried to kill your wife and why that somebody is now dead. And mark my words, Friend, I will find out. I'll be back in action next week. And you know that old Psalm about the Valley of the Shadow of Death?"

"What?"

"I'm just serving notice that if anybody tries another hit on me or if something should happen to Myra, I'll personally show you that I'm the meanest son of a bitch in the valley."

Windom's voice rose in pitch, "Man, you're nuts." Pleading now. "Why tell me? She's my wife and I'm the one protecting her, not you! And I'm not trying to hurt her. I swear."

"I wish I could believe that, Windom. I really, really do wish I could believe that. All I know for sure is that the jerk who attacked her sure as hell wasn't trying to steal anything. He was after her. But somehow, I think you know that and I suspect you knew the attack was coming. Hell, you probably hired him."

"No way, no how, you bastard! I knew no such thing."

"Herb, I'm an old investigator. I've interrogated lots of people over a lot of years. You got to be careful about those dramatic denials. They're a sure tip-off that you're concealing something. You had to know, Herb! Somebody told you the attack failed, otherwise you wouldn't have raced to the station to get Myra home before she said too much to the cops."

Windom started to sputter that nobody had called him.

"Oh? So maybe you have a mind link with the 911 Dispatcher like Dr. Spock on Star Trek? For sure nobody called you from the station."

An idea struck Powers. He wanted to think. "Herb, I was bored when you came in and I'm really bored now, so I'd take it kindly if you would get out. Just leave."

Windom seemed to shiver. "I'm not through with you," he said, as he turned to scuttle out the doorway.

"Yeah, yeah, yeah. Goodbye."

The idea: Maybe somebody at the police station actually did call Windom; an ally; somebody Windom wouldn't want identified.

Like, maybe the chief himself.

Chapter 46

Daniels sauntered in to visit late the next morning. "Here you go, Brad," he said, dropping *The White Tecumseh* on Powers' bedside table.

"Great! Thank you so much," Powers said, getting up from the bed. "I was only past the first chapter when all this happened. Say, guess who came up here yesterday to threaten me?"

"Windom?"

"Right, and it took about two minutes to scare him off. I think he is a little light in the guts division."

"Yeah, I got that impression," Daniels said, perching on the bed. "I don't think he's stupid, but he ain't what I'd call a criminal mastermind, either. He doesn't seem to have the force to match those macho looks. So what are you thinking?"

"Well, first off, what if it was the chief that tipped him about Myra being at the station?"

Daniels looked down and thought. "Damn! That seems to fit."

Powers wheeled his IV stand over to the window. "As far as Windom is concerned, I agree. Not a lot of force there. He acted like he was going to attack me, but the .45 warned him off. And when I started totting off everything that's going wrong for him, it overwhelmed him. He really got flustered when I asked how he knew Myra was at the police station.

"Sooo, what I'm starting to wonder, Bob, is whether he's somebody's puppet. Maybe it's his squeeze, Carlene, who's pulling the strings."

Daniels said, "Ahhhh, yes. The rich, acquisitive widow with the heaving bosom?"

"The same." Powers chuckled. "We should be getting something soon from my buddy and I included her on his list. According to old Mrs. Medlin, she was a pretty hot number and always was, shall we say, cherchez le homme."

"What?"

"I mean she's always on the lookout for guys. She's got herself on constant exhibit. And she supposedly has a pretty hot lifestyle – new cars every year, lots of travel to faraway places. Buying lots of foreign goods and antiques. That stuff doesn't come cheap."

"Yeah, but so what, Brad? Maybe Windom is milking the company for her. I hear it happens all the time. It might violate some federal pension laws, but it ain't the kind of crime we're interested in."

"Yeah, maybe." Powers said. "But how often does milking the business also involve a failing company on one hand and a majority owner-heiress with a big trust fund -- an heiress who touches a real sore spot when she starts talking to the trustee about plans for twin daughters to attend top-notch colleges? Does that make your pointy little ears quiver?"

"Hmmmm." Daniels' eyebrows rose as he mulled the idea.

Powers frowned. "Bob, my worry is that even though you rattled Windom's cage, maybe Carlene's cage isn't rattled at all. He might have gone to her – probably did – about your meeting with him and Myra. But if she's the driving force back of all this, she maybe just gave ol' Herby a treat, scratched his ears and got him all pumped up and ready to try something new."

"So, Brad, you think she needs to be rattled?"

"That's the way it looks to me."

"Wow, man! Well, let's both give it some thought. I can't do any cage-rattling the rest of this week because I'm swamped, but maybe over the weekend."

"By the way, Bob, what's turning up in Forrest's murder?"

"Right now it's starting to look like a dead end. He showed up at a local watering hole, the Hey Diddle Diddle Tavern out on the highway south of town. It has those breeding rooms upstairs where a fella can go get some honey on his stinger.

"But Forrest never got that far. He had a couple of beers by himself and then some guy came in and they got into a booth and split a pitcher. Then they both stepped out back for a smoke and never came back.

"So maybe 10 or 15 minutes later somebody else went out and found him face down on his own cigarette. The other guy's gone. Tells me he was surprised by somebody he knew."

"Whacked for real, eh?"

"Yep. Blunt force trauma to the occipital bone . . . right hand side. Great big blood puddle."

"Any description of the other guy?"

"Pretty vague. Better than middle height, pretty stout. Maybe middle aged. Glasses. Grubby work clothes, quilted jacket and a ball cap."

"Could have been the guy who drove the truck into my car next day."

"Maybe. Could have been anybody."

"Cell phone?"

Daniels stood up to leave, "If Bluto had a phone, it was gone."

They heard a knock. "Eh, Senor Powers? It is okay if we can come in, no?"

Powers called out, "Hey, Rosa! Do come in, por favor."

Grinning, Rosa walked into the room, a slightly nervous Myra in tow. Powers walked toward Myra, steering the IV stand around the bed and past the chair. "Oh, man, am I glad to see you."

Chapter 47

Myra knit her eyebrows as she reached out to gently touch Powers' black eye and then traced the cheekbone below it.

"Oh, Brad, your poor face is starting to look like a piece of modern art. We could title it Saffron Morning. I hope it's not too painful."

"Milady," Powers said, "it feels better already. You have the royal touch. But how 'bout we just call it Brad's Boo-Boo and let it go at that?" Myra chuckled and started to give him a big hug.

He stiffened. "Ahhhhhh. Easy! Easy! Please, don't ye squeeze me. These ribs are trying to knit."

"Ooops. Sorry. Okay, how 'bout just a little gentle cuddle?"

"Great! How about a kiss, too?"

"Don't push your luck, big boy." Then she gave him a peck on the cheek.

Over Myra's shoulder, Powers caught a quick glimpse of Rosa beaming. "Thank you both for coming to see me," he said as Myra broke the hug. "And thank you for coming with her, Rosa."

"Ah, de nada. Hey, Brad, this is one very nice lady."

"I know," Powers said. They awkwardly stood back from each other, Myra conspicuously avoiding looking at Daniels.

"Who sent the roses?" Myra asked.

"Funny you should ask. We think they're from Carlene Purdy."

In unison Myra and Rosa exploded, "What?"

Powers hastily explained the meeting he described to Daniels . . . and Carlene's parting words which appeared on the card.

With a sneer, Rosa demanded, "Why you were in a bar with that puta?"

"I wasn't with her, Rosa. I was in the bar eating lunch when she came in. She acted like she wanted to get frisky and I gave her the brush-off."

"What is this brush-off?" Rosa said, frowning.

"I showed that she didn't interest me," Powers said. "Not now, not ever."

"That's good, Brad," Myra said vehemently. "She is vicious and pure poison."

"Si! You should never see that puta again."

"Ladies, don't worry," Daniels said. "That bouquet isn't a love gesture. We think it's a warning . . . or maybe a threat."

In icy tones, Myra asked, "Exactly what do you mean by that, Detective?"

"Hey, ease up Myra," Powers said. "Bob's is very much on our side. We're beginning to suspect Carlene's involved in a lot of this trouble. Rosa tipped us off to some things about her."

"Detective Daniels," Myra said, "please accept my apologies. I've been a bit rattled lately, and your little interview with us didn't help." Daniels nodded and smiled.

"I think Rosa is a very special friend," Myra added. "She's making one of her apartments available to me and the girls. After we leave here, I'm going to see my lawyer about filing for separate maintenance and maybe we can move over the weekend."

Powers said, "Oh." He lowered his eyes. "Oh boy!"

Myra looked stricken at his reaction. "Is something wrong?" she asked with an edge to her voice.

Powers grasped her hands. "Myra, I'm glad you want to take this step – very glad. But I hope your lawyer has no relationship with Herb or with Purdy Precision Castings – in fact, I hope he's an out-of-town guy."

She looked perplexed.

Daniels chimed in. "Mrs. Windom, I think Brad is giving you some damned good advice. Southland is a very small town. You know the motto: 'Ten Thousand Friendly People' and everybody is in everybody else's back pocket.

"You say 'Boo!' around here," he added, "and in 10 seconds the cocktail circuit knows all about it."

"Amen," Powers said. "Second, we still aren't quite sure who our real opponent is. So please find you a good out-of-town lawyer and get him up to date.

"And give us a few days and we'll know what we're facing . . . and we may be able to bring in some troops of our own.

"Meanwhile," he looked up with a smile, "let me take a guess at what apartment Rosa found for you."

She smiled back.

Chapter 48

On his noon visit three days later, Daniels brought Powers a manila envelope. It was hand-addressed in block letters and bore no return address.

"Ah-ha! It looks like old Bevis came through for us," Powers said, pulling out three typewritten sheets and a hand-printed note.

> Found these papers on the sidewalk. Somebody's been squeezing this little cash cow awfully hard. And if you start interrupting, they're likely to get really pissed off, so you'd best watch your six, buddy.

He scanned the papers, handing them one-by-one to the detective. "Wow, this seems to crystalize things a bit."

After five minutes, Daniels looked up from reading. "Man, what a scam. Yeah, it tells us who's who. Myra's definitely the victim to the tune of a couple million bucks or so. I think it shows a pretty clear motive for Chet Purdy's murder."

"Yep, Bob. And I'd say it shows that poor stupid old Bluto was just a loose end."

"Brad, do you mind if I copy this?"

"Not a problem. Just keep it strictly between us for now. It has no legal standing, anyway, and no source information so it's not much use."

"Right, Brad, but Myra's new lawyer sure as hell ought to know what's going on. He can ask the court to order a discovery and that brings everything out into the open for civil proceedings. And . . ." Daniels added, "it mightn't hurt if a little bird tipped off the county prosecutor. He could get a subpoena for all this material."

"This really makes me want out of here," Powers said. He told Daniels the doctors were supposed to remove the chest tube and release him that afternoon.

"How are your ribs?" Daniels asked.

"They're sore. It hurts a bit to sneeze or cough, but that's how it is and all. It's the knee that's really painful."

"Sorry to hear it," Daniels said. "Be right back." He went out to the nurses' station to make copies. Minutes after the detective returned, the pulmonologist sailed into the room, introducing his preceptor who was with him on rounds.

Daniels started to leave.

"This won't take long, so it's okay to stay," the doctor told Daiels as he lifted Powers' bed jacket to examine the tube and incision. "This probably will take about two minutes."

Murmuring medical jargon to the preceptor looking over his shoulder, the doctor examined the site again.

"Okay, Mr. Powers," he said at last. "I'm going to pull out the tube and then I'll tighten the sutures to close the incision. Then I'll bandage it and you can be on your way. We'll supply you with some pain meds. I just don't want you to do any showering until you check with your own doctor in three days.

"Now, I want you to take a deep breath. I'll count three before I pull the tube out.

"So when I get to 'three' I want you to expel air as hard as you can with your lips pursed. That causes back pressure which expands the ribs and helps the removal.

"Ready?"

"Ready, Doc." Powers inhaled as deeply as possible. When the doctor reached three and pulled out the tube, Powers blasted out air as hard as he could, and then tried to imitate the *brudden-brudden!* of a starting lawn mower, as if the doctor had yanked on a starter cord.

Daniels and the preceptor both laughed aloud. The doctor, stone-faced, turned the tube back and forth in his hand, viewing it from all angles.

"Great job, Doc," Daniels said. "I didn't even feel it come out."

"Good, but you'll sure as hell feel it when I snug up your sutures."

❧   ❧   ❧

Chapter 49

Late the next afternoon, Powers pulled out a chair for Myra at his kitchen table. As they seated themselves, he laid a large legal pad filled with figures at his right hand. He looked at her briefly, not knowing quite where to start.

"Myra, I've got some good news and some bad news."

"Well, don't fudge around about it, Brad. Tell me what's going on."

"There's so much here," he said, drumming with his pencil on the tablet, "that it's hard to know where to begin. Bottom line: for almost 20 years, Herb has systematically looted your trust, apparently funneling most of that money to Carlene.

"The bad news, Myra, is that the trust -- which should contain minimum $3 million by now -- actually has just under $300,000.

"The good news is that you've got enough in the trust to finance the girls' college."

She gave a sigh of relief. "Thank God at least for that."

"I'm no finance man," he added, "but beyond that I doubt the remainder can support your current life-style."

"That's the least of my worries," she said. "I lived rough while I was a runaway and I can do it again. I certainly don't need a 4,000-square foot house or cleaning ladies or yard service. The girls are the main thing."

She lowered her head into her hands.

"Lady," he said, "you have more than your share of plain old guts."

"My God, Brad," she said quietly, "this raises about ten thousand questions . . . the most important one is what stops him from raiding the rest of the trust bright and early tomorrow morning?"

"Right. I think we need to call your lawyer first thing," Powers said. "He's got to move fast in court for some kind of order or an injunction for a full accounting of the trust and to freeze its activities, and to strip Herb's trust authority.

"I also think you should talk to the lawyer about filing a criminal complaint against Herb and Carlene – fraud and conspiracy at the very least, tax evasion probably, and I think there's more."

"He and Carlene did all this together?"

"Yep," Powers said. "They're a team. They've known each other since her childhood in Philadelphia. He never attended Wharton, by the way. He only went to a junior college and one year at a business college. And it looks as if he's been sleeping with her since before your father's death."

"Oh, my God! I knew she was poison . . . Wait, Brad, how did you find all this out?"

"Daniels and I worked it together. The finance part, I can't tell you."

"What do you mean, you can't tell me?"

"Myra, I got this information in confidence from a former Army colleague. I can't reveal his identity or it would destroy him."

She stared at him for a minute. "You know, Brad, Herb told me crap like that for 20 years. 'There, there, Little Lady, don't bother your pretty head about it.' It sounds like the good ole' boy network all over."

Powers flushed and took a deep breath. She held her head in her hands again for a moment and then stared back up at him.

"Myra," he said, "I am trying to draw the clearest possible picture for you. Whenever this goes to trial, all this information will be brought out officially, right down to the last penny."

"How do I know I can trust you . . . or any of this?"

He look at her flabbergasted. "Well," he said finally, "I guess you don't."

She stood up. "It sounds like a damned set-up to me, Mr. Powers. You win my confidence and trust and then all this . . . I don't know what to think about you right now."

"Are you serious, Myra!" he snapped. "Think for a minute! Do you believe I just dreamed up Rae's garden and the story about my late ex-wife? You're acting like you think it's all a well-rehearsed soap opera . . . or a *Mission Impossible* movie. Maybe you think all the folks in the nursing home dining room were extras . . . and that Burt and Gywn are back in Hollywood right now sucking down vodka gimlets while waiting for their next gig."

He stood up, facing her over the table.

"Oh, yeah, and of course the studio hired a stunt man to play Bluto, so I could put on that fake ninja act. And Officer Hasselbeck's real name is Bob Foonman and he's from Acting Central, too.

"Of course Bluto's supposed to be dead now," Powers added, "so you can't check with him personally, unless maybe you can locate him on his slab in the morgue through his agent in Actors' Equity."

"Brad, I . . ."

"Yeah, it's confusing," he said. "I hope you haven't forgotten that Bluto and your father were murdered in exactly the same way: blunt force trauma to the right base of the skull? Maybe you think I staged that killing, too."

"Stop it!" she screamed. "Stop it!" She clapped her hands over her ears and sobbed, rocking forward and back in her chair. He knelt and put his arm around her.

"Don't touch me, damn you!" she sobbed, but soon leaned against him as the storm subsided.

"Brad, please forgive . . ."

"Hush," he said, "I shouldn't have snarled at you like that. I guess this is getting to both of us." He kissed her cheek and, with a grunting effort, got back to his feet and returned to his chair.

She blew her nose and gave a weak chuckle. "Foonman, Brad? Foonman? Where did you ever dream up a name like that?"

"I think I remember it from an old edition of *Mad* magazine about 30 years ago."

They talked more than an hour, she questioning him minutely and he answering as precisely as he could.

She finally asked whether there were any chance of recovering any of the money. Powers doubted it, but said the courts would decide.

"Was daddy's death part of this?"

Powers said, "I think so. It seems to fit the pattern. But we don't have concrete evidence about it."

"You think Herb may have done it?"

"Myra, I just can't say at this point."

"My God," she said, "this is overwhelming . . . but somehow none of it really surprises me."

∽ ∽ ∽

Chapter 50

Leaving his notes on the table, Powers got up. "Sorry, Myra. I can't sit this long without my knee locking up. I'm going make a few circuits around the room."

She nodded, staring at his notes as he limped in slow circles.

She was ignoring the coffee by her elbow. He turned back toward her. "Is the coffee cold? Do you need a refill?"

Silence.

"Myra?"

"Sorry. Coffee's fine," she said, looking at him. "I've just been thinking . . ." her voice trailed off.

Pausing in his walk, he stood and stretched for a moment in front of his son's photo. *How're you doing, Boy?*

He resumed pacing and glanced at Myra. She was looking directly at him, holding his eyes, her face lowered so that he could barely discern her pupils below her brows.

"Myra? You okay?"

"No," she said in a whisper, still locking on his eyes.

Powers' breath suddenly thickened in his throat. He circled behind Myra, placing his hands on her shoulders. She raised her shoulders as if to trap his hands against the sides of her neck.

He leaned over and pulled her hair away from her right ear. As he nuzzled her there, she relaxed her shoulders. He lowered his face to kiss her neck, then moved his lips, barely touching her skin, from her neck to the well of her collar bone and then back up to her ear.

She tilted her head back and murmured. Then in a rush she arose and turned into him and they both were breathing like sprinters. His heart began to sledge in his chest.

"This is stupid," he murmured, his voice quivering.

"Quiet," she said, holding his face in her hands and gently fitting her lips to his. She reached around his neck and pulled her body to his.

He broke the kiss and panted, "Let's go to the couch."

153

"No, Brad," she said. "Your bed."

And then they were in the little bedroom.

He fumbled with her shirt buttons. She helped. He turned her away and slowly pulled the fabric off her shoulders easing it tenderly down her arms, kissing her bare right arm and feeling the goose bumps rise.

His fingers felt like thumbs and it took him a long clumsy time to undo the little bra latches. She murmured, "You seem to be out of practice."

Slowly easing the bra straps down her arms, he said. "I think I'm starting to remember."

He reached around to cup her breasts, pressing his hands up against their solid weight, pulling her against him. She arched to him, taking in a huge white gasp and then releasing it. "Ohhhhhhh."

They led each other to the bed. She said, "Brad, I forgot about your ribs and your incision. Maybe we should wait . . ."

"Be quiet, woman."

She gently pulled his golf shirt up over his head. He stepped out of his bermudas.

Still standing, they pressed their bodies together. If she looked trim and fit when dressed, now he found her achingly voluptuous and incredibly soft to his touch.

Still facing, they lay down slowly, to knees, to elbows, to their sides. He gave a quiet grunt at the pain in his ribs when he collapsed to his full length, but he dismissed it.

He buried his face in her bosom. She held a hand on each side of his head, guiding his mouth first to one breast, then to the other. He kissed and nibbled her nipples and gently sucked at them

He looked up to see her face tensed, head tilted back and mouth yawning. He inched upward in the bed to kiss her and she enfolded him in the most warming, welcoming, healing embrace he could ever remember. He clung tightly to her, shuddering with joy and wonder, tears beginning to roll from his eyes.

"Myra," he whispered hoarsely, "I've so wanted to hold you and to be held by you. This is so wonderful. It's a miracle."

"Yes. Yes," and she muffled him with her insistent mouth.

So intent were they on each other they didn't hear the squeal of the screen door spring. Bowser crouched, staring at the door with saucer eyes.

But cats don't bark.

Chapter 51

Later, she turned her head lazily to him. "Brad, tell me a story."

He lay for a minute looking at the ceiling. A glance through the bedroom door at the kitchen window curtain showed him it already was nearly dusk. He looked back at the ceiling, saying nothing.

"Dear, I don't mean to disturb you," she said. "I just want to know something more about the man who made such wonderful love with me."

He turned onto his right side, facing her and propping his head onto his hand, resting his other hand on her waist. "Such a beautiful girl," he said softly. "And I don't feel in the least disturbed." he added, smiling. "It's a serious request and deserves a serious answer.

"Now, here's a story," he said, relating a time when he was convalescing in a second-story hospital room in Germany. It overlooked a small snowy lawn.

"The lawn was maybe only 30 yards long and, oh, maybe 10 wide. It edged a wooded area with a lot of brush and brambles and fallen logs."

She closed her eyes and moved lower in the bed to lay her ear against his chest, enjoying the resonance of his voice. She pushed her knee between his legs.

"Whoa Myra," he gulped. "Now *that's* disturbing. It makes it a little hard to concentrate on telling my story. Gee, I don't know if I can go on, now."

She chuckled and he hugged her and pressed his lips into her hair, inhaling her scent. Combing her hair over and over with his fingers, he said, "Well, as I was trying to say . . . what was I trying to say? Oh, now I remember."

He told her that every dawn a grumpy German janitor with a wide push broom came out and shoved the night's snow from an area on the lawn about the width and length of a pickup truck.

Then the old man sprinkled seeds and cracked corn all over the place. And a couple of steel shepherd's crooks held bird feeders – one with suet and one with something else.

"Anyway, when he was finished, he'd hoist the broom over his shoulder just as if it was a rifle and he'd do an about-face and march right back indoors."

Powers lifted his hand and snapped his fingers.

"When he closed the door, it was like a signal. The birds started showing up. Titmice on the feeders, finches of all sorts.

"They literally were just falling out of the trees, braking in flight at the last inch above ground. Snow buntings. Jackdaws – great birds, those Jackdaws, a little bit like our crows, but much more tame acting. Anyway, they just seemed to show up in flocks."

As he talked, he lowered his hand back to her hip and then slowly moved it to her waist causing a huff of breath on his chest.

"If I opened the window a crack very, very slowly . . ." his hand began a slow journey upward to her ribs ". . . I could hear all the twittering and the whir and rush of their wings. I'd just sit back and watch and marvel," he said, whispering, as if not to startle the birds he remembered.

"Every few minutes the whole flock would take off all together into the brush. You could see them perched in there like so many Christmas tree ornaments. And then slowly, in twos and threes, they'd start fluttering back.

"I could sit and watch for hours. It was so restful and peaceful. And I often thought how wonderful it would be to be able to reach over and hold my lady's hand, right there beside me sharing and savoring . . . ." She smiled at the image.

"Anyway, darling Myra, that's a story I'd love to live over and over with you."

"I'd love it too," she yawned. "Sounds like the best way to awaken in the morning."

"Ohhhhh, I don't know," he said.

He gently tilted her to her back, and with his knuckles gently angled her face upward. He kissed her lips as he moved his palm back to her ribs and then upward to caress her breast. Her body gave a slight quiver.

"I think it's the second best way to wake up."

"You devil," she chuckled, and reaching up, she pulled his face to hers.

Chapter 52

Bowser began an insistent whining which slowly deepened to a series of loud yowls. Myra shook Powers' shoulder and he awakened with an "Ouch!"

"Oh, my God, Brad. I'm sorry! I forgot your ribs. I think Bowser wants out. I'll go." She started to stand up from the bed but so did Powers.

"Dammit, cat!" Powers mumbled. He reached out to grasp Myra around the waist, gently restraining her. "No sweetheart," he said, and then pulled her back into the bed. "You stay here and I'll let the mooch out."

Their movement had pulled the sheet from Myra's body. He got out of bed and bent to give her several gentle kisses. "You just lie right here and keep looking as beautiful as you do now."

He stumbled briefly pulling on his bermudas and then padded toward the living room. He turned around in the doorway to look back at her. "I love you!"

He disappeared through the door and returned immediately, grinning. "And I'll call you in the morning – and every morning!"

As he disappeared again, she stretched and smiled.

"I love you, too," she whispered, as she heard the screen door squeal open. She heard him say, "Raus, cat! And don't bring your furry butt back here for at least a week!"

A pause and then came the sound of paper ripping as the door closed.

"Oh no! Oh, my God!"

Myra jumped from the bed and ran into the living room. "Brad! What is it?"

His face was dead white. A FedEx folder lay on the table and he was rereading a single sheet of paper.

He looked up. "Matt's wounded."

Scrambling into her shirt, she asked, "How bad is it?"

"Don't know. Says here they tried to call. I guess it was bad enough. They evacuated him all the way from the Mid-East to Walter Reed, the Army medical center. It's in Bethesda, outside Washington, D.C.

"It says that his condition is guarded, whatever that means. Damn! The best day of my entire life suddenly is also the worst. Couldn't happen at a worse time with all that we're trying to accomplish here in Southland."

He slapped the table in frustration. "Son of a bitch!"

"Brad, you've got to go to him."

"I know, but I won't leave you here in danger. I just won't. Not now! Especially not after this . . . and us discovering each other today. And don't forget that we've got to meet with your lawyer first thing tomorrow."

"Please excuse me," he said, and sat down at the phone, punching in the patient information number from the letter. Myra went to dress, listening as he worked through the folderol of identifying himself as the letter's recipient and the patient's nearest – only -- relative.

He spoke in occasional monosyllables. Once he said, "Well, can I speak with him?" Later he asked, "What does that mean, sir?" And then, "I know this is not a fair question, but based on what you've seen in similar cases, how would you rate his chances?"

Finally he said, "Thank you very much for your help and patience with me, Captain. I really appreciate it. And, sir, you'll have somebody call if there's any change, right?"

He replaced the phone in its charger and looked up at Myra.

"Well, he's got all his fingers and toes but he has a closed head injury and he's in a coma." He dropped his head into his hands. "Ah, God!" and his shoulders began shaking.

Myra stood beside him and pulled his head against her stomach and rocked him. He put his arms around her hips and pressed his head into her.

A few minutes later he pulled back, looked up and said, "Thank you, Myra. And bless you for being here."

"Brad, I have an idea."

"What?" he said, sitting back and grinding the heels of his hands into his eye sockets.

She sat down to face him.

"Look, we've got to go to Indianapolis tomorrow morning to meet with my lawyer, right? And if you're going to Washington, you've got to catch the plane in Indianapolis. So why don't we go right now? Tonight!"

"What?"

"Herb, think about it. We can get an airport motel room – Comfort Inn or something like that. You can brief the lawyer first thing in the morning and be on your way to see your son, and I can come home when I'm through."

He reflected briefly. "Great idea. And rather than send signals by taking your car, I'll call Bob see if I can get him to rent one and bring it over. What about clothes and things for you?"

"There's a Meijer's in Moorseville right on the way to the airport. It's open all night and I can get everything I need in 20 minutes."

"And what about the girls?"

"Oh, I didn't tell you? They're in Chicago staying with their great-uncle . . . my dad's kid brother."

For the first time since he received the letter, Powers smiled. "Gee, Myra, this is almost like you planned to spend tonight with me."

She smiled back and shook her head. "No, Brad. I didn't. I just wanted them out of town and away from Herb while we find out what's what from the lawyer."

She paused and then bent down to give him a long kiss. "But it did work out sweetly, didn't it?"

"Very, very sweetly! When we get to the motel I figure on registering us as Mr. and Mrs. Brandon H. Powers."

"It has a nice sound, doesn't it? I know I feel more like I'm married this minute than I have for 15 years."

He pulled the .45 from his dresser. "Let's go, Babe."

She eyed the pistol.

"I'm just giving it to Bob for safe-keeping."

Using the alley behind the property, they walked to a nearby service station.

Daniels met them 45 minutes later with a rental Lincoln.

None of them saw the man concealed in the bushes and watching them from across the street – the man who followed them on foot from Powers' apartment.

Chapter 53

Powers later looked back at the flight from Indianapolis to Reagan Airport as the worst three hours of his life, worse than wounds or seeing squad mates shredded in Iraq.

Not counting the security search lines, it was three solid hours of unremitting sweaty anxiety about whether Sergeant First Class Matthew James Powers would end up a vegetable on life support; anxiety that Myra wasn't with him to cushion his fears; anxiety that he was separated from Myra; anxiety whether Myra could be in danger; anxiety whether in his absence Myra might lose her feelings for him.

I guess Gwyn was right. I was alone too long. And now I'm alone again.

He chuckled derisively at himself for wracking his mind into a mental stew. It reminded him of stories he heard about the orientations soldiers received when they arrived at Tan Son Nhut Airport in Vietnam.

A special services sergeant holding a mike had paced the stage, warning that any bicycle, any Renault taxi, any Lambretta tricycle auto, any motor scooter, any rickshaw and any ox cart could be filled with plastic explosive. "If somebody parks one of them bikes or Honda scooters or rickshaws or one of those little Renaults outside your hooch, get OUT! Because its tubing or its trunk is probably loaded with plastique just waiting to detonate!"

Then as they filed aboard the waiting busses after the lecture they went slack-jawed at the sight of a huge parking lot. Hundreds of Honda motor bikes packed it – along with Renault taxis, civilian jeeps, rickshaws, Citroen sedans, bicycles, scooters and Lambrettas.

"Well," a corporal announced, "it's either a case of go crazy or forget about it."

Powers thought back to his meeting with Myra and the lawyer, a testy little bulldog of a man who kept interrupting. Powers finally told him, "Look, dammit, I've got a plane to catch . . ."

Myra interceded. "Mr. Schoener, Brad just found out his son is wounded and he's at Walter Reed Hospital. He only has a few minutes before he has to catch his plane."

"Sorry, Mr. Powers," Schoener said. "I'll shut my yap right now. Please proceed."

Powers quickly sketched the indications of fraud, theft and conspiracy on the part of Herbert Windom and Carlene Purdy and an unknown party or parties.

He urged the attorney to take legal steps to immediately protect and preserve what remained of the trust fund and to even obtain restitution from certain possible overseas accounts.

As he left the office, he was pleased to see Schoener drop his hard-case attitude and begin questioning Myra slowly and in great detail, making notes on a yellow legal pad. Powers caught a taxi to the airport, leaving the Lincoln rental for Myra.

# # #

Powers thought himself mentally prepared for ruby-numbered monitors, IVs, wires, crawling heart-rhythm charts, tubes and beeping devices, but it still wrenched him to see his son virtually buried in medical technology.

He was relieved to learn that the doctors had artificially extended the coma to give Matt's brain time to recover from the shock of his head injury. The cause of the injury was a non-penetrating strike either by bullet or shrapnel. Matt's Kevlar helmet had saved his life and prevented a skull fracture.

Nonetheless, he sustained a wound to the left scalp. The laceration looked superficial, but whatever struck him had severed the upper arc of the ear. Thanks to the respirator mask, it was impossible to see much else of Matt's features, but the left side of his face appeared bruised far worse than Powers' own shiner.

The nurses told Powers to speak to Matt as much as possible.

He drew up a chair by the bed and, holding Matt's free hand, began reciting the same Yeats poem with which he lulled his son to sleep as a child.

Where dips the rocky highland of Sleuth Wood in the lake
there lies a leafy island where flapping herons wake

164

the drowsy water rats. There we've hid our faery vats
full of berries and the reddest stolen cherries . . .

From time to time Matt's hand twitched. Occasionally a slight
frown knitted his brow. The neurosurgeon said Matt's vital signs
were excellent and they were reducing the coma medication. He
might regain consciousness the following morning.

Powers also learned Matt's condition actually wasn't as grave as
implied by medical evacuation to the United States. The Army
returned him to the U.S. because his tour of duty in Afghanistan –
which he already had extended once -- was near its end.

Parched after three hours of poetry recitation, Powers was
getting a drink when Myra called. Cell reception inside the mammoth
hospital was bad, so Powers went outside to return her call.

She was excited but tired after a day with the lawyer.

"Dear, I've got so much to tell you," she said. "But first how's
your son?"

Hearing her say "Dear" gave a glad squeeze to Powers' heart. He
told Myra he felt much more optimistic than when he boarded the
flight that morning. "And we'll know a lot more tomorrow. So I'm
doing something I haven't done in a long time. I'm praying. Now,
Myra darling, how are things with you?"

She said Schoener felt that tomorrow he could obtain a
temporary injunction freezing all disbursements from the trust.

"Boy, is that good news. And then what?"

Myra said Schoener planned to follow up with a motion to
transfer control of the trust to the holding bank's trust department.

"I don't understand everything else," Myra said. "Mr. Schoener
said something about scheduling a hearing for a permanent
injunction and filing motions for discovery of the trust's activities, of
Herb's assets and Carlene's assets. He also introduced me to a
divorce attorney in his firm. He says she's topnotch and I've got a
meeting with the two of them tomorrow so they can coordinate."

"Oh, boy. Well you can bet their meters already are running, but
artillery is expensive and they are our artillery. So, you say you're not
driving home tonight? I think that's good a very good idea."

"Right. Mr. Schoener thought I should stay here until you get back or until I could arrange some kind of protection through Sergeant Daniels."

"Good thinking," Powers said. "The only thing wrong now is that I really, really miss you. It was horrible flying to Washington without even being able to hold hands."

"I'm sorry," Myra said. "But I'm glad that you miss me as much as I miss you."

"Listen to us," he said. "We sound like two high school kids. And I love it. And you don't know how much better that makes me feel. I've got to sign off now and get back to my boy. I love you."

"I love you," she replied, making a smooch noise in his ear.

Chapter 54

Powers dozed at Matt's bedside, awakening when nurses came in to change his IVs and check his vitals.

He kept watching his son for some signs of consciousness and was rewarded once when the patient slid his free hand upward to his chest. The only sounds, however, came from the monitors, the IV pump and the motor slowly canting Matt's hospital bed side-to-side.

When the neurosurgeon arrived at 5:30 a.m., a groggy Powers said, "Damn, Doc! It looks like your reveille is at Oh Dark Thirty, just like it is for the troops."

"You bet," the surgeon smiled. "Got to get here early in this business. I hit the sack at night right after my kids go to bed."

He warned Powers that his son wouldn't emerge from the coma by just awakening; that it was a gradual process. "The point is, you and your boy aren't going to be catching up by lunch time today. Being on a respirator, of course, he can't speak."

"That's okay, Doc. During Desert Storm I went through some of this myself at Landstuhl Medical Center in Germany, so I've got some feel for what's going on. There's no rush as long as he can recover and be himself again."

By noon, Matt actually seemed to be stirring.

When Powers went outside to walk and to phone Myra, she told him the divorce lawyer was a female counterpart of Schoener – short, grim, blunt and hard-bitten. Myra said the lawyer was planning to have papers served on Windom tomorrow.

Myra also had talked with Daniels who was ready to arrange for off-duty cops to escort either her or Windom into the home depending on who would be moving out.

By that same evening, the staff took Matt off the respirator and he began opening his eyes and occasionally muttering though nothing was coherent.

About midnight a whisper brought Powers to the surface of consciousness like a trout to a fly. Matt was staring at him. In a raspy voice he asked, "Who are you?"

Powers felt the tears sting as he scooched his chair closer. "Hey, Sarge, how you doing? I'm your father." He pushed the call button and then gripped his son's hand for a moment.

"Oh." Matt swallowed repeatedly. "Throat hurts. Where am I?"

"You're back in CONUS . . . the good old US of A."

"Hospital?"

"Yep. Walter Reed. Don't worry about it for now."

"If you say so, sir" Matt shook his head and winced. "And you're my dad. Somehow, I kind of remember."

A younger nurse bustled in, "Oh, Sergeant Powers, you're with us. Wonderful! Would you like to have some ice chips for your throat?"

Matt nodded, immediately wincing. He then winked at her. As she left, he held his head still but turned his eyes to Powers. "Man, she's a beauty." By the time the nurse returned, he was asleep snoring faintly.

"Is falling asleep a good or bad sign?" Powers whispered.

"Oh, it's a very good sign. He'll probably do a lot of napping. The great news is that he seemed coherent."

"Yes. When you left to get the ice he said, 'Man, she's a beauty'."

She laughed. "That's a very good sign."

"You bet," Powers said, grinning. "It at least shows his powers of observation are unimpaired. Oh, and by the way, he's a bachelor."

She laughed aloud. "Let's not get ahead of ourselves here. Don't be surprised if he has some amnesia. And keep that ice handy for him because being on a respirator really makes the patient's throat sore."

"He didn't recognize me."

"That often happens. The doctors tell us that's partly due to the injury, and partly to the anesthetic. It takes time."

∽ ∽ ∽

168

Chapter 55

For three days Powers delighted in seeing his son learn to walk again. His balance was bad at first, but he soon was able to navigate, only needing occasional aid from a cane.

The medical staff was pleased with his physical progress, but were concerned about his temper, which tended to be short, and the loss of some memory.

Worse was his initial stubborn refusal to focus on some basic exercises such as word and math puzzles. They said his deficits called for some fairly intensive neurological therapy. That they'd keep him at least three weeks and perhaps longer.

"The good thing," a psychologist told Powers, "is that he's really willing to work. He gets snappish about what we ask, but then after some grousing he buckles down to it. I wish more of our patients had his determination."

Powers spoke three to four times a day with Myra who said she felt increasingly overwhelmed by legal complexities. She was lonely for Powers and for her daughters.

On the phone the evening of the sixth day she said her divorce lawyer reported that Windom would vacate the home with his personal property the following day.

"It almost seems too easy to me," she said. "His lawyer called mine, relaying a message that Herb wanted to talk about the girls and visitation. I refused, saying I couldn't because I was out of town. I don't want to speak with him about any of that. Not right now."

"Have you spoken with the girls?"

"Yes. They're fine. Their uncle has had them out on Lake Michigan on his sailboat. They live right on the shoreline north of Chicago, so he's got his own boat basin. He's very active for his age and they said he has just about worn them out crewing for him. But the upside . . ." Powers could visualize her rolling her eyes ". . . is that they've met some 'real neat' boyyyys."

Powers told Myra the psychologists said it would be better for Matt if Powers left now that he was assured of Matt's survival. He told her he was catching a plane to Indianapolis the following day. He asked her to meet him at the airport so they could drive back to Southland together.

"Brad, maybe I, ahem, shouldn't check out of the Comfort Inn quite yet. Hint. Hint. Hint."

She laughed when Powers said, "Gulp!"

"Wellllllll," Powers went on, "I guess there's no real rush to get back, is there? I mean, it doesn't matter if we delay an hour or so – or maybe six or eight hours."

"Now don't get carried away, Big Guy. I'm not exactly a spring chicken anymore."

"Oh, I don't know, Myra. You sure seemed to have more stamina than me. All that walking, you know."

"Well, Mr. Powers, I guess we'll just have to find out, won't we."

"You bet . . . er . . . Dear. Sorry, Myra. I haven't used endearments for years so they don't come easily. It's a nice novelty that I'm going to have to practice a lot. Meanwhile, I'll call you as soon as I line up my flight reservation. Is that okay . . . Honey?"

"That's great, Darling. I'm nibbling my lower lip just thinking about us together. Please hurry."

Powers spent most of the rest of the day lining up a late morning Southwest flight from Reagan to Indianapolis via Atlanta.

He hit the sack to take a nap and slept the night through.

Chapter 56

Powers dialed Myra's room phone about 8 a.m. to give her his arrival time.

No answer.

He tried her cell phone.

No answer.

He called the desk to leave a message for Mrs. Powers. "Oh, sir, Mr. and Mrs. Powers checked out about 5 a.m."

Powers' stomach went hollow. He felt sick. "What do you mean, 'checked out'?"

"Sir, I was here on the desk when Mr. Powers checked out."

"Well, that's really kind of odd seeing's how I happen to be Mr. Powers. I'm the Mr. Powers who checked us into your establishment last week. I'm calling from Washington, D.C. to notify my wife, Myra, to pick me up at the airport at 3:30 this afternoon."

"Well sir, I don't know what to tell you. A man identifying himself as Mr. Powers checked himself and his wife out."

"Did you see her?"

"No. She must have gone to their car separately."

"Describe him," Powers snapped.

"Sir, I don't think I should do that."

"Well, I'll tell you something, Miss. Within seconds I'm going to be on the phone to the police and they're going to descend on your establishment like a wet blanket – in fact, a soaked, dripping, absolutely sodden drop cloth -- unless you just give me this little bit of information. I'm very, very serious."

"Well, he was tall and good-looking."

"A full head of iron gray hair?"

"Yes sir, now that you mention it."

"And he was driving a white Lincoln?"

"I wouldn't know about that. The registration shows a license plate number but I didn't see the car. He just walked out the door and, of course, it was still pretty dark outside so I couldn't see much."

"Okay, thank you very much. I urge you to tell your manager about this call and to keep this all carefully in mind, because the police are going to be in touch and they'll want to know every detail you can remember.

"And I advise you not to let housecleaning touch that room. I suspect it's a crime scene. Again, thank you very much for your cooperation. My wife's life probably depends on it."

Powers called Daniels to tell him what happened. He also advised that Herb Windom had been served divorce papers and was supposed to be moved out of the family home tomorrow.

"Bob, I suggest you put out an APB for that rental Lincoln . . ."

Daniels interrupted. "Brad, stop trying to tell me my job. First, I'm gonna ask Sheriff Crockett to get the state bulls to see whether the Lincoln is still at the motel. If it is, then we have a problem trying to intercept him, not knowing what he's driving.

"Meanwhile, we'll keep an eye on the Windom residence. I recommend you get back here ASAP."

At 9, Powers called Schoener to say he believed Myra Windom possibly had been abducted.

Schoener said he hoped the authorities could locate her quickly. "Without her, Mr. Powers, we lose standing in court. We're dead in the water. You can't proceed if you have no plaintiff. Please keep in touch on this. And I hope you find her quickly because she's a very nice lady who's suffered some grievous injustices."

"For starters, Mr. Schoener, I just hope she's alive."

Chapter 57

When Powers walked up to Daniels' desk just before 5 p.m., the detective raised his hands and dropped them against his thighs.

"Definitely looks like kidnapping, Brad. We've got nothing. The state police said the rental Lincoln was still at your motel. They went through it and found nothing but your prints, my prints, Myra's prints and the prints of the rental staff.

"When they went through your room, though, they found some possible indications of a struggle. A slipper was found beneath one of the beds and a tube of some kind of make-up was on the floor behind the toilet.

"No blood, but a pillow case was missing and so was one of the top sheets. They also found powdery linen debris, as if the sheet had been torn or cut to make ties or a gag.

"At my request, the FBI is getting involved unofficially even though the mandatory three days isn't up. They want an interview with you."

"Face-to-face?"

"No, at my recommendation they already checked with Walter Reed so they know you were there when all this happened. Just give Special Agent James Hadden a call. I've talked with him twice today and he sounds very competent and like a straight shooter."

The call to Hadden's number went to voice mail.

"Agent Hadden, this is Brandon Powers returning your call at 5:05 p.m. regarding the disappearance of Myra Windom. I'm at this cell number at all times. You also can reach me through Detective Daniels of the Southland PD. If I don't hear from you by 10 a.m. tomorrow, I'll try to reach you again."

As Powers looked up from the phone he found himself looking into the eyes of Chief Ackers. The man looked purple with rage. "What the hell are you doing . . . in my police department?"

"Blow it out your gargantuan ass," Powers barked, coming to his feet. "I'm here in connection with an investigation of a kidnapping of a citizen of your damned city . . . and maybe a murder. If you don't like it you can . . ."

Daniels muscled Powers aside and snapped, "Back off, Powers!" He turned to Ackers.

"Chief, the bastard has information we need. Just let me handle it and I'll get him out of here as soon as I can. Okay? Yeah, we were buddies once, but that was 20 years ago. But he's a person of interest even if he is a piece of shit, but it'll be fine. I'll get rid of him."

Powers, now seated on a chair facing away from them, heard the chief. "Fine. You handle it again, but I don't want that son of a bitch hanging around here. He's just a goddam troublemaking hotdog."

The chief, turned away, grumbling and returned to his office. Daniels moved to Powers' chair and very loudly said, "Now, look wiseass, we're getting a little tired of you trying to throw your weight around. So shut up and stay put. I'm gonna get to you in a minute."

As soon as the chief left the room, Daniels took a chair and pretended to take notes on a legal pad as he told Powers the state police also found a gauze pad in the room and asked the state lab to test it for chloroform and for DNA. He said they speculated that Myra could have been anesthetized and then tied and wrapped in linens and transported in a car trunk.

"That bastard, Windom," Powers gritted. "Has he surfaced?"

"Oh, yes. Herby Windom seems to be spending the day with the movers, getting out of the house, per Myra's divorce filing. He put a lot of things in one of those rental storage units and moved into a motel. I called and asked him to come down and make a statement.

"He said that based on how I treated him and Myra two weeks ago he wouldn't come near the station without his attorney . . . that I was welcome to call his lawyer.

"So I did. Howie Feiler said he'd be happy to bring Herb to the station at any time I wish. So I told him 9 a.m. tomorrow. He said he didn't think the interview would be very productive – that Mrs. Windom has been depressed and overwrought, taking up with another man, yadda yadda yadda . . . disappeared, filed for divorce, irrational, forcing Mr. Windom from his home of 18 years, yadda yadda yadda . . . perhaps a repetition of her runaway teen years."

Powers let out a very convincing growl and clenched his fists until his knuckles cracked. "So that's the line the assholes are taking. That she's unstable or irresponsible. So what the hell are you going to do next?"

"Brad, dammit, I know you're stressed but calm down for Christ's sake! I'll have Windom here tomorrow and you're welcome to witness the interview – but through the one-way mirror and only – Only! -- if you promise you'll keep your mouth shut."

"Okay. I promise. Now are the state cops checking on the sexual harassment investigations being brought against Windom?"

"I made sure today that they know about it. They'll be checking."

"Good," Powers said, "I want to see you sweat this SOB as much as possible. I want to break him and find out what he's done with her. I hope some criminal charges can be filed against him, too – you know, fraud, conspiracy, assault, kidnapping, maybe murder."

"Brad, he's a person of interest, not a suspect. Not yet. So we can't get a warrant for his financials. We're doing everything we can. Now, do I have your promise about keeping quiet tomorrow?"

"I promise, Bob," Powers said. "And, thanks. I know you're doing all you can."

"Thanks. Now why don't you go home and get a shower and read or something."

"Okay, Bob. I'll get out of your hair – well, I'd get out of your hair if you had any."

"Up yours! And get out before I arrest you!"

Chapter 58

Powers was unlocking the door to his apartment when Rosa pulled into the driveway, looking at him through the passenger window of her car.

"Hi, Rosa," he said, trying to pronounce it correctly.

"Mr. Brad," she said, "I am so sorry about what is happened to Myra. Bob called me and said you were coming home, so I brought you some dinner."

"Oh, thank you so very much, Rosa, but I'm too depressed to want food."

She alighted from her car carrying a large wicker basket and a long-necked bottle. "Don't be an estupid gringo, Brad. You must eat to be strong for Myra. So let me in and I give you dinner."

Powers sighed and opened the door for her. The squawk of the rusty door spring grated on their nerves.

Once into the apartment, she set the basket down and give Powers a quick hug and kissed him on both cheeks. "Senor Brad. I promise I get you a new screen door that don't screech. Now," she ordered, "go unpack your bags and shower and get on nice clean clothes and I have dinner ready for you."

Powers, feeling numb, obeyed orders. When he returned to the front room, the table was set with a plate of steaming enchiladas and a glass of chilled sangria. Rosa was sitting on the opposite side of the table, her eyes fixed on him. "So, tell me what you think has happened to Myra."

"He either has her prisoner or I'm afraid he's killed her."

She slammed her hand on the table hard enough to rattle Powers' silverware. "No, Senor Brad! I do not believe it! I know she is alive. I feel it in here in my heart. She is a prisoner and we must find her."

With the first bite of food he discovered he was ravenous. She nodded approval as he devoured her food and sipped the sangria. He listened to Rosa speculate that Myra must be tied or chained in the basement of the Purdy house.

"When my Luisa worked there, the puta didn't want her going to the basement. The puta told her it had many espensive things all locked up. I think they lock Myra down there."

"That's a thought, Rosa. I'll be sure to tell Bob."

"Okay. Meanwhile, tomorrow I clean the apartment upstairs for Myra and her girls so that they can move in."

Suddenly, Powers found himself nodding. "Rosa," he said, "I'm sorry, but I'm about to fall asleep right here on the table."

"Si," she said. "Some good food and a little wine. I go home now so there will be no noise upstairs and you can go to bed and sleep! Okay? Be ready tomorrow to help, yes?"

"Okay, Rosa. And thank you so much."

She gave him another hug and left. He barely had time to shuck his clothes before discovering Rosa had turned back the sheets for him.

He collapsed into sleep.

Chapter 59

Powers awakened about dawn to the slow rhythmic pricking of needles in his chest. He tilted his head up from the pillow. Bowser's golden eyes, pupils vertically slitted, were fixed on him. The cat was purring and making biscuits right on his pecs.

"What the hell are you doing here?"

The cat showed off its needle teeth with a gaping yawn. Then it looked Powers in the eyes and said "Arraaowww."

Powers dropped his head back to the pillow and closed his eyes and the cat only dug in deeper. Powers wanted to shove the big feline off his chest. But the bushy tail lashing back and forth on his stomach told him that Bowser's temper was changing. The cat's mood dial was moving up from Somewhat Impatient to Condition Red.

Painful experience told Powers any sudden move would lead to a sudden hard push-off, with all 10 back claws digging in deeply.

"Okay! Okay. I guess Rosa must have let you in when she left."

He stroked the spot between the big tabby's ears where the frown lines merged. Bowser pushed his head against the stroking for a minute and then jumped down to the floor.

Yesterday's events came flooding back – along with a deep-freeze chill of fear for Myra. Powers swung his legs over the side of the bed.

The cat, tail high, walked to the door and turned back to give him The Look: Failure To Comply would result in a bitten ankle.

"I'm coming, you fuzzy bastard. Don't rush me."

Standing back out of view, he opened the living room door. Bowser shouldered the screen door open, stalking out into his world of hedges, yards and birds.

As Powers closed the door, the phone rang.

"Yeah!"

"It's me," Daniels said. "You better get your ass down here to the station because I think we may have gotten a break."

"Okay, Bob. I just got up. I'm gonna grab some coffee on the way. Should I bring you some?"

"Yeah, man. With cream. And some Twinkies."

"Twinkies? Seriously?"

"I been here all night. I need Twinkies."

# # #

Powers walked straight to Daniels' desk and set a large coffee on his desk.

"They were out of Twinkies, so I got these things." He dropped three plastic-wrapped confections on the desk. They thudded when they landed beside the coffee.

"Jesus, Brad, these damned things look like frosted cow pies."

"Gee, Bob, life's a bitch, you know? Now, what's the break?"

Biting into a Speedway Danish, Daniels said, "Well, Myra's alive. They allowed her to call her daughters very briefly. And the girls noted that it's an 812 area code. That narrows it down to the southern third of the state."

"That's our break?"

"Well, one of the girls – I think her name is Jennifer – noticed something else, but she'll only tell it to you. Something about some French words her mother was using."

"And she wants to talk to me? I'm not one of her favorite people and the only French I know is 'oui'."

"Yeah, well, call her anyway. Right now."

"I left Hadden from the FBI a message to call for me," Powers said.

"Don't worry. I'll take care of Hadden. Just make the damn call."

Powers punched in the numbers and Powers identified himself to an old man's husky voice. "Hold one," the man said.

A young woman came on asking, "Is that you, Mr. Powers?"

"Yes. Please call me Brad. Are you Jennifer?"

"Yes . . . Brad. I didn't want to call you, but I know Mom trusts you and we're really worried about her."

"I am too. Now Detective Daniels said something about your mother speaking some French."

"She did. And I think she was trying to tell us something that the people beside her could not understand."

Jennifer explained that when talking with her daughters, Myra often used the phrase 'entre nous'.

"It more or less means 'just between us'," Jennifer said, "or something like 'just between you and me'.

"But," Jennifer stressed, "when Mom spoke on the phone, she distinctly said 'entrepo nous' not 'entre nous' and later said something that sounded like 'day stoh-kazh'."

"I'm sorry," Daniels said. "I don't speak French, so none of that means anything to me."

"At first, it didn't mean anything to us, either," Jennifer said. "But then we looked up the words in my French-English dictionary."

Jennifer's voice now gained excitement.

"We think the words she was using were -- I'll spell this out for you so you can write it down -- e-n-t-r-e-p-o-t and d-e s-t-o-k-a-g-e. Both translate pretty directly to 'storage warehouse' in English. She also said 'local de stokage' which means 'storage room'."

"Oh, really!"

Jennifer's voice now was racing. "Yes, and she also said that she was reading lots of 'magazine' – but she used the singular not plural, and she pronounced the first two syllables 'mah-gah' which made it sound French – and the French word m-a-g-a-s-i-n . . ."

"Yes," Powers interrupted with excitement now paralleling Jennifer's, "that also relates to storage. Most armies have borrowed that word from the French. Fantastic work, Jennifer! Anything else?"

"No, that was all."

Powers asked Jennifer to repeat the story slowly and finally said, "You're really sharp. You're your mother's daughter. Now, anything further?"

Only, Jennifer said, that her Mom said she'd probably get to call again in a day or two.

"Brad, those were her words -- 'get to'. That sounded to us like she has no choice; like somebody else decides when she can or cannot call. And, Mr. Powers . . . sorry, Brad . . . her voice sounded well, kind of sluggish or maybe a little slurred like maybe she'd been doing a lot of drinking. But Mom hardly ever drinks. We're really scared. Maybe they're drugging her."

"I'm scared too, Jennifer. I'll confess that I love your mother and I'd either kill to help her or die to help her."

"Mom told us earlier in the week that your son was wounded in Afghanistan."

"He was, but I think he's going to make a good full recovery."

"Well, we hope so."

"Thanks, Jennifer. But let's all concentrate on finding your mother. If you think of anything else, anything at all, please call. If you can't reach me, ask for Detective Daniels. He and I are old friends from way back . . . and he's your Mom's friend, too. Now, can I speak to your uncle again?"

When Purdy came back on the phone, Powers urged him to be prepared to keep the girls indefinitely. "I think Jennifer just gave us a good lead and we're going to work it for all we're worth. But I know you want them to be safe. So, for Myra's sake, keep them there no matter what, even if their father comes for them.

"We'll keep them here especially if the SOB comes for them!" the uncle snapped. "We've got five acres here with an excellent alarm system. Plus that, he's going to have to come through two husky fully-armed private guards."

"Good," Powers said. "I don't think he's got the guts to face that."

"I don't either. He's a wimp . . . always has been."

181

Chapter 60

When Powers related Jennifer's report to Daniels, the detective gave a wry response. "Gee, that's better. Now it's narrowed way down to a warehouse that's somewhere in the southern third of Indiana."

"Don't joke about it, Bob. It ain't funny."

"No, it isn't. It's just that we've got a hell of a search ahead of us."

As the pair sat down to drink coffee and strategize, the chief wandered out of his office.

"Anything yet?"

Powers was about to speak but Daniels said, "Nothing yet, chief." He gave a hard stare at Powers who decided the look meant Keep Quiet. The chief grunted and spotted the two remaining confections Powers brought in. "Anybody want these?"

"Nahhh," Daniels said, "help yourself."

The chief nodded, peeled the cellophane from one of the rolls and bit into it. He picked up the other roll and turned toward his office. "Keep me up to date," his voice muffled by a second bite.

"Jesus," Daniels said, shaking his head. "What a worthless piece of crap." He suggested that they ought to give Jennifer a Yes or No question for Myra which might hint the warehouse location, and whether Windom was her captor.

"That's a good idea," Powers said, "but we've got to be pretty subtle. I can't believe they'd let her call without having her on speaker so that they can hear both ends. And they'll keep the calls short to avoid tracing."

"Mmmm." Daniels said. "Maybe we ought to just cool it until I've had a chance to interview Windom, though I don't expect to get a thing from him with his lawyer there."

"Is his lawyer a good one?"

"Oh, he's a competent shyster."

"Okay, Bob, but what I mean is whether he is a good and decent man. Will he represent his client to the bitter end even if he knows his client might kill Myra?"

"I guess we'll find out. I'll direct all kinds of questions at Windom and he'll tell Windom not to answer, but maybe the questions will make Feiler think. Maybe I can get him to put some pressure on his client."

"Okay, have at it. Listen, I don't think I could stand to watch the interrogation without trying to kill him. So I'm going back to the garden. Something that Jennifer said is nagging at me and I can't put my finger on it. Maybe getting my mind off it will let it surface. Why don't you give me a call on my cell when you wind up with Windom?"

"Will do, Brad."

#

Attacking weed sprouts, Powers crawled among emerging hosta stalks in Rae's garden. In his mood, the sprouts were tiny enemy infantrymen popping up in soil that earlier was a perfect granulated brown. He pulled them up by the roots with thumb and forefinger. As he worked, the garden bench kept catching his eye and he repeatedly turned his head toward it, reflexively expecting to see Myra and her smile.

Each time, his heart sank.

The sight of a white tail tip wagging among the plants told him Edna and Cooper were arriving. When Edna asked where Myra was, Powers curtly said the whole police department wanted to know the same thing. It was news to Edna and she obviously wanted to talk.

Powers didn't.

He made it clear he appreciated her call and her grandson's quick response the day of the abduction attempt.

"But now, Edna, it's happened again and I've got to think."

She took the hint. "I understand, boy. I hope you figure it out quick. Come on, Cooper."

It was 11:30 before Daniels called to summon Powers back to the station.

When Powers arrived, Daniels looked exhausted.

"Well," Daniels said, "like I told you, the lawyer let Windom answer little more than his name and new address. So I spent the whole time probing about what could happen to someone convicted of fraud, let alone kidnapping. I really pounded it at him and said I felt we had just about enough to get the prosecutor to call a grand jury who would order a discovery and question dozens of people about everything, and without their friendly lawyer present. Well, he tripped up. He said he had destroyed most of the trust's records.

"Feiler told him, 'Shut up. Herb!'"

"And I said. 'Too late, Mr. Feiler. Your client has just admitted engaging in anticipatory obstruction of justice. That's a 20-year felony in this state.'"

"Feiler said, 'I'm sure my client misspoke.'"

"By now Herb was sweating. I allowed as how I wasn't too worried about the obstruction charge since other issues like murder and kidnapping were involved. "It's abduction that has us worried," I said.

"And then I started grinding Windom again on every little detail of Myra's attempted abduction. The atmosphere changed a just little bit. Feiler perked up about Herby showing up at the station to get Myra when supposedly nobody had called him.

"He started looking at me kind of speculatively. He knows me and he knows I'm a pretty straight cop and I think this brought up some factors that he didn't know about his client. A lawyer doesn't like it when his client lies to him. It's okay to lie to the cops, man, but not to your own legal eagle.

"Finally, Feiler told me 'We're done here, Detective. This is all sheer speculation. You don't even know that Mrs. Windom is being held against her will somewhere.'

"I looked him right in the peepers and quietly said, 'Yes, counselor, we do'. I think that sent him a signal he didn't like.

"And then I turned back to his client and said, very slowly, 'The fact – the *fact*, Mr. Windom – that you came to the station to get your wife when no law official called you – that's an issue of grave suspicion. The fact that you just confessed to obstruction of justice and the fact that you now are more than a person of interest in this matter means that you can expect a grand jury summons. I warn you not to leave town'.

"When they got up to leave, the lawyer winked. I think I may have brought him over to our side a little bit."

"Yeah," Powers said, "I doubt if he wants to feel like he's part of the cover-up on a series of felonies, let alone murder. Now, is there anything we can do to accelerate the state's sexual harassment action?"

"I think they're working on that. By the way, there's a message that Agent Hadden called to speak to you."

"I better get back to him right now."

Chapter 61

The call with Hadden demanded patience. The agent queried Powers in a low, dull tone with endless, methodical questions.

Hadden seemed prepared to spend all day on the phone to fill in a perfect picture of all events leading up to and subsequent to Myra's disappearance.

The plodding interview started with Powers' and Myra's departure from Southland, taking them every inch of their drive to the Mooresville Meijer's store, to what they bought there and how they paid for it, to the motel at Indianapolis International Airport, to Reagan Airport, to Walter Reed and then back.

Powers answered Hadden's questions in exhaustive detail. As Hadden started over the same ground, he broke in. "Look, Agent Hadden, I know what you're doing and I suspect you're planning to go over it all a third time just to see whether my story is consistent. I've been in this business, too.

"But first you should know that all of this ties to some earlier and very significant events."

He carefully described the foiled attempt to abduct Myra, the murder of her would-be kidnapper, the surveillance on Myra and then his own injury in what appeared to be a deliberate collision. Powers referenced the Southland police investigations and interviews with witnesses.

Finally he described Daniels' account of how Windom came to pick up his wife at the police station without apparently being notified of her presence there.

Hadden was quiet for a minute. "I'm mulling this over and it seems to me some things are missing."

"Oh, yeah," Powers said. "A very great deal is missing."

"What?"

"Officer Hadden, were you ever in the military?"

"Yes. I did my hitch with the Office of Naval Investigations."

"Good. I was in the same business with the Army. I was a counterintelligence investigator for about 10 years and then I double-dipped as a civilian investigator for another four or five years. Now, how are you about letting someone discuss situations that are, shall we say, hypothetical?"

"I can go along to a point."

"Well, let's just say hypothetically that an unofficial search of financials was done on one Herbert Windom and his long-time paramour, Carlene Purdy, who also was his late superior's spouse. And these relationships that definitely are not hypothetical. Be patient because it's confusing."

"Take your time, Mr. Powers."

"Okay," Powers said. "Item One: Carlene Purdy is the widow of Chester Purdy, Herbert Windom's former supervisor. And Item Two: Chester Purdy was the father of Myra Windom, who is Herbert Windom's estranged spouse.

"Item Three: It's Myra who now is missing and presumed kidnapped. And, Item Four: Herbert and Carlene both come from Philadelphia and have known each other since her childhood.

"Now, Item Five: all three of these people are stockholders in Purdy Precision Castings, Myra being the majority stockholder.

"Item Six: Myra also is the sole beneficiary of a trust established by Myra's late father, who designated Myra's husband, Herbert -- Item Seven -- to be its trustee and manager.

"Now, let's say that hypothetical financials show that over a period of 20 solid years, Herbert Windom dipped into the corpus and interest of his wife's trust to the tune about two million bucks and change, much of it going to Carlene.

"Oh – and these are facts now – Item Eight: the man who attempted to abduct Myra three weeks ago was released on bond and murdered that same night in exactly the same way as Myra's father 20 years earlier – baseball bat to the base of the skull."

Hadden gave a long, low whistle. "This is all hypothetical, eh?"

"No, Agent Hadden. Only the financials are hypothetical – and then only until somebody can get a court order to bring them out in the open. I think there's also a case of milking the company for Herb and Carlene's benefit, but that's a whole other story."

The agent suddenly dropped his dullard pose. "Mr. Powers," he asked crisply, "just what is your interest in all this?"

"First, Hadden, I'm an investigator and by nature very nosey. Second, and much more important, I am enamored of Myra. We've known each other through plain old chit-chat for about three months. She wants to divorce Windom and, if all goes well, I hope she'll marry me one day. But everything I've told you about Herb Windom and Carlene Purdy all arises from me breaking up the kidnap attempt three weeks ago."

"Mr. Powers," Hadden said, "I'll see if I can work on that financials warrant. I think we might be able to get it under the federal RICO statute."

"Thank you, sir."

"One more question, Mr. Powers. Have you seen anything more of the man who wrecked you and is there any chance he's the man who murdered Forrest?

"No, Mr. Hadden, he hasn't surfaced as far as I know and, yes, there's a good chance he did the number on Forrest."

"Well, keep that in mind and you and Daniels keep me in the loop, okay?"

"Damn right. And vice versa. In fact, Daniels is here right now if you want to speak to him."

"Good idea, Mr. Powers."

Powers handed the phone to Daniels.

As he did, he stared down at the floor of Daniels' cubicle and began nibbling the tip of his thumb.

There's something I'm missing or forgetting. So what the hell is it?

৩ ৩ ৩

Chapter 62

After speaking with Hadden, Daniels hung up. He and Powers were just starting to talk when the phone rang again.

With a look of exasperation, Daniels answered but quickly sat forward and thrust the phone toward Powers.

It was Jennifer.

"Brad, Mom just called us again. Only this time it was a 317 area code – that's Indianapolis -- so I asked her if she was traveling. Well, she said, 'No, I'm planted . . .' and she gave a little scream, like she was hurt, and the connection broke." Jennifer began sobbing.

The light dawned on Powers. "Sweetheart, I think you and your mom just gave us the clue we needed. I think I know where she is. In fact, I think I've known all along but just didn't realize it. We're going to move on it today, Jennifer. I know this is scary, but have faith."

"Brad, please call us the minute you know anything for sure."

"I will, Jennifer. You'll absolutely be the first to know." He hung up and looked at Daniels. "Bingo!"

"What?"

"Okay, look. Myra just called Jennifer again and this time it was a 317 area code."

"Oh, great! So they've moved her."

"I don't think so, Bob. I think it's a ruse. Jennifer asked Myra if she was traveling and she answered something like, 'No. I'm planted,' at which time somebody cut her off and apparently hurt her doing it. Bob, I think they were using an out-of-town burner cell and they've got her stashed right here in town."

"How do you know?" Daniels asked.

"Look, Bob, do me a favor. Call Windom on his cell. Tell him to relax. Tell him you're sorry . . . that you came down on him way too hard this morning . . . that the investigation has taken a whole new turn. And while you're pretending to reassure him, just ask him casually how business is at the plant today."

"Why?"

189

"Trust me. Just do it."

Daniels made the call, spoke at length with Windom, and hung up.

"Okay, wise guy, now what?"

"Okay, now call Purdy Precision Castings and ask to speak to Windom."

"Brad, what the hell?"

"Just do it, man. Please!"

Daniels made the call. After a minute later he hung up looking mystified. "The gal at the switchboard said Windom isn't in today and won't be back until late tomorrow. But when I talked to him on the phone he told me they were working like crazy at the plant today on a materials inventory."

"Okay, Bob," Powers said, "I think he is present on the plant grounds but not in his office. I think he's currently Myra's jailer."

"What the hell are you talking about?"

"This is what has been nagging at my memory. When I was talking with Jennifer it finally dawned on me – duhhh! I think they've got her locked in a custom-made storage facility right inside that old office building just off the main gate on Riverside Drive."

Powers slowly and carefully told Daniels about his conversation three weeks earlier with Charles Jefferson, the retiree who had been retained by Windom as a janitor-caretaker.

"This guy agreed to stay on as kind of a part time janitor and go-fer but then he got stuck for working directly for Carlene Purdy. He had to wall in a big climate-controlled storage area – I think he said it was something like 4,000 square feet -- for the treasures she's been bringing home from overseas.

"He built it inside the ground floor of that office building off the main plant gate. Jefferson said Carlene was a real pain in the ass when it came to putting a feminine bathroom in the place – pink tile and all – and even a little kitchenette. Almost a high-end survival shelter like back in the cold war days. He even had to tie a sheepskin cover on the toilet seat for her.

"Jefferson also said she had him install the best locks money could buy." Daniels was grinning as Powers talked, but then his face fell.

"Well supposing she is in there," Daniels said. "I don't see that there's a damned thing we can do about it. We have your speculation, but not one ounce of evidence that Myra's on the property. Or even that somebody's holding her against her will. We've got no probable cause to get a warrant to enter those premises."

Powers slumped back in the chair beside the detective's desk. "You've got to be kidding me."

"Pard," Daniels said, shaking his head, "I'm sorry, but right now there's no legal way this police department can get in there."

Powers just stared through him for a minute. "Yeah, well," he murmured. "I guess I just have to do it myself."

Chapter 63

Daniels looked at Powers and said, "Whoa! Hold on just a damn minute."

Powers grinned. "I guess I better not say anything more because you might think I was about to commit a breaking and entering."

"I believe you'd better give some serious thought to any hare-brained rescue-the-damsel-in-distress fantasy."

"Bob, for sure it ain't a fantasy," Powers said. "But what would you say to having a cruiser patrolling in the neighborhood of Purdy Castings tonight . . . and maybe an ambulance on alert?"

Daniels looked his friend straight in the eye.

Powers lowered his voice and leaned close to Daniels. "Dammit, Bob, don't look at me that way. Myra is the best thing to happen in my life since Matt was born. Christ knows what they're doing to her but I'm not just going to sit on my ass and wait to find out."

Daniels sighed. "My friend, I'm an officer of the law. You break into that place and I'll cheerfully arrest your ass and throw it in jail. And that's that!

"Of course," he added, "if such a stupid unlawful act happened to disclose that Myra *is* being held in there against her will, then that would be held in your favor. You might not get sentenced to prison for the rest of your natural life . . . maybe."

"Okay, so be it, Bob." Powers frowned. He thought for a long moment and then his face lightened. "Say, Bob, on another subject, I wonder if you can give me a hand with some research."

Daniels gave Powers a suspicious look. "Jesus, Brad, I'm really tired. I've been up all night. What kind of research?"

"If you'll bear with me," Powers said, "it'll take about an hour, and I think you'll be grateful. You just need to take a break and go with me for a short drive with me.

"We'll get coffee to keep you awake. Maybe we can find you some Twinkies."

With a sour look, Daniels said, "Gee, thanks pal."

Once they were in his new rental car, Powers drove Daniels right past the entrance to Purdy Precision Steel Castings. He slowed when passing the old office building. "There, Bob, that's the place and . . . wellll, now . . . would you look at that?" he said.

"What?" Daniels asked.

"The last time I drove by nearly three weeks ago," Powers said, "those old double front doors were just hanging open. In fact, one was dangling from a single hinge. Looks like they've been repaired and locked."

"So?"

"Be patient, Bob."

Powers drove three blocks to the residence of Charles Jefferson who was seated in a wicker chair on his front porch, with a beer on a matching table by his knee.

"Come on, Bob," Powers said. "I want you to meet somebody."

Jefferson came down the front stoop to meet them. "Mr. Jenkins?" he said.

"Nope, Mr. Jefferson, I lied to you about that."

He pulled out his temporary private investigator I.D. "My name actually is Brandon H. Powers. I'm a private investigator. This here is my old Army buddy from Panama, Detective Sergeant Robert Daniels, of the Southland PD. Show him your badge, Bob."

Daniels did so, giving Powers a nasty look.

His voice rising, Jefferson said, "Just what the hell is this all about?"

Powers said, "The short version, Mr. Jefferson, is that Myra Windom has been kidnapped and I believe her husband and Carlene Purdy, are at the bottom of it. I also am convinced they've got her locked in the storage facility that you constructed inside the office building at Purdy Castings."

"Jesus, Brad!" Daniels said. "You call this research?"

Jefferson looked from one to the other. "What outfit was you with in Panama?"

Daniels gave an exasperated sigh. "Oh shit, what the hell? We were in the same squad in First Battalion, 9th infantry. Brad was the M-60 gunner and I was a rifleman and grenadier."

Jefferson said, "Yeah, I was out of the Corps by then, but my boy was with the third battalion, Sixth Marines at Panama." He gave the two men a dirty look. "He got hurt pretty bad three days after Noreiga quit. Some Army puke in a jeep."

"Sorry to hear it. Were you in Vietnam?"

Jefferson nodded. "I was there with Third MAF, that's Marine Amphibious Force, in '66 and '67."

"You jarheads were at Cape Batangan, right?" Powers said.

"Yep, but we called it Chu Lai. But now what's all this about Myra Purdy?"

Powers started to explain about how Myra's trust had been looted by Windom and Carlene Purdy.

"Wait." Jefferson said. "Why don't you come up here on the porch and set. You want a beer?"

"Thanks, but I can't," Daniels said. "I'm on duty."

"So this call is official," Jefferson said as they climbed the stoop.

"Well, sort of," Powers said. "Detective Daniels is here under protest. I brought him along so you'd understand that I'm serious and this issue about Myra is real, but the police can't do a thing because they can't get a warrant to enter that building."

"Yeah, so?"

"So I want to break in myself after dark and get her out, and I need you to tell me how to go about it because from the way you talk, it's probably locked tight as a drum."

"Well Jesus H. Christ! You want me to be an assessor . . ." He glanced at the policeman. "What do they call it?"

Grim-faced, Daniels said, "Accessory. Don't feel bad, Mr. Jefferson. By just sitting here listening I'm in the same boat. Right now I ought to arrest all three of us for conspiracy."

Jefferson laughed and slapped his knee. "But you ain't read us our rights so the arrest wouldn't stick, right?"

Daniels gave a tight smile. "Well, that's what I'm hoping," he said. "And just call me Bob, by the way."

Jefferson laughed again. "Okay then. Friends call me Charlie."

Jefferson turned to Powers. "Now, getting in that old place to where they are wouldn't be no thang at all. But I can't just tell you how. I'd need to do a map for you and I don't have any construction plans. They was just my rough sketches anyhow, you know."

Jefferson took a long pull on his beer. He squinted. "Guess I just have to take you in myself."

Powers and Daniels both looked at him open-mouthed. After a moment, Powers said, "I'm very, very grateful. I don't know what else to say."

"Well, why the hell not?" Jefferson grinned. "Ain't got nothing else to do, and I always liked that girl. Just like her Momma and Daddy -- real good folk. Besides, this would be a little payback for that Purdy bitch."

"Well . . ." Powers started to speak.

Jefferson raised a hand. "Hold on, now. Gots to think on this for a minute." He closed his eyes and gave an occasional slight tilt of his head first to the right, then to the left.

At length he opened his eyes and said, "Looka here, you want dark clothes and a hat, say a baseball cap. Dark one. Stout work boots, no damn tennis shoes. And gloves, leather ones. And a couple of them teeny flashlights, you know what I mean? We gots to go in through the basement and climb around lots of rusty equipment and old cabinets and shit in that basement afore we gets to the locker."

"The locker?"

"That's what I calls it . . . that storage area I built. Now, the front doors by the plant gate? That's the east end of the building. But we go in through the west end . . . through a old, broken down stairwell. Then we gots to work forward though the basement and come up through a place in the floor that I never bothered to fix. It's real rotten flooring – sagging -- behind a big tall stack of some of them paintings she bought. I'm surprised nobody's put a foot through it yet."

Jefferson mused again. "Powers, you best come back here about 10:30. It's good and dark by then. Pull into the alley and right on to my back yard next to the garage. I'll be out there to guide you. We'll walk from there along the alleys."

"Won't your neighbors spot us?"

"Hell, no," Jefferson said. "They too damn busy watching TV. Now . . . I got a nice long crowbar. You happen to have bolt-cutters or wire-cutters?"

"No, but I'll buy them," Powers said. "And I'll bring along my .45."

"Well, damn, Powers, I believe I'll tote mine along, too. You can't never tell."

Daniels gave a grim shake of the head. "I hope you stupid bastards don't shoot each other in the dark."

"Oh, I ain't worried about that," Jefferson said. "Being a black man, it's so dark in there I can't even see myself, so cain't nobody see to shoot me. The damn VC never could . . . well, except oncet right here."

He patted his right chest.

Chapter 64

It was raining heavily when Powers, using only parking lights, let his car coast down the alley. Spotting Jefferson, he pulled into the yard, shut off the car, got out and eased the door shut. The rain rattled loudly on his vinyl jacket.

"Right on time," Jefferson said. "Got them bolt cutters?"

"Yep. The handles were yellow and I spray-painted them black."

"Cool, man. Let's go."

In ten minutes they crossed Riverfront Drive about a block west of the office building. They had to splash through a shallow drainage ditch to reach the fence which lay about 20 feet from the pavement.

"Cut us a little gate down low to the ground," Jefferson said. As Powers knelt, they spotted oncoming headlights. They scrambled back to hunker down in the ditch water until the car passed. Returning to the fence, Jefferson pushed aside a cluster of sumac saplings giving Powers working space at the foot of the fence. "Just about two foot high and two foot acrosst. We can just tilt her down flat and crawl right over it. But don't cut the tension wire at the bottom."

"Got it," Powers said. "This is going to sound all along the fence," he warned.

"Nahhh. Don't worry," Jefferson said. "This old fence already been cut in a dozen places. Don't make near so much noise as a new one."

Cutting the first chain-link wire made a loud snap, but the fence didn't reverberate as Powers feared. Once finished, Powers wiggled through the hole, Jefferson right behind. "Follow me," Jefferson said. "Bring them cutters. Might need them for the padlocks."

He set a slow pace through the soaking brush inside the fence. As they reached the west end of the building, Jefferson turned left, walking even more slowly, keeping his right hand on the wall. Daniels kept hearing a faint high-pitched squeak.

"What is that noise? Rats?"

"Yeah, maybe," Jefferson said. "Maybe something else, too."

"Maybe what?"

Jefferson stopped.

"Gots to look out here and keep quiet," he said over his shoulder. "There's a sloping pit in front of us where the old wooden stairs went down into the basement. It's our way in, but it's all rubble now – broken brick and cement blocks. Feel your way just like in the jungle -- weight on your back foot, and feel with your front."

Crumbling concrete walls edged the stairwell and fragments of mortar and other rubble filled its bottom – along with thick brush.

"Shit!" Powers said when he blundered against a tall nettle, setting his right ear and cheek ablaze.

"Quiet!"

Picking their way through the broken masonry and brush, they reached the door. The wood was so rotten Jefferson broke through it with one twist of the crowbar. Then they were in the basement, out of the rain, but standing ankle deep in water. "Now for some damn light."

Both turned on their miniature flashlights. "I'll lead," Jefferson said. "Keep your light on the floor ahead of us. In some places the water might be a foot deep, but remember, there's tons of scrap and old machinery and lumber down here too, so keep steppin' careful like."

Powers answered. "Lead on, Marine."

Jefferson chuckled. "Semper Fi, Mac."

In seconds they were wiping spider webs from their faces and sloshing through the water, trying to be as quiet as possible. Powers whispered, "Place smells like a skunk . . . a very dead skunk." Jefferson snorted.

As they zig-zagged between and sometimes had to climb over heaps of scrap wood and junked machinery, the squeaks become louder and more protracted.

"Those are screams," Powers said.

"Yep. I think it's Myra."

They twice ducked beneath tilted old timbers and rusty I-beams. Powers' light caught rats swimming ahead of them and then scuttling to disappear into the scrap piles. Some of the rodents squeaked angrily.

Jefferson turned left at a high pile of lumber blocking their path. With his back to the basement wall and stomach sucked in, he pressed past the edges of jagged refuse. "Not far now."

Three more steps and he stopped. "More screams?"

"Damn right," Powers said. "Let's move, dammit!"

Jefferson speeded up, banging his head against another beam. "Watch out -- low bridge," he said. After six or eight more steps, Jefferson pointed his light straight up, illuminating wood that looked water-stained and splintery. "This is it."

Another scream, a long one, came to them. "God damn it," Powers said, "what are they doing to her?"

"Come on," Jefferson said. "Quick."

With their flashlights in their mouths, they shifted the pedestal and table of an ancient drill press directly beneath the rotted flooring. Urged on by more screams above, Powers climbed up onto the table so that he was crouching in the cobwebs between two floor joists.

"Hold on a second," Jefferson whispered, just as another high-pitched scream erupted above them.

"Listen, man, when we break through there, we'll come up behind a big rack of paintings or some crap like that. So I'll go to the left and you go to the right."

Impatiently, Powers said, "Make it so." He pulled back the slide on his .45, jacking a round into the chamber. He heard Jefferson do the same. Then he pushed the sharp end of the crowbar upward and it penetrated easily through the rotting floor boards.

Powers inverted the tool, shoving the curved head through the hole and then hauled downward. The flooring resisted at first and then gave suddenly, causing him to lose balance and fall off the table into the water below. "Fuck!" Powdery wood fragments dusted them both.

Jefferson scrambled up on the drill press table and used his hands to yank down sections of crumbling wood. With a body-sized opening in the floor they heard Windom's voice. ". . . either start cooperating and sign the request, you bitch, or we're just going to go on till you wish you were dead . . ."

Myra screamed, "You slime. I already wish I was dead!"

A snarl and the sound of a slap followed. Jefferson yanked furiously at the floor boards and a large section gave way with a loud crack.

As Jefferson placed his hands either side of the hole to pull himself up into the room, a form loomed above them, silhouetted against the room's lights. "Who the fuck are you?"

Jefferson and Powers both reached to pull their pistols from their belts.

Windom fired first.

Chapter 65

Powers heard the bullet smack into Jefferson and suddenly his arms were full as Jefferson collapsed onto him from the pedestal, he in turn splashing back down onto the basement's watery floor.

Windom pulled a lit cigar from his mouth and said, "Hah. Nailed you!"

Jefferson groaned, "Ahhhh, shit! You motherf . . ." just as Powers fired three shots past him up through the hole.

The .45's reports were ear-splitting, but they heard Windom collapse.

"Good!" Jefferson gasped. "You hit the bast. . ." A high-pitched shriek interrupted Jefferson. And another. And another.

Powers splashed as he eased himself out from under Jefferson. Jefferson coughed. "By God I think you got him good -- real good!" The shrieks continued and now they could hear bumping and thumping above them.

"I better get up there," Powers said.

"Do it, man. Call 9-11 and then look to her. I ain't hit that bad."

"I'll get back as soon as I can," Powers said. He boosted himself onto to the table and stood upright in the hole. Windom was five feet away tossing in agony. A pencil-thick stream of blood was arcing through a hole in the left pant leg and, despite Windom's frantic motions, the lower leg lay inert, as if amputated.

"Myra," he yelled. "I'm coming. I'll be with you in a minute."

"Brad? Oh, thank God, Brad. Please help me!"

"I will, Dear!"

Powers pulled himself up to the floor and yanked the belt out of his pant loops. "I'll be there as soon as I save this sorry bastard from bleeding to death."

He knelt to loop the belt around Windom's thigh. Doing so, he saw a raw fist-deep exit wound at the back of the thigh, so he had to move the belt up near the man's groin. If possible, Windom's screams grew louder as Powers yanked the belt tight. Windom clawed at him. Ducking away from the wounded man's hands, he saw that the .45 slug had virtually amputated the lower leg at the knee, leaving it attached by mere strands of flesh and ligament.

Windom kept shrieking.

Powers looked around past the stack of paintings to see Myra tied to a high-back chair. Her neck was taped to the chair back as were her wrists either side of her head. Her blouse was pulled open and the bra dangled at her waist.

Powers kicked Windom's pistol across the floor and dialed 911 on his cell as he walked toward Myra. He was in the midst of requesting two ambulances when he got his first real look at her.

"Oh, my God," he said to Central Dispatch. "This is horrible. Make it three ambulances! Stat!"

Myra's eyes were closed tight. She was shuddering.

"Oh, God," he said again at the sight of quarter-sized, bloody blisters the cigar had burned on both breasts and – still with ash clinging to it -- on her right cheek. He trembled as he dropped the phone and began cutting the duct tape that held her neck against the back of the chair.

"Oh, goodness," he said, "Oh, God love it," reverting to phrases he once used to soothe his little son when he had hurt himself.

She was breathing in little gasps as Powers cut away the last of the neck binding, but Windom's shrieks overwhelmed the sounds.

Eyes still closed, she let her head fall forward, but she was still held upright by the tape binding her wrists to the chair back. He pulled her blouse shut and fastened the one remaining button. When he cut the duct tape from her left arm she started to hug herself, but cried out at the pain of her burns. Powers kissed her forehead and barely heard her say, "Brad," as he went to work on the other binding.

He knelt to cut the tape around her ankles, and as he freed her she said, "Help me lie down. Please." Holding her shoulders, he eased her to the floor and she drew herself into the fetal position.

With Myra released, he became more aware of Windom screaming, "Help me! For God's sake, help me!"

Powers got up and walked back to the paintings. He roared at Windom, "You can just keep on screaming for a while. You miserable, sick son of a bitch. How the hell could you do that to anyone, let alone your wife? I want the EMTs to take care of Myra and Jefferson first. You're last in line, you sick bastard!"

He leaned over the hole in the floor. Jefferson had managed to get back up on the drill press table.

Powers reached down. "Grab my hand, Charlie. Let's get you up here."

Jefferson nodded and seized Powers' hand and wrist. "Owwwww, Dammmm!" he yelled as Powers pulled him up so his knees were level with the floor.

Jefferson sat onto the floor, lower legs dangling into the basement. He carefully pulled off his shirt and wadded it against his left side. "Thanks man. I be okay for now." He looked over at Windom arched in agony, blood vessels standing out in his neck and forehead.

Jefferson yelled, "Hey, Herb! Herb! Will you please shut the fuck up? You sound exactly like a pig squealing. If it's anything like when I was hit in 'Nam, you ain't going to feel the real pain for another half hour. Think on that, you rat bastard."

Powers returned to Myra and seated himself on the floor beside her.

"Come here baby," he said, grasping her shoulders and pulling her to him. He pillowed the undamaged side of her face on his thigh. She pressed her fingers into her ears to mute Windom's screams. Powers tried to soothe her by rubbing her shoulder. "God, Myra, I'm so sorry this happened. So sorry. But it's going to be okay, Sweetheart. The ambulance will be here soon."

They heard a tremendous crash and seconds later, a policeman with a steel battering ram bashed open the storage room door. Headlights and pulsing blue-and-red flashers of the cruiser in the building's main doorway were blinding, but as the vehicle backed out, Powers saw the silhouettes of other officers scrambling through the entrance.

Officer Pratt leaned over him, raindrops beaded on his cap visor. "Powers, are you okay?"

"I'm fine, officer, but this lady really needs medical care. So does Jefferson over there. Likewise, that asshole with my belt around his leg."

"They're on the way. Where are the firearms?"

Powers handed his pistol to Pratt. "Careful, it has a round chambered. I kicked Windom's over there by the far wall. Jefferson had his own .45, but never got the chance to fire it. It's probably down underwater in the basement."

Powers combed Myra's hair with his fingers. "There, there, baby. There, there. God love it, I know it hurts. We'll get you to the hospital and get something for the pain in just a few minutes."

Daniels came in a minute later and knelt beside Powers. "You okay, Brad?"

"Bob," he said, "I waive my rights to an attorney and confess to this breaking and entering. Just get an ambulance for Myra. She's been horribly tortured."

"They're on the way, Brad," Daniels said. When the first ambulance took Windom away and the warehouse became quiet.

"Oh, thank God," Myra sobbed.

Chapter 66

At Daniels' urging, the EMTs let Powers ride in Myra's ambulance. Lying on the wheeled stretcher, Myra clung to his hand but kept her eyes shut until the last few minutes of the ride. She met his gaze and whispered, "Nightmare."

"I know," he nodded, trying to smile. "It's over now, Sweetheart. As soon as I can, I'll call the girls and let them know you're safe and that you're going to be okay."

"Thanks, Brad. Please tell them I love them."

"I will. First thing."

She closed her eyes and then opened them wide. "You're not leaving, are you? Brad?"

"No way am I leaving you."

She sighed and closed her eyes again. "Sleep, if you can," he told her. She nodded again and seemed to sink into the stretcher's mattress.

The EMT, a blond lad with weight-lifter shoulders, whispered to Powers, "I'm not clear what her injuries are."

"See that burn on her cheek?"

The EMT nodded.

"Well, it was torture by cigar while she was tied to a chair. I'd say she has maybe another dozen identical burns all over her chest. I don't know how long it was going on, but I recommend checking her neck. Her neck was taped to the chair back and I know he slapped her hard at least once, so I bet there could be some muscle tears."

"I'll tell the ER people."

"Yeah, well . . . never mind, friend. I'll tell them. I'm coming in with you."

"The docs might not like it."

"Tough shit."

# # #

Windom's screams filled the ER as a nurse began taking Myra's vitals. Powers left to call her daughters. He told them their mother was utterly exhausted and sleeping under observation in the hospital. He promised to drive her to Chicago as soon as the hospital released her. He said he thought she'd be able to call them tomorrow.

When he sat back down by Myra's bed, Windom was sedated and the ER was quiet again. A doctor had ordered pain medication for Myra and she was sleeping. They let Powers stay with her while they worked on Windom at the other end of the ER treatment bay. After two hours, a tired-looking doctor pulled aside the privacy curtain to ask Powers what happened.

Powers gave him a flinty look. "I shot the bastard with my .45."

The doctor recoiled.

"He was torturing this lady – his wife," Powers said. "He was burning her with a lighted cigar."

"Jesus," the doctor said. "Well, he's lost the leg for sure. Right now I don't know if we can save him. He lost a lot of blood and he's shocky."

"I could give a damn," Powers said, "but good luck anyway." The doctor left.

Powers stretched and yawned and discovered Myra gazing at him.

He smiled. "Hi there, Sweetheart."

She gave him a tired smile. "Just checking," she whispered, and went back to sleep.

Perhaps an hour later the doctor returned. "We got him stabilized. Tomorrow we'll see if he's strong enough to send him off to Indianapolis. They're equipped to handle that kind of trauma."

He gave a Powers quizzical look. "Weren't you in here two or three weeks ago?"

"Yeah," Powers said, "but I was out like a light from a car wreck, so I don't remember you."

"Welcome back," the doctor said. "Now I've got to take a look at her so I'd like you to leave."

"Doctor, she and I are lovers so you'll need Security to drag me out, and I'll fight the whole way."

The doctor peered at him. "You look like you can handle yourself."

"Believe me, Doc, I can."

"Okay. Have it your way." The doctor pulled back the sheet and opened Myra's blouse. "My God," he hissed. Myra stirred but did not awaken. "Any idea how long he was doing this to her?"

"No clue. I just wish we had broken in this morning. By the way, how's my buddy, Jefferson?"

With his head, the doctor signaled Powers to step away from the bed, walking him out to a bench in the hallway. "It's a nasty flesh wound. It lacerated some muscles and then gave him a long crease along the outside of his hip and thigh, but it didn't penetrate the gut. He'll be fine in three weeks or so."

"Great. Can I see him?"

"How about tomorrow morning?"

"Fine, but can we go back? I'm uneasy being away from Myra."

"Mrs. Windom is in no danger," the doctor said. "Those burns are acutely painful, of course, but they're superficial. She'll have some scarring, but plastic surgery can take of that. The main thing is that her burns don't constitute a threat to her life."

"I figured that," Powers said, "but she's been through a hell of an ordeal and I think she needs the reassurance."

"Right. I've handled a few other torture victims and they require a lot of emotional support."

"She'll have all the support I can give, plus some friends. And her twin girls."

"And that bothers me a bit," the doctor said.

When Powers started to interrupt, the doctor went on. "Let me explain . . . I'm worried about clinical depression. There's the threat of the victim becoming so dependent on another person – say a care-giver or a rescuer, like you -- that she can remain passive . . . even catatonic in some cases; unable to make decisions of any kind."

The doctor said he recommended at least a two or three-day stay which would include some counseling.

"Now, don't worry, Mr. Powers. You can be right next to her the whole time. But first I think you should go get cleaned up. You look like you've been rolling in mud and spider webs. They're all over your head and shoulders. Blood on your hands. Same with Jefferson. And the right side of your face . . ."

"Nettles, Doc," Powers said. "Don't ask."

"I'll get you some ointment for that. You can shower in the physicians' locker room. We'll give you some scrubs because your clothes look like the mice have been at them."

"Thanks, Doc. I'll do that. But first, I have one more worry. I believe Myra's life still could be in danger and that she needs to be under a round-the-clock watch."

"Why?"

"Her husband's partner in all this – maybe two partners -- is still unaccounted for. With Windom in the hospital and under arrest, the partner's money spigot has closed. And, of course, the law wants to have a long talk with her. I think the partner could be desperate. I wouldn't put it past her to try something right here in the hospital." Powers felt a hand on his shoulder. He looked up to see Daniels.

"Thanks, Doc," Daniels said. "Why don't you let me take it from here?"

As the doctor returned to the ER, Daniels said the police were putting a 24-hour guard on Myra. He nodded toward a uniformed policeman coming into the corridor. "Meanwhile, you and I need to talk."

"Are you going to read me my rights and arrest me?"

Chapter 67

"Hell no, I'm not arresting you. Come on. Let's go get coffee before I collapse."

As they walked toward the little hospital's cafeteria, he said. "You know, now that you mention it, I should arrest you because of all the paperwork I've got to do now."

"Aww, too bad. Here I do all the heavy lifting, and you're *still* bitching. Maybe you need a Twinkie."

Daniels snorted. "Well, I have a right to bitch. I got no sleep last night and I don't think I will tonight."

"Actually, Bob, I guess I'm lucky you haven't jailed me for homicide. I've never wanted to kill anyone as much as I did that bastard. My God, how could anybody . . .? Ah, well . . . let it go."

Daniels nodded and said, "I think I know how you feel," as he slipped a five dollar bill into the coffee machine and punched Cream. He fed change back into the device and signaled Powers who punched Black.

As they began sipping, Daniels made wry face. "God, I hate the coffee out of these machines. It tastes just like sludge."

"I think you're wrong, Bob. I never drank any sludge that tasted this bad."

Daniels took out his notebook and began questioning Powers about the encounter with Windom. He soon focused on Windom's demand that Powers had overheard for Myra's cooperation. "And you think Jefferson heard those same words?"

"I'm sure of it. The slap we heard galvanized him and he yanked open that hole in the floor and next thing we know, Windom shot down through it at us. You'll have to ask Charlie."

"I will."

As Daniels took notes, Powers said, "The only thing I can figure is that he wanted her to request a final withdrawal from the trust. Maybe that's the only way he could get his hands on the lump sum left in the trust. I thank God that he didn't kill her."

"Hell, he didn't dare," Daniels said. "With Myra dead, everything would be tied up in the estate. And the girls probably are the beneficiaries. So what's he going to do, wait a year and then kidnap and torture them, too?"

"I just hope I get to question him again," Daniels said. "But I doubt if Howard Feiler, esq., would go along with that."

"Well, Bob, maybe Feiler would be helpful if there was some plea offer. And I bet Windom could rat out Carlene for fraud and you-name-it . . . maybe even murder."

Daniels nodded. "We'll check with the county attorney." He looked Powers in the eye. "What are you going to do?"

"Well," Powers said, "if there's ever a trial I'm going to testify for the prosecution, of course.

"But in the meantime, I wonder where the other guy is – the man that wrecked my car and probably killed Bluto. Until he's found and locked up, I'm staying as close to Myra as possible. I told her girls that I'd try to get her up to Chicago to see them soon. First, though, the doc wants her to talk with a psychologist."

"Damn good idea," Daniels said. "Torture isn't something you just forget after a good night's sleep. For one thing, the nightmares don't let you sleep. It's suffering that you just don't peel off like a sock."

"Say, Bob, can I get my pistol back?"

"Hell, no. It's evidence."

"Shit!"

"I've got a 9 mm I can lend you. It's one of the early Rugers -- 15-round magazine."

"Better than nothing."

Doris Arends walked up to their table. "Bob? Brad? I thought I'd let you know that we got Myra cleaned up and her dressings applied. She's in Room 235 and the guard's outside the door. She's asleep and you can go sit with her any time you want."

They simultaneously answered, "Thanks, Doris."

Daniels called after her, "Is Jefferson awake?"

"Yes," she said. "And I bet he wants to know what's going on."

"Okay Brad," Daniels said, "I think we're done for now. I want to see him while things are still fresh in his mind."

"I think I'll go shower," Powers said, "and then see if I can find Room 235."

Chapter 68

As Powers came down the hall toward Myra's room, he spotted Officer Hesselbeck seated in a wing-arm chair outside her door. He was writing in an aluminum notebook.

He glanced up and did a double take. "Hey, Mr. Powers!" he whispered, "for a minute, you being in scrubs, I thought you were a doctor. Say, I hear you're a dead-eye shot."

"Please call me Brad. And the shot was pure blind-assed luck, but at least it gave the dirty bastard a taste of his own medicine."

"Damn right," Hasselbeck said.

"Now, Denny, do you know who you're keeping an eye out for?"

"Not sure. Maybe some blond lady."

"Well, she's not just some blonde. She's green-eyed, about 5-8 and got huge jugs. But the rest of her is all hardbody. Her butt looks so tight that when she sits, her cheeks wouldn't cover more than a quarter's diameter. She's strong and meaner than rhino in heat.

There also could be a guy – pretty good-sized and beefy – who's an out-and-out murderer."

Hasselbeck looked grim. "I've got the picture. I'll let my relief know."

"Thanks."

Once in the room, Powers pulled the recliner next to Myra's bed. Her hospital gown concealed the burns on her chest and a Telfa dressing covered the burn on her cheek. Her face looked drawn.

He eased into the recliner, conscious for the first time in hours of his aching ribs and the incision in his left side. *But nothing like what you've been through, Myra my dear.*

The day's tension and pressure took their toll and he fell asleep.

Later, Hasselbeck awakened Powers to introduce him to his relief, a 10-year veteran. The cop gave Daniels' pistol to Powers with an extra loaded magazine and a nylon belt holster. Powers strapped on the Ruger as they chatted briefly in the hallway. Then he returned to the recliner.

# # #

Pressure on his hand brought Powers awake with a jerk. Myra was sitting on the side of the bed touching him. Her eyes foggy with sleep. "You didn't leave me," she said.

"I never will, Myra," he said, bringing the recliner upright. "But I don't think you should be getting up."

She gave a grin. "I've got to get to the john . . . bad," she said, "and I hate bedpans. So I'm trying to figure out how to do it with all this." She held up her left arm with its IV connected to a bedside stand

Powers got up and wheeled the IV stand around to her side of the bed. "Don't look at my fanny," she said.

"I promise. I won't." He grinned and steadied her as she walked to the bathroom. She closed the door behind her.

She stayed in the bathroom some time after the toilet gave its hospital roar. Finally he called, "Myra, are you okay?"

"No," she said.

He pushed the door handle down, "I'm coming in . . ." but the door opened. Tears were streaming down her face. "Oh, Brad, I'm going to be so scarred."

Taking her hand, he said, "Myra, do you still love me?" She nodded rapidly, her eyes huge. "Of course, I do."

"So do you even see this scar on the side of my face?"

She shook her head. "Now that you mention it, I do."

"But when we made talked or when we made love, did you notice it or the scars on my arms or my leg?"

"No," she said.

"I know you don't like your injuries," he said. "But they don't change you. You're a beautiful, wonderful woman and your scars don't matter to me any more than my scars matter to you. I didn't fall in love with your cheek or your breasts. I fell in love with the whole

Myra and I'm aching now because you're hurting. I wish to God I could make it all go away."

"Oh Brad," she said, tears starting to stream. "I need a hug."

He gently pulled her to him, her uninjured cheek to his. He kissed her tears. "Aren't we a mess?" he said. "You can't hug because of your burns, I can't hug because of my ribs."

Gazing into his eyes, she whispered, "Let's have a contest."

"What?"

"To see who recovers first."

"Damn right," he said, smiling and bobbing his head for emphasis. "So what's the prize?"

She brought her forehead to his. "Well," she said with a throaty chuckle, "if we put our heads together – like this – something ought to occur to us."

"And we'll both be winners?" he said.

"For a poor old knuckle-dragger, you catch on pretty quick."

Powers helped her lie down and then returned to the chair.

They watched each other's eyes and gradually fell asleep.

# # #

Powers began flinching to the crash of grenades and bullets cracking past his foxhole. He yanked back on the M-60's cocking handle and grabbed the weapon's pistol grip, trigger finger pointing downrange, ready to hit the trigger.

But swiveling his eyes in the dark, he saw no target. A Degtyaryov machine gun stuttered, overridden by the repeated thumps of grenades. *Assault? Rag heads inside the wire?*

His eyes opened and he recognized Myra's dim hospital room. His ears retranslated the rattle and thump back into something hitting the wall out in the hallway. A peculiar metallic ring brought him fully awake. Myra was awake, too, sliding from bed, the gown riding up above her knees.

Powers jumped up and pulled the Ruger from the holster as he moved between Myra and the door. "Stay behind me." He jacked a round into the chamber and pointed the 9 mm at the open door. His finger was on the trigger.

A clown dashed in through the doorway and stopped cold, staring at his pistol.

A Ronald MacDonald wig and a giant baseball cap turned sideways topped the skin-tight pinstripe uniform which emphasized a very female figure.

She carried a cluster of balloons in her left hand. Half-concealed among their bright ribbon tethers was an aluminum hardball bat. A huge crimson smile, triangular eyebrows and giant red cheek patches accented the dead white makeup.

It didn't disguise the snarl on Carlene Purdy's lips.

Chapter 69

Aiming at her face, Powers shouted, "Try me! Just take one more step!" Myra cried out in pain as Powers backed into her, forcing her against the bed.

Carlene slowly started to raise the bat higher. "Move that bat so much as another half inch and I'll plug you right between those big green eyes!"

She snarled, "Shit!" and darted out the door. Powers followed, seeing balloons, wig and hat flying from the sprinting figure.

He aimed at her back and took up the trigger slack. She skidded to dodge into the stairwell where she careened into a janitor pushing a bucket and mops. Both fell, knocking over the bucket with a crash and a cascade of soapy water. She was up like lightning, but slipped in the mop water, falling again. The janitor grabbed her foot and, by that time, Powers arrived to fall on her just as she tried to hit the janitor with the bat.

It was like trying to seize a big slimy fighting fish. Suds made it almost impossible to grip her. She raked her fingernails across his face twice before he could pin her face-down and wrench her arm into a hammer lock.

"Call the cops," he yelled to the nurse's station.

"What the hell's going on?" the soaked janitor said, using the door to get to his feet.

"She's a murder suspect and I think she half-killed a police guard just up the hallway. Do me a favor and get his handcuffs for me."

"Will do, mister. Right now."

Carlene continued kicking, squirming, sputtering and trying to bite, her clown make-up adding a red tint to the suds and mop water on the floor. Only after he tightened the cuffs to the point that it must have been agony did he subdue her.

He dragged her by the collar up the hallway where a nurse knelt, trying to disentangle the unconscious policeman from his capsized chair.

Blood from a scalp wound was puddling inside the blue uniform hat on which his head lay. Powers snatched up the cop's shoulder mike. Depressing the key, he asked "Is Sergeant Daniels on this circuit?"

"You're not authorized to use this radio." Powers recognized Hasselbeck's voice.

"This is Powers. Your replacement here at Bledsoe Memorial has been injured by Carlene Purdy. We have her in custody."

Hasselbeck ordered Powers off the circuit saying there were other problems at the hospital and officers were on the way.

# # #

When a soapy, dripping Powers finally returned to the room, he expected to find Myra terrified. She was spitting mad.

"Brad, why the hell didn't you shoot her?"

"Because I don't want to kill anybody or go on trial for murder or even manslaughter."

"Right," Myra gritted. "Stupid of me."

She winced as she raised her arms in exasperation, "God, how I hate that bitch! She's so unbelievably greedy – she's beyond greedy! Before Herb started burning me yesterday, he dragged me on a tour – with my wrists and my mouth taped – to show me all of the plunder she stored there.

"It's more than she could ever use in that house or even look at. She's just a pathological hoarder . . . an insatiable thief, a complete klepto. Stuff is all she that values and he was bragging about it! To me! As if he were proud of what they stole! How could she control his brain so completely?"

"Myra, I don't think his brain was what she was controlling. But in any case, now she's in a sling. She assaulted a cop and will be in jail for a long time to come."

"There's more than that," a distraught voice came from the door.

Powers and Myra looked up to see a shaken Doris Arends. "She beat in Windom's skull after she cold-cocked Bob with her bat. They think he's concussed."

"Who, Bob?"

"Right."

"But Windom's dead?"

"I've never seen anyone so dead," she added with a shudder.

"Well, now she's really in a sling." Powers said. "Meanwhile, I hate to be crude," he added, turning to Myra, "but it looks like Carlene just arranged your divorce."

"Oh, my," Myra said. She paused, staring down at her hands. "I don't know quite how to react to that," she said.

"It will be hard on the girls. They didn't really know what he was. But after what he did to me, I guess I'm not all that upset. I suppose that makes me a bad woman."

"No!" Doris snapped. "You're a good woman. That sadistic bastard tortured you. Be glad that he can't do that ever again to anyone!"

When Powers asked Doris about her ex-husband, she said she'd heard that with the aid of an ice pack, Daniels had recovered consciousness. She gave a wry grin. "He's so hard-headed, I didn't think he could really be hurt by a blow to the head."

"Doris," Myra said, easing herself back into the bed, "I'm sorry, but these burns are really starting to hurt again. Do you suppose I could have another pill?"

"I'll check the doctor's orders and be right back," she said.

From the bed, Myra held out her hands to Powers.

"Thank you again, my knight in rusted armor. I'm just kind of shocked," she said, as he took her fingers in his. "I've been through the most awful two days of my life. That awful helplessness – you don't know how I prayed for you to come . . . Lord, how I prayed . . . and now this. I don't know what to say or do except to thank God."

He bent to kiss her forehead. "Myra, dear, you don't have to say or do another thing right now. It's easy for me to say this, but you should just lie back and relax. After what you've been through, you need rest.

"In a few days, we'll go see your girls. I told them we'd come up soon – that you were in the hospital for observation. I also told them it was their reading of your signals that enabled us to find you."

Doris bustled in with a pill in a tiny paper cup and a larger cup with water. "Here you are, Dear. Now try to sleep."

"Very well," Myra said. "I'm following both your orders." She chased the pill with a gulp of water.

Powers stayed with her until she drifted to sleep and another policeman was posted at the door. Then he went in search of Daniels.

Chapter 70

Powers found Daniels sitting owl-eyed on a bed in the ER. His tie was pulled away from his blood-stained collar and the right side of his head had been shaved to make room for sutures and surgical dressing.

"How you doing, Bob? And why aren't you in a hospital gown?"

"Don't give me any crap, Brad. I've got a hell of a headache and I'm in a *real* bad mood. Even Doris is giving me a wide berth."

Powers grinned and patted Daniels' shoulder. "Bob, I'm just glad you're still among the living."

"Yeah, me too," Daniels said. "Truth is, I feel like a damned fool, falling for that clown act. My God that bastard was fast.

"One minute I'm telling him to go peddle his balloons somewhere else and Bam! Next minute I'm on the floor . . . and he's standing by the bed slamming that bat down onto Windom's head, blood and brains flying all over. He must have hit him 20 times with that bat."

"What do you mean, 'He'?"

"What do you mean, what do I mean? I'm talking about the guy in the clown suit who killed Windom."

"Guy? You're saying the clown who killed Windom was a man? Bob, did you see any other clowns?"

Daniels groaned. "No, except the one I'm looking at right now."

"Well, it was Carlene Purdy who came into Myra's room – clown outfit, make-up, balloons, ball bat. I aimed your Ruger at her and she took off running but piled into a janitor and his mop bucket. So we caught her."

"Good. So they must have been working together," Daniels said.

"Who must have been working together?" Power said. "Buddy, I think you got hit on the head too hard. Just try to get some sleep."

Daniels closed his eyes and lay back. "Killing Windom really was a stupid move," he said. "Utterly psychotic. I'm gonna sleep now."

"I think she always was psychotic," Powers said as he started to leave,

Daniels raised himself on his elbow. "Brad. Wait! I forgot to tell you -- before the clown showed up, Windom did some talking . . . a lot of talking. Between his injury and shock and sedative, he was almost hysterical. Anyway, he said he and Carlene had a hell of a running fight when he kidnapped Myra."

Daniels related that Carlene wanted Myra killed, but Windom refused because he needed her so he could empty the last few hundred thousand dollars out of the trust.

"Oh, I almost forgot this, too," Daniels said. "Windom solved another mystery for us. He came to the station that day – you know, after you rescued Myra from Forrest – because he was called and warned by none other than our police chief."

"That's what I guessed," Powers said. "It explains why Ackers didn't want me to do any nosing around."

"You bet," Daniels said. "Apparently Carlene seduced him when he took her home after she ID'd Chet's body, and she kept screwing him for years after that. That's at top of my call list tomorrow with the sheriff, the DA and state cops."

"So he's been running interference for them the whole damn time?"

"Yeah, if for no other reason than to protect his mammoth ass." Daniels' eyebrows rose, "Anyhow – get this -- Windom said what he was really trying to do in that torture chamber was save his wife's life. If she'd just signed the request for the remainder of the money in the trust, then he wouldn't need to kill her. They could just go their separate ways."

"Right," Powers said. "He was trying to save her by taping her to a chair and playing tic-tac-toe on her tits with a lit cigar. I'm glad I made him squeal like a baby."

"Where did you learn to shoot like that, anyway, Brad?"

"Bob, like I told Hasselbeck, it was pure blind luck. I just pointed and yanked the trigger. Too bad the bastard isn't alive to suffer longer."

Daniels closed his eyes for a long time. "I think the clown did you a hell of a favor by killing Windom."

"Yeah, Myra doesn't need to divorce him, now."

Daniels was starting to wind down with weariness, but he gave a sputter of exasperation.

"Powers, use your brain. With Windom dead, I bet Myra can make a valid claim to all that high-class art and stuff in the warehouse. It's on company property and she's the controlling stockholder. If she can't actually recover a nice chunk of her own heritage, there might be enough value in that place for her to bring in a real manager and rescue her daddy's factory."

"Damn," Powers said. "I didn't think of that. I'd better get ahold of Myra's lawyer and get him up to speed."

"Yeah, Brad, and I think I'd tell him about Feiler, too -- Windom's lawyer. He's got to have some information nobody else does . . . no more attorney-client privilege when the client's dead. So . . . since I've done all your thinking for you and I see through the window that it's dawn, I need some sleep. Now get out of here."

"Good idea, Bob. It's a much better dawn than yesterday's."

"Damn tootin'."

Powers stopped in the doorway. "Say, Bob?"

"God, what now?"

"Was the clown right-handed?"

"Nope. Southpaw."

"I guess that cinches it, Bob. We had two clown-murderers. One's in custody. The other is still at large."

# # #

Powers' feet literally dragged as he trudged down the hall to the stairwell and climbed to the second floor.

He peeked in at Jefferson and the sight of him sleeping made Powers long for the recliner in Myra's room.

He recognized Officer Pratt standing guard outside Myra's door.

"How you doing, Mr. Powers?"

"Officer Pratt, I'm whipped. I'm climbing in that recliner in Myra's room and catching some Z's. Now don't let any clowns get near you."

"Don't worry. I'm not even going to let any nurses get near me."

"Gee, I don't think I'd go that far."

"Mr. Powers, I'm a newly married man."

"Oh, okay. I see your point." Powers chuckled and walked into the room. Myra's face looked peaceful. The recliner beckoned.

Powers dropped into the recliner and was asleep before he could kick back.

Chapter 71

He became dimly aware of voices, female voices. He seemed to recognize Myra's words and he smiled and drifted from a doze to deeper sleep. Later he rose back to the surface of consciousness. The voices now seemed to speak about him, about his hair. Myra wanted his hair longer, so he'd look like a violinist or maybe an orchestra conductor.

"Huh? What's that?" He opened his eyes and rubbed them. Myra was sitting up in bed, freshly made up. A gray-haired woman in a lab coat perched on a corner of the foot of the bed and Doris stood beyond the far side of the bed. All three were grinning at him.

"What's that about my hair?"

The three women laughed. "I knew that would wake you up," Myra said.

Powers rubbed his hands on his bristly cheeks and chin. "I must look like hell," he muttered. Then he smiled. "Well, ladies, if I were to grow my hair long – and I'm not saying I would – but if I did, with all this bald acreage on top, I could do one of those real oily comb-overs."

Lab Coat said, "Eewwww!" and Doris shook her head vigorously side to side. Myra said, "Yechhh!"

"That won't do? Okay." Powers stood up from the recliner and stretched. "Instead I could let it grow it out to shoulder length and develop a lisp. I could change my name to Percy Sugartonsils, speaking very softly and standing like this." He crossed his left foot over his right and put one hand out, wrist bent, and the other on his hip, fingers forward. "Dahlings, I could be sooo *very* sensitive."

"See," Myra told the other women, "I said he could take teasing."

The woman extended her hand to Powers. "I'm Nancy Elgin, psychologist."

"Pleasure to meet you, Doctor."

"Please, just Nancy. Anyway, Myra and I have been talking about these ordeals, and her daughters and . . ."

"And you," Myra added.

"Yes, Brad, the knight in shining armor."

"No, Nancy. No knight. Just a guy who loves this woman."

"I disagree," the doctor said. "I think you've been a genuine white knight, a bona fide, Grade A, USDA-inspected hero. And I want you to know, thanks in part to you, I think Myra is coming through this extremely well. She's a strong woman. But I think there's a danger that . . ."

"A danger of dependency?" Powers asked.

"Well, yes, and then some. But here's the point: I think the two of you potentially could be good for each other. Or you might not. You come from very different backgrounds – very different. So with that in mind, and all this crisis and stress, I also think you both need some separation and to take some time apart. You need to wait six months for some of the dust to settle before you make any major moves or relocations."

"Well, would this mean we couldn't date?"

"Oh, no. You absolutely could see each other. You should get to know about each other outside of this constant crisis. Go out to dinner and a movie. But I don't think you should rush things by moving in together as soon as Myra's discharged."

"What about if I were to drive her to Chicago to see her daughters? I kind of promised them that I would do that."

The doctor waved dismissively. "Not a problem, Brad. But when you get there, I think you should leave Myra with her family and check yourself into a hotel. Keep that separation. It will give you both time to decompress, and that's very important, especially for Myra at this stage. And, Brad, you certainly wouldn't want to rush pell-mell into the girls' lives."

Myra was looking at Powers with a question in her eyes.

Powers nodded. "You're the doctor," he said. "You make a lot of sense." Myra gave him a look of relief.

"But," he added with tones of mock severity, "I don't want to carry this separation thing *too* far. And, I have my reasons." Turning

225

to Myra, he said, "You know you have thanked me several times for coming to you and finding you. Well, you shouldn't thank me. I did it for me.

"I was miserable the whole time in Washington," he said. "Sure, I wanted to see my boy and be with him. But I was miserable because you weren't there with me. Each time I heard your voice on the cell it was like sipping an ice-cold lemonade in the desert. And then when I called for you at the hotel and you were gone . . . well, it was just like something fell out of my life. Scariest thing I've ever experienced.

"Myra, I needed to find you because without you I think I would just crawl in a hole and die. Over the past three months I've gotten to know you pretty well and I discovered I just flat need you. Period."

Tears started rolling down Myra's cheeks.

"So we'll do some separation," Powers said, wiping his own eyes and walking over to put his hand on her shoulder.

"But . . ." he leaned down and kissed her head, and then looked at the doctor, ". . . well, I just want you to know I believe in moderation in all things – very, very, very strict moderation!"

Doctor Elgin was dabbing at her eyes. She gave a chuckle.

Myra put her hand on his shoulder. The motion made her wince. "I'd hug you if I could."

"Patience, my dear," Powers said. "Patience. We each must heal. Meanwhile, I'm way overdue for a shave and a change of clothes. I'm headed back to the apartment and I've got to stop and see Jefferson. He's the real hero in all this. Without him I'd still be sloshing around in that basement trying to find you."

"Brad?" She smiled. "Come back soon. Remember what you told us about not overdoing separation."

# # #

Once in the apartment, Powers flopped his mail on the table and started pulling the scrub top over his head. That's when he caught the barest glimpse of the clown just as a bat speared into his solar plexus.

226

Chapter 72

Powers dropped like a rag doll.

Legs splayed, the side of his face flat on the carpet, he gasped like a landed fish. Vivid vein patterns streaked his vision.

A pair of black Nike runners appeared before his nose as the assailant yanked the shirt the rest of the way off Powers' arms and head. He pulled the Ruger from Powers' holster. "You won't be such a big man without this," he said, walking away from the table to place the weapon on the bookshelf.

Powers began to recover and started to rise, but the clown rapped his left ribs with the bat, convulsing him with pain. It took a good minute to master the agony. As he hissed trying to get his breath, he raised his head slightly. The clown jabbed the bat against his ear and pushed his head back to the floor. The bat kept his head pinned to the carpet.

He had never felt so utterly helpless.

"Please," he gasped. "I just want to sit up."

"Mmm, okay, tough guy." He removed the bat and stepped back. "I seen you handle yourself with Forrest, so sit on your hands."

Powers pushed himself upright and rocked first right then left to shove his hands under his butt.

He looked up.

The clown makeup was half gone. The man used Powers' scrub top to wipe at the red greasepaint around his mouth. It smeared the make-up, turning the whole lower half of his face pinkish.

"You look familiar," Powers said. "Who the hell are you?"

"I'm Billy."

"Billy who?"

"Billy Price."

Powers shook his head in exasperation. "Okay, Billy, give me a little help here. Why are you dressed in a clown suit that looks like it has Herb Windom's blood and brains all over it?"

227

Price looked surprised and finally said, "Well, what do you think? It's because I did him."

"The same bat you used to do Forrest and Chet Windom."

"Well, the same one on Charlie, but . . ." Billy's eyes went saucer. "How did you know?"

"Because you just told me. And now I recognize you. You're the guy that Carlene made get out of the chair so I could sit next to her at that tavern."

"Yeah, she was real mean about that. Really pissed me off."

"And then you drove that pick-up into my car."

"Yeah."

"And you did that because Carlene told you to?"

"That's right, Mister. It was part of the plan."

"What plan?"

"Carlene's plan for her and me to retire from here on."

"Retire?" Powers chuckled. "My God, you've got to be kidding me."

"No, man. See, she's my cousin and she's real smart. She has this plan for us to live on . . ."

"Let me guess. You're going to live on Easy Street? And you killed Herb and Charlie and Chet because she told you to?"

The man rolled his eyes. "You're making it sound stupid, but we grew up in the projects in Philadelphia. Her mom took me in after my mom was killed by her pimp. And it was always food stamps and handouts and getting beat up for our lunch money . . . if we had any. And they beat us up when we didn't have no lunch money."

"Billy?" Powers said quietly.

"Yeah?"

"What are you going to do now that Carlene's in jail? Do you want to go see her so she can tell you what to do?"

"Can't. She's dead."

"No, she's not. They took her in to the lock-up from the hospital last night."

"Yeah, well, the chief was taking her to the courthouse this morning and she just happened to fall off that platform behind city hall. Except she didn't fall. She was in handcuffs and he just reached down, grabbed her ankles and tilted her right over that railing. She fell one story and landed on her head."

"I can't believe . . . how do you know, Billy?"

"I watched from the car. I was trying to think of some way to get her away from the cops. But the chief just fucking killed her. And then there was a rumble right there on the platform. I think the other cops cuffed him."

"Jesus," Powers said. "I knew Ackers was a bastard, but I didn't think he was a cold-blooded murderer just like you."

"Screw you, Powers! And what do you care? Come dark, I'm going to bash your head in and take your car and drive out of town."

It took Powers about a minute to convince Price that the state police, city police and sheriff's department would have cruisers out stopping cars at every intersection.

"But I've got an idea that I think might work," Powers said.

"Oh, sure, like you're going to help me after I hit you."

"Look, Billy, I don't want you to kill me. I want to live. So let's make a deal. I can get you out of state. The cops around here know me and they're not going to stop a car I'm driving. Or if they do, they know who I am and they'll let me through. Then when we get wherever you want to go, you can tie me up and take off."

"I don't know . . . that might work."

"But Billy, what will we do for money? I've only got about 15 bucks on me."

Billy grinned. "Oh, that's no sweat. Carlene's been saving money. Got lots of it just in the basement at the house . . ."

"Carlene's house?"

"Yeah. And she's got all them checkbooks for the money she's been stashing away in banks so we can go on cruises and the settle down in South America some place. She's even got fake driver's licenses and those passport things for us. I'll be Charlie Wright. She was going to be Annie Wright, my wife."

"I don't know, Billy. I bet the cops will be watching her place like a hawk."

The grin disappeared. Billy rapped the bat hard against the point of Powers' right shoulder. The pain exploded down his arm into his hand as he rolled onto his left side. He couldn't so much as twitch the elbow or wiggle his fingers. "Ahhhhhh, shit!" he said, levering himself upright with his left arm, "Damn, Billy! How am I supposed to steer when you paralyze my arm?"

"Well, just let it be a lesson, smart guy."

"Okay! Okay! Tell me, though, why did you kill Windom?" As he spoke, he heard the screen door spring give a slight creak. He coughed to mask the sound and caught a glimpse of motion beyond Billy. "Was it because he refused to do in his wife?"

"Yeah. But that was just the last of his screw-ups. As long as he followed orders, we was working this deal real good. He knew the numbers stuff. Carlene was the looks and brains and I'm the muscle.

"But this past year Herb was really starting to lose it, you know? He was doing stupid things -- like he was dipping his wick in too many places at the plant."

"That make Carlene jealous?" He coughed again.

"Hell, no. She didn't give a rat's ass who Herb screwed. But messing around with the help right there in the office was pissing people off and they were getting the state labor jerks all riled up. Carlene said you can only pay off those assholes for so long. It was bad enough having to give that fat-ass cop his $3,000 a month.

"But with Herb it was just getting to be one damn thing after another. Like when I told how you took down Forrest, he just went ape shit!

"Carlene told him to just leave well enough alone. But, no! He had to get his Myra away from the cops. Even then, the three of us still could have just taken Myra and disappeared and left her in a ditch somewhere and it would be weeks, months maybe, before anyone realized we all had gone.

"And then those rich bitch twins of hers could go live in the fucking projects.

"But the thing about Herb, Carlene would come up with a plan. I'd follow it. But he'd do his own thing, you know, and screw it all up. Of course, you didn't help things any with all your prying and getting all cozied up to Myra. Not that I blame you. For her age, she's a sharp chick. But after I took old Forrest out of the picture, your cop friends came around to talk to Herb about it, he really started getting, like, weird."

Powers spotted more movement behind Billy and resumed coughing.

"Will you quit that noise?"

"My ribs are broken," Powers said, "and when you hit them I think it may have reinjured them." He coughed again, and then extended the coughing spasm for all it was worth.

"Sorry about that," Billy smirked.

"Don't mention it. So, let me guess," Powers said. "You're three kills for three times at bat. Nobody left on base."

Billy grinned again. "Yeah, good one. Three times at bat. Three clean kills. Batting 1.000."

"My God in heaven," Powers said. "You don't have any regrets? None at all?"

Billy chewed his lip for a minute. "Oh, maybe at first, you know. Like after Chet. He was a good old boy. But a few drinks and you can handle that. After that, it just got easier to forget about it because we made out so well. Carlene kept the chief on a string once he figured out what happened, but then he got so bloated up he didn't care anymore as long as he got his money."

"But don't you feel anything?"

He gave Powers a blank look and shrugged. "It is what it is."

"And that's it?"

"Well, I sure am going to miss Carlene. She was real good to me."

"Was she a good fuck, Billy?"

Billy's eyes trained on Powers like guns in a turret. He crouched into a batter's stance. "Brad, I think I'm gonna try for a grand slam." The end of the bat twitched like an angry cat's tail. He tightened his hands on the grip and coiled back to swing.

Powers glanced past Billy, widening his eyes. Billy started to pivot away from Powers, lashing with the bat at chest level. But Rosa Hinojosa was too far away. And too fast. As Billy swung the bat, she jacked a round into the Ruger's chamber and fired. The 9 mm slug exited in a gout of blood through his left shoulder blade. Billy said "Ahhh!" and went up on his toes, upper torso bending back. He dropped the bat with an aluminum clang.

Rosa fired again, this time blowing the back of Billy's skull and a fair amount of his brains onto Powers' bedroom door. As he collapsed, a spurt of blood leapt from Billy's ruined face, leapt again, again and dwindled to nothing.

Rosa crossed herself and spat at the corpse.

Chapter 73

Unable to use his right arm, Powers found it a chore to get back onto his feet.

"Rosa," he said, "thank you. Thank you for my life. I hope you don't feel upset about this."

"No, Senor Brad, this is not my first time," she said. "It is sad to do this, but I am not upset."

"Really?" Powers raised his eyebrows.

"When I was a young girl," she said quietly, "I must kill a coyote. You understand 'coyote'? This man is paid money – big money -- to help us come from Mexico to the States. Only before they arrive, he rapes and kills those people. I am 15 and he tries to rape me, so I put my knife into him – I stab him -- many times. He was evil just like this man. That's why I kill him, too."

"No! Rosa, when the police ask why, you only say you killed him to save me, because he was hitting me with that bat."

She nodded and gave a small smile. "Okay, Senor Brad. That is what I tell the police."

"Good. And thank you again, Rosa. And God bless you," he added, as he dialed Daniels' cell phone.

Daniels sounded beyond groggy when he answered. "Bradley H. Powers, this call better be good because I'm still without sleep. We've got a hell of a mess here at the station and I'm really feeling pretty rocky."

"Well, Bob, I've got good news. The man who clobbered you with the bat and beat Windom to death is lying on the floor of my apartment."

"No shit?"

"No shit, Bob. And as we used to say in the desert, he's tits up. He was taking his bat to me and Rosa saved my life with your Ruger."

"Damn! Are you kidding? No. Hell, no! Okay! I'll call the uniforms. Get them over there right away. How did Rosa happen to be there?"

"I don't care and I haven't asked. She may have been upstairs getting the apartment cleaned up for Myra. Rosa and I will just wait out on the driveway for your boys. We haven't touched anything."

"Good. See you soon."

# # #

Detective Subczek arrived first with the uniforms to do the scene investigation. She had Rosa and Powers cuffed and locked in separate cruisers. Before he was shut in the cruiser, Powers asked her to call the medical examiner's attention to the blood and brain tissue on the dead man's uniform – that it stemmed from the hospital murder.

An ambulance took the body after Subczek had the scene photographed from two dozen angles.

Daniels arrived and asked Subczek to escort Rosa to the ground floor apartment to take her statement.

Daniels freed Powers' hands and interrogated him at length. Daniels could see the circular bruise in Powers' midsection and the bruise darkening his right shoulder. Daniels called the ER to arrange for X-rays of Powers' shoulder and an orthopedic surgeon to verify that the shoulder was injured.

After an hour with Detective Subczek, a furious Rosa came out to the driveway. "Why do the police not believe me, Roberto? Why do you question Brad? He is a good man and this man injured him! He is ready to kill Brad. So why?"

Holding both palms toward her, Daniels said, "I do believe you, Rosa, and I do believe Brad. But we must make sure there are no questions -- no questions at all. This is to protect you and Brad."

He turned to Powers rolling his eyes. Powers said, "One question, Bob."

"What?"

"Any chance I could go to my bathroom and shave and shower and get a change of clothes on before I go back to the ER? I'd like to be cleaned up when I give Myra the news."

"Naa. I'll go in and get some clean clothes and you can clean up at the station. Then I can tell you about the madhouse down there. Mainly it's that Ackers is under arrest for the felony murder of Carlene Windom and meanwhile, the city manager named me temporary acting chief."

"Holy shit! I want to hear all about that. Well, I guess I should say congratulations, too. Hey! Need a detective?"

"Don't push me, Brad."

Chapter 74

Powers, right arm in a sling, rapped on the door before entering Myra's room.

She was in the recliner reading. "Hey, Brad!" She gave a bright smile, stood up gingerly and then stopped. "What's wrong with your arm?"

"Carlene's cousin – the guy that wrecked me -- ambushed me at the apartment and gave me a shot with his bat. But he's not ever going to bother us or anybody else again."

"They arrested him?"

"No. He's dead."

"Dead?"

"Yes. Rosa saved my life by shooting him."

"Good Lord!" She paused. "That must have been horrible for you, but I can't say I'm sorry about the guy. Now is Rosa in trouble? Have they got her in jail?"

"No. Nobody is pressing any charges against her. They're saying it's justifiable homicide because if she hadn't killed Billy Price, he would have batted my ugly skull into the next county."

"Well, thank heavens for Rosa and good riddance," Myra said. "By the way, I'm being discharged the day after tomorrow . . . so what's with the arm?"

Powers explained that the orthopedic surgeon found that he had severe bruising, probably some rotator cuff and nerve damage, possibly temporary. "He said I might need surgery, but first they want to try physical therapy."

"Well, I hope you don't need surgery. Tell me, do you think can turn your sling away from your body?"

Acting the innocent, Powers asked, "Now why would you want to know that?"

She gently pushed his slung arm apart from his chest. "I don't care if this hurts," she said, and pressed herself against him, hugging gently. "I'm on pain meds so it's not too bad . . . and I'm so glad you're back . . . and I'm so glad you're okay."

"Myra, I'm glad we're both alive and mending." They were silent for a long minute. Then Powers said, "But we do have a problem."

"What now?"

"Well, I'm so short and you're so tall, that I need a foot stool or maybe lifts. Otherwise, one of these days I'll smother in your chest."

"Oh, man up, will you?"

"Well, Myra, that's exactly what starts happening every time we hug."

She laughed and hugged him again. "Prove it."

He lowered himself slightly and began mumbling into her bosom. As she pulled back, laughing, he said, as if continuing a statement ". . . and the other problem is that I'm not fit right now to drive us to see the girls."

"Not a problem, big guy," she said. "I think the trust can afford to hire a limo and a driver."

"Let's get serious a second," he said, "How are you planning to break all this to the girls? It's going to be several massive shocks for them."

"The question is not how am *I* going to break it to them but how you and I together will do it. Dr. Anglin and I have talked quite a bit about it." She paused.

"Brad, we're going to tell the truth. If necessary, I'll open my blouse and show them the truth. And," she added. "I want you beside me. They need to know you saved my life – twice. If it weren't for you, I wouldn't be able to speak with them at all."

"But aren't they likely to resent . . ."

She interrupted. "Brad, for years I've bottled up a lot of anger and frustration. So don't argue with me on this or I'm likely to do a Mount St. Helens right here."

"Yes, Dear."

Chapter 75

As they settled into the back seat of the limo, Myra asked about Daniels' story concerning Carlene and the chief.

"Well, Bob was still at the hospital when they booked her, but he told me that she was screaming to see Chief Ackers and he was refusing. So she began yelling at the top of her lungs that the chief was part of her conspiracy to defraud your trust and to cover up your dad's murder, and your attempted murder, and Forrest's murder and Herb's murder."

Powers said nobody at the station took her seriously . . . except the chief, who ordered her brought in shackles to his office for a private but very noisy interview. "Bob said the chief ordered no recordings, so nobody knows exactly what transpired except she finally calmed down and was taken back to her cell.

"By then, Bob was home catching up on lost sleep, but later he found out that the chief announced he personally would take this high-profile prisoner to the courthouse next morning for her arraignment.

"Daniels also said the chief had disabled the catwalk surveillance camera.

"Anyway, he said that as the chief took Carlene from her cell, she was calm . . . cocky actually, even though her legs were shackled and her hands were cuffed to her waist.

"Daniels thinks the chief convinced her that he would help her escape. But once he got her out on the catwalk deck, he tilted her head-first over the railing, held her just a second and then released her for a straight, head-first fall onto that concrete wall surrounding the basement entrance. It snapped her neck and shattered her skull."

"Unfortunately for the chief," Powers said, "there were two witnesses."

"Who?"

"Denny Hasselbeck and a young cop intern who is an electronics whiz. Just as the chief took Carlene out the door, Hasselbeck noticed that the TV monitor was blank. So he asked the intern to come with him to check the camera. They stepped onto that platform just as the chief let Carlene drop."

"How awful," Myra said.

"Yeah. A real mess. The chief tried to draw on Denny, but Denny had him in cuffs immediately. So they called to wake up poor Daniels to come in and take charge. The last I heard, the state cops were handling the investigation and Bob is getting to do what he loves best."

"What's that, Dear?"

"I love hearing you call me 'dear,' Dear."

"I'm glad, Dear," Myra said. "But what does Bob love best?"

"Paperwork. Actually he hates it more than anything in the world. But that's his problem, now. You and I have a problem of our own to think about. At least when we come back from Chicago."

"Oh, Lord! What now?" she said.

"Well, darling, you have no place to live."

"What do you mean? I've got the house."

"Nope. It's part of the investigation," Powers said. "The police and the FBI's forensic accountants are going over all of Herb's records. He didn't take them when he moved out."

Myra gave an icy reaction. "Probably because the SOB counted on moving back in after my disappearance became permanent."

"Chilling thought," Powers said. "And I bet you're right. Anyway, the house is bordered by yellow tape – you know, 'Crime Scene – Do Not Enter.' They'll be working there for weeks. And the same for your parents' house. They're going to inventory everything Carlene had on display there plus everything at her storage unit in the old office building.

"And that's not all," he added with a grin.

"My God, what else?"

"That same tape is stapled across the door of my apartment. So I can't stay there, either."

"Well, gee," she said, batting her eyes, "what are we going to do, Brad?"

"Well, temporarily," Power said, "I guess we could stay in that upstairs apartment Rosa was getting ready for you."

"Together?"

"Yep."

She smiled broadly. "Well, so how do we handle the separation we're supposed to have?"

He put his hands either side of her face and pulled her lips to his.

A moment later he said, "Shut up, woman."

"Yes, dear."

~ The End ~

About The Author

J. Scott Payne is a retired journalist who began his career as a cub at the Kansas City Star. He then took Lyndon's shilling to serve with the U.S. Army in Korea, Vietnam and – worst of all -- Washington, D.C.

Subsequently, he worked as reporter and editor for an assortment of Midwest newspapers and magazines. He and Jane now are retired to a little college town in Michigan enjoying the mornings, the woods, their rescued pooch and cat and (at a safe distance) the birds.

Jane predicts that the photo on the back cover will win the Mr. Congeniality Prize in the Josef Stalin look-alike contest.

If you enjoyed this story please give it a quick review at its listing on Amazon.com. This and Scott's first book, *A Corporal No More — a Novel of the Civil War*, are available on Amazon in both ebook and paperback forms and also may be ordered through Barnes and Noble or any other book store.

Other Titles From Argon Press –

Return To Mateguas Island
A Tale of Supernatural Suspense, by Linda Watkins

The Universe Builders
Bernie and The Putty, by Steve LeBel

Mateguas Island
A Novel of Terror and Suspense, by Linda Watkins

The Short of It
Poetry and Short Stories, by H. William Ruback

Bargain Paradise
A tender, amusing novella, by Darlene Blasing

Secrets
Mateguas Island Series Prequel – By Linda Watkins

A Corporal No More
A Novel of the Civil War – By J. Scott Payne

For details on these and other novels that are in the works, please visit Argon Press at www.ArgonPress.com

Made in the USA
Charleston, SC
17 July 2015